ZANE GREY

RANGLE RIVER

LEISURE BOOKS NEW YORK CITY

A LEISURE BOOK®

May 2005

Published by special arrangement with Golden West Literary Agency.

Dorchester Publishing Co., Inc.
200 Madison Avenue
New York, NY 10016

ISBN 0-8439-5212-1

Printed in the United States of America.

Visit us on the web at www.dorchesterpub.com

RANGLE RIVER

TABLE OF CONTENTS

Amber's Mirage

Now that it was spring again, old Jim Crawford slowly responded to the call of the desert. He marked this fact with something of melancholy. Every winter took a little more out of him. Presently he would forget it, when he was once more out on the lonely and peaceful wasteland, hunting for the gold he had never found and for which he had given the best years of his life.

Still, Jim seemed a little more loath to bring in his burros and pack for the long trail. He sat on the sunny side of the shack and pondered. The peaks were glistening snow-white, the lower slopes showed patches and streaks of snow under the black pines, but the foothills were clean and gray, just beginning to green and purple over. High time that he be up and doing, if he were ever to find that treasure at the foot of the rainbow.

"Reckon I've grown fond of this lad, Al Shade," soliloquized the old prospector, as he refilled his pipe. "An' I just don't want to leave for the desert with things the way they are for him."

Jim Crawford's shack stood at the edge of the pinewoods on the slope opposite the lumber mill and was the last habitation on the outskirts of Pine, a small town devoted to lumbering and cattle raising. The next house toward town was a picturesque log cabin, just up in the pines and within plain view, as Jim had found to his sorrow. Jim's neighbor, Seth

Low, was a millhand, a genial and likable fellow with only one fault—an over-fondness for drink, which had kept him poor. He had a complaining wife and five children, the eldest of whom, Ruby Low, seventeen years old, red-haired and red-lipped, with eyes of dark wicked fire, had been the cause of no little contention in the community.

Jim had seen Ruby carrying on with cowboys and lumberjacks in a way that amused him, even thrilled him a little for his pulses were not yet dead to the charm of beauty and youth. But when Ruby attached Al Shade to her list of admirers, the circumstances had grown serious for Jim. And he was thinking of that now, while he listened to the melodious hum of the great saw, and watched the yellow smoke arise from the mill stack, and felt the old call of the desert in the spring, something he had not resisted for thirty years.

Long ago, in a past slowly growing clear again in memory, he had been father to a little boy who might have grown into such a fine lad as Alvin Shade. That was one reason why he had taken such a liking to Al. But there were other reasons, which were always vivid in mind when Al appeared.

A cowboy galloped by, bright face shining, with scarf flying in the wind. Jim did not need to be told he would stop at the Low cabin. His whistle, just audible to Jim, brought the little slim Ruby out, her hair matching the boy's scarf. He was a bold fellow, unfamiliar to Jim, and without a glance at the open cabin door or the children playing under the trees, he snatched Ruby off the ground, her heels kicking up, and, bending, he gave her a great hug. Jim watched with the grim thought that this spectacle would not have been a happy one for Al Shade to see.

The cowboy let the girl down, and, sliding out of his saddle, they found a seat on a fallen pine, and then presently slipped down to sit against the tree, on the side hidden from the cabin.

They did not seem to care that Jim's shack was in sight, not so very far away. Most cowboys were lover-like and masterful, not to say bold, but this fellow either embodied more of these qualities than any others Jim had seen with Ruby, or else he had received more encouragement. After a few moments of keen observation Jim established that both possibilities were facts. He saw enough not to want to see more, and he went into his shack sorrowing for the dream of his young friend Alvin.

Straightway Jim grew thoughtful. He had more on his hands than the problem of getting ready for his annual prospecting trip. If a decision had not been wrung from him, it certainly was in the making. Dragging his packsaddles and camp equipment out on the porch, he set morosely to going over them. He wasted no more glances in the direction of the Low cabin.

Eventually the mill whistle blew. The day was Saturday, and the millhands got off at an early hour. Not many minutes afterward the old prospector heard a familiar quick step, and he looked up gladly.

"Howdy, old-timer," came a gay voice. "What you-all doin' with this camp truck?"

"Al, I'm gettin' ready to hit the trail," replied the prospector.

"Aw, no, Jim. Not so early! Why, it's only May, an' the snow isn't off yet," protested the young man, in surprise and regret.

"Set down a while. Then I'll walk to town with you. I'm goin' to buy supplies."

Al threw down his dinner pail and then his old black hat, and stood a moment looking at Crawford. He was a tall, rangy young man, about twenty-one, dressed in overalls redolent of fresh sawdust. He had a frank, handsome face, keen blue eyes just now shaded with regret, and a square chin cov-

11

ered by a faint silky down as fair as his hair. Then he plumped down on the porch.

"I'm sorry," he said.

"It's good of you, Al, if you mean you'll miss me," replied the prospector.

"I sure mean that. But there's somethin' else. Jim, you're not growin' any younger, an' you . . . well, these eight-month trips on the desert must be tough, even for an old desert rat like you. Forgive me, old-timer. But I've seen you come back . . . four, five times now, an' each time you seemed more done up. Jim, you might die out there."

" 'Course, I might. It's what I want when my time comes."

"Aw! But that should be a long while yet, if you've got any sense. Jim, you've taken the place of my dad."

"Glad to hear it, son," replied Crawford warmly.

"Suppose you come live with mother an' me," suggested Al eagerly.

"An' let you take care of me?"

"No, I don't mean that. Jim, you can work. We've got a little land, even if it is mortgaged. But if we cultivate it . . . if we had a couple of horses . . . the two of us. . . ."

"Al, it's not a bad idea. I've thought of that before. There's plenty of work left in me yet. But I'd only want to tackle that after I'd made a strike. Then we could pay off your debts, stock the place, an' farm right."

"Jim, you've thought of that?" asked Al.

"Lots of times."

"I didn't know you thought so much of me. Gosh, wouldn't it be grand!" Then his face fell, and he added ruefully: "But you old prospectors never make a strike."

"Sometimes we do," replied Jim, vehemently nodding.

"Aw, your hopes are like the mirages you tell about."

"Al, I've never told you about Amber's mirage."

"Nope. That's a new one. Come on, old-timer . . . if it isn't too long."

"Not today, son. Tomorrow, if you come over."

"Well, I'll come. Ruby has flagged me again for that Raston cowpuncher," rejoined Shade with a touch of pathos.

"Raston. Who's he?" queried Jim, looking up.

"Oh, he's a new one. A flash cowboy, good-lookin' an' the son of a rich cattleman who has taken over the Babcock ranches."

"Uhn-huh. Reckon I remember hearin' about Raston. But he hasn't paid for those big range interests yet. Al, is young Raston sweet on Ruby?"

"Sure. Same as all those other galoots. Only he's the latest. An' Ruby is powerful set up about him."

"*Humph.* Does she encourage him?" asked Jim, bending to pick up a saddle cinch.

"She sure does," burst out Al in disgust. "We've had rows over that often enough."

"Al, you're deep in love with Ruby?" asked Crawford suddenly.

"Head over heels. I'm drownin'," replied the lad, with his frank laugh.

"Are you engaged to her?"

"Well, I am to her, but I guess she isn't to me . . . at least, not all the time. Jim, it's this way . . . I just know Ruby likes me better than any of them. I don't know why. She's sure been thicker with other fellows than with me. But that's not so much. Ruby likes conquest. She loves to ride an' dance an' eat. She's full of the devil. There's been more than one fellow like Raston come along to take her away from me. But she always comes back. She just can't help herself."

"Uhn-huh. What does your mother think of Ruby?"

The boy hesitated, then replied: "Ruby often comes over

13

to our house. Mother doesn't exactly approve of her. She says Ruby is half good an' half bad. But she believes if I could give Ruby what she craves . . . why, she'd marry me, an' turn out all right. Jim, it's my only hope."

"But you can't afford that on your wages," protested Jim.

"I sure can't. But I save all the money possible, Jim. I haven't even a horse. Me . . . who was born on a horse! But I'll get ahead somehow . . . unless somethin' awful happens. Jim, now an' then I'm blue."

"I shouldn't wonder. Al, do you think Ruby is worth this . . . this love an' constancy of yours?"

"Sure she is. But what's that got to do with it? You don't love somebody because she or he is so an' so. You do it because you can't help yourself."

"Reckon you're right at that," replied Jim slowly. "But suppose a . . . a girl is just plain no good?"

"Jim, you're not insinuatin' . . . ?" ejaculated Al, aghast at the thought.

"No, I'm just askin' on general principles, since you make a general statement."

Al's face seemed to take on an older and yet gentler expression than Jim had ever observed there.

"Jim," he said, "it oughtn't to make no difference."

"*Humph*. Mebbe it oughtn't, but it sure does with most men. Son, there's only one way for you to fulfill your dream . . . if it's at all possible."

"An' how's that?" queried Al sharply.

"You've got to get money quick."

"Lord! Don't I know that? Haven't I lain awake at nights thinkin' about it. But, Jim, I can't rustle cattle or hold up the mill on pay day."

"Reckon you can't. But, Al Shade, I'll tell you what . . . you can go with me!"

"Jim Crawford! On your next prospectin' trip?"

"You bet. The idee just came to me. Al, I swear I never thought of it before."

"Gosh almighty!" stammered Al.

"Isn't it a stunnin' idee?" queried Jim, elated.

"I should smile . . . if I only dared!"

"Wal, you can dare. Between us, we can leave enough money with your mother to take care of her while we're gone. An' what else is there?"

"Jim . . . you ask that!" burst out Al violently. "There's Ruby Low, you dreamin' old rainbow chaser! Leave her for eight months? It can't be did!"

"Better that than forever," retorted Crawford ruthlessly. He was being impelled by a motive he had not yet defined.

"Jim!" cried the young man.

"Al, it's you who's the rainbow chaser. You've only one chance in a million to get Ruby. Be a good gambler an' take it. Ruby's a kid yet. She'll think more of fun than marriage yet a while. You've just about got time. What do you say, son?"

"Say! Man, you take my breath."

"You don't need any breath to think," responded the old prospector, strangely thrilled by a subtle conviction that he would be successful. "Come, I'll walk to town with you."

On the way the sober young man scarcely opened his lips, and Jim was content to let the magnitude of his suggestion sink deeply.

"Gosh. I wonder what Ruby would say," murmured Al to himself.

"Wal, here's where I stop," said Jim heartily, as they reached the store. "Al, shall I buy grub an' outfit for two?"

"Aw . . . give me time," implored Al.

"Better break it to your mother tonight an' come over to-morrow," returned Jim, and left Al standing there, his mouth open, his eyes dark and startled.

Seldom did the old prospector answer to unconsidered impulse. But he seemed driven here by something beyond his immediate understanding. Through it flashed the last glimpse he had taken of Ruby Low and the lover whom Jim took to be young Raston. Jim felt that he was answering to an inspiration. One way or another—a successful quest for gold or failure—he would make Al Shade's fortune or spare him inevitable heartbreak. Some vague portent of Amber's mirage ran like a stream through Jim's thought.

He bought supplies and outfits for two, and generously, for he had ever been careful of his meager funds. Leaving orders for the purchase to be sent to his place, Jim started back with quickened step.

It was a great project. It had a flourish and allurement that never before had attended his prospecting trips, although they all had fascination enough. He tried to evade queries and rest content with the present, well knowing that, when once more he had been claimed by the lonely desert, all his curiosity and doubt would vanish. Then came a rush of impatient sensation—a nostalgia for sight of the long leagues of lonely land, the bleak rocks, the solemn cañons, the dim hazy purple distances, ever calling—smell of the cedar smoke, the sifting sand, the dry sage, the marvelous fresh fragrance after rain—sound of the mournful wind, the wailing coyote, the silence that was appalling, the cry of the nighthawk.

These passed over him like a magic spell. A rapture pervaded his soul. How could he have lingered so long?

A gay voice calling disrupted Jim's meditation. Already he had reached the outskirts of town, and he was opposite the Low cabin with Ruby waylaying him at the gate. Her red hair flamed, and her lips were like cherries. She transfixed him with a dazzling smile.

"Uncle Jim, I was layin' for you," she said archly. "I hate to ask you, but I've got to have some money."

Ruby sometimes borrowed, and on at least two occasions Jim remembered she had paid back.

"Wal, lass, I'm about broke myself," he replied. "But I can rake up five wagon wheels. Will that help?"

"Thanks, Uncle Jim. It'll sure do. I just want to buy somethin' for tonight. I'm goin' to a party," she said, as she took the silver, and then ran her arm through his. "I'll walk over to your house with you."

Jim could not reproach Ruby for any indifference to him, that was certain. She liked him and often told him her troubles, especially with the boys.

"Another party, huh? I reckon this time you're goin' with Al," rejoined Jim.

"No. He didn't ask me, an' Joe Raston did. Besides, Al an' I have fought like cat an' dog lately. Al's jealous."

"Wal, hasn't he cause?" asked Jim mildly.

"I 'spose he has, Uncle," she admitted. "But I'm not . . . quite . . . altogether engaged to Al. An' I do like the other boys, 'specially Joe."

"I see. It's pretty hard on you an' Al. Say, Ruby, do you really care about the boy? Tell me straight."

"Uncle Jim!" she exclaimed, amazed.

"Wal, I just wondered. I seen you today over back of that pine log, an' it looked to me. . . ."

"You saw me . . . with Joe?" she interrupted confusedly.

"I don't know Joe. But the cowboy wore a scarf as red as your head."

"That was Joe. An' you watched us! I told the big fool. . . ."

"Ruby, I didn't mean to spy on you. I just happened to be lookin'. An' when you slipped off that log, I sure didn't look long."

17

She had no reply for this. Ruby was nervously clinking the silver coins in her hand. They reached Jim's shack, and Ruby sat down on the porch steps.

"Uncle, did you give me away to Al?" she asked, and a tinge of scarlet showed under her clear skin. She was ashamed, yet no coward.

Jim gazed down upon her, somehow seeing her as never before. He realized that he had reason to despise her, but he did not. At least he could not when she was actually present in the flesh. Ruby had seen only seventeen summers, but she did not seem a child. Her slim form had the contours of a woman. And like a flaming wildflower she was beautiful to look at.

"No, Ruby, I didn't give you away to Al," replied Jim presently.

"You're not going to, Uncle?"

"Wal, as to that. . . ."

"Please don't. It'll only hurt Al, an' not do a bit of good. He has been told things before. But he didn't believe them. An' he thrashed Harry Goddard. Of course, he'd believe you, Uncle Jim. But it wouldn't make no difference. An' . . . an' what's the sense?"

"Ruby, I reckon there wouldn't be much sense in it. Not now, anyway, when I'm takin' Al with me on a long prospectin' trip."

"What?"

Jim motioned to the packsaddles and harness strewn upon the floor, the tools and utensils.

"Oh, no! Don't take him, Uncle," she cried, and now her cheeks were pale as pearl. She caught her breath. The sloe-black eyes lost their wicked darts. They softened and shadowed with pain. "Oh, Uncle, I . . . I couldn't let Al go."

"Wal, lass, I'm afraid you'll not have anythin' to do with it."

"But Al would never go . . . if I begged him to stay."

Jim believed that was true, although he did not betray it. He felt gladness at a proof that Ruby cared genuinely for Al, although no doubt her motives were selfish.

"Mebbe not, lass. But you won't beg him."

"I sure will. I'll crawl at his feet."

"Ruby, you wouldn't stand in the way of Al's coming back home with a big lot of gold."

"Gold!" she echoed, and a light leaped up in her eyes. "But, Uncle, isn't prospectin' dangerous? Mightn't Al get killed or starve on the desert?"

"He might, sure, but he's a husky lad, an' here I've been wanderin' the desert for thirty years."

"How long would you be gone?"

"Till winter comes again."

"Seven . . . eight months! I . . . I don't . . . believe I could bear it," she faltered weakly.

"Ruby, you'll make a deal with me not to coax him off . . . or I'll tell him what I saw today."

"Oh, Uncle Jim," she retorted, although she winced. "That'd be mean. I really love Al."

"Uhn-huh. You acted like it today," replied Jim dryly. "Reckon you're tryin' to tell me you love two fellows at once."

"I'm not tryin' to tell you that," she flushed hotly. "If you want to know the truth, I love only Al. But I like Joe . . . an' the other boys. I'd quit them in a minute, if Al had anythin'. But he's poor. An' I don't see why I should give up havin' fun while I wait for Al."

"Did Al ever try to make you give them up?" queried Jim curiously.

"No. He's pretty decent, even if he is jealous. But he doesn't like me to go with Joe."

"Wal, do we make a bargain, Ruby?"

Her red lips quivered. "You mean you won't give me away, if I don't try to keep Al home?"

"That's it."

"Wh . . . when are you leavin'?"

"Wal, I reckon tomorrow sometime . . . late afternoon."

"All right, Uncle, it's a deal," she replied soberly, and with slow reluctance she laid the five silver dollars on the porch. "I won't go to the party tonight. I'll send for Al."

"Wal, Ruby, that's good of you," said Jim warmly. "I'm goin' over to Al's after supper to see his mother, an' I'll fetch him back."

"She'll be glad to have Al go," rejoined Ruby bitterly. "She doesn't approve of me."

Jim watched the girl walk slowly down the path, her bright head bent, and her hands locked behind her. What a forlorn little creature. Suddenly Jim pitied her. After all, vain and shallow as she was, he found some excuse for her. Under happier circumstances the good in her might have dominated.

The old prospector's mind was active, revolving phases of the situation he had developed, while he prepared a hasty supper. It was dark when he started out for town. The lights were flickering, and the wind from the peaks carried a touch of snow. Al lived on the other side of town, just outside the limits, on a hundred-and-sixty-acre farm his father had homesteaded, and which, freed from debt, would be valuable some day. Jim vowed the prospecting trip would clear that land, if it did no more. A light in the kitchen of the cottage guided him, and, when he knocked, the door appeared to fly open, disclosing Al, flushed and excited, with the bright light of adventure in his blue eyes. Jim needed no more than that to set his slow heart beating high.

"Come in, old-timer," shouted Al boisterously. "No need

to tell you I've knuckled. An' mother thinks it's a good idea."

Al's mother corroborated this, with reservations. She seemed keenly alive to the perils of desert treasure seeking, but she had great confidence in Jim, and ambition for her son.

"What's this Amber's mirage my boy raves about?" asked Mrs. Shade presently.

"Wal, it's somethin' I want to tell Al," replied Jim, serious because he could never think of Amber in any other way. "I knew a wonderful prospector once. An' for twenty years I've looked for his mirage on the desert."

"Gracious, is that all? How funny you gold hunters are. Please don't graft any of those queer ideas on Al."

"Say, Jim, haven't you seen this Amber's mirage?" asked Al.

"Not yet, son. But I will this trip. Wal, good night an' good bye, Missus Shade. Don't worry about Al. He'll come back, an' mebbe rich."

"Alas! I wonder if that is not the mirage you mean," returned the mother, and sighed.

Al accompanied Jim back to town and talked so fast that Jim could not get a word in, until finally they reached the store.

"No, don't come in with me," said Jim. "You run out to see Ruby."

"Ruby! Aw, what'd you want to make me think of her for? She's goin' out with Joe Raston tonight."

"Al, she's stayin' home to be with you this last night."

"Gosh!" ejaculated Al rapturously, yet incredulously. "Did you tell her?"

"Yes. An' she sure got riled. Swore she'd never let you go. I reckon she cares a heap for you, Al. An' I'm bound to confess I didn't believe it. But I talked her into seein' the chance for you, an' she's goin' to let you go."

"Let . . . me go," stammered Al, and he rushed away down the street.

The old prospector lingered to watch the lithe, vanishing form, and, while he stroked his beard, he thought sorrowfully of these two young people, caught in the toils of love and fate. Jim saw no happy outcome of their love, but he clung to a glimmering hope for them both.

An hour later, when he trudged homeward, thoughts of Al and Ruby magnified. It was youth that suffered most acutely. Age had philosophy and resignation. Al was in the throes of sweet, wild passion, fiercer for its immaturity. He would be constant, too. Ruby, considered apart from her bewildering presence, was not much good. She would fail Al and, failing, save him from ruin, if not heartbreak. Yet she, too, had infinite capacity for pain. Poor pretty little moth. Yet she seemed more than a weak, fluttering moth—just what, Jim could not define. But they were both facing an illusion as tragic, if not so beautiful, as Amber's mirage.

Jim felt tired when he reached his shack and was glad to sink upon the porch. The excitement and rushing around during the day had worn upon him. He bared his head to the cold, pine-scented wind. The pines were roaring. The pale peaks stood up into the dark blue, star-studded sky. To the south opened the impenetrable gloom of the desert. A voiceless call seemed to come up out of the vast windy space, and that night it made him wakeful.

But he was up at dawn, and, when it was light enough to see, he went out to hunt up his burros. They never strayed far. With the familiar task at hand again there returned the nameless pleasurable sensations of the trail. High up on the slope he found the four burros, sleek and fat and lazy, and, when he drove them, the first time for months, he had strange, dark, boding appreciation of the brevity of life. That succumbed to the exhilaration of the near approach of the solemn days and silent nights on the desert. In a few hours he would be headed down the road.

The supplies he had ordered came promptly after breakfast, and Jim was packing when Al bounded in from the porch, so marvelous in his ecstasy of flamboyant youth that Jim's heart almost failed him.

"Howdy, son," he managed to get out. And then: "I see you come light in heart as well as in pack."

"Old-timer, I could fly this mornin'!" exclaimed Al fervidly.

"Uhn-huh. Ruby must have sprouted wings on you last night," ventured Jim.

"Gosh, she was sweet. I'm ashamed to death of the things I felt an' thought. We said good bye nine hundred times . . . an' I sure hope it was enough."

"Wal, she'll be over before we leave, you can bet on that."

"Aw, no. I stayed late last night . . . gosh, it was late. Mother waited up for me. Jim, old-timer, that red-headed kid was hangin' on to me at one o'clock this mornin'." Al delivered that amazing statement with a vast elation.

"You ought to have spanked her."

"Spank Ruby? Gosh! It would be like startin' an avalanche or somethin'. Now, Jim, you start me packin', an' you'll think an avalanche hit this shack."

Jim did not require many moments to grasp that Al would be a helpful comrade. He was, indeed, no stranger to packing. But they had just gotten fairly well started when Ruby entered like an apparition in distress. She wore her white Sunday dress and looked lovely, despite her woeful face and tearful eyes.

"Aw . . . now Ruby," ejaculated Al, overwhelmed.

"Oh, Al!" she wailed, and, throwing her arms around his

23

neck, she buried her face on his breast. "I didn't know I loved you so . . . or I'd been different."

Jim turned his back on them and packed as hurriedly and noisily as possible. But they had forgotten his very existence. And presently he proceeded with his work almost as if these young firebrands were not present. But they were there, dynamic, breath-arresting with the significance of their words and actions. Jim was glad. Al would have this poignant parting to remember. He sensed, and presently saw, a remorse in Ruby. What had she done? Or did her woman's intuition read a future alien to her hopes and longings? Perhaps, like Al, she lived only in the pangs of the hour.

Nevertheless, in time he wooed her out of her inconsistent mood and kissed away her tears and by some magic not in the old prospector's ken restored her smiles. She was adorable then. The Ruby that Jim had seen did not obtrude here. She entered into Al's thrilling expectancy, helped with the packing, although she took occasion now and then to peck at Al's cheek with her cherry lips, and asked a hundred questions.

"You'll fetch me a bucketful of gold?"

"I sure will, sweetheart," promised Al with fire and pride.

"A whole bucketful, like that bucket I have to lug full of water from the spring. Al, how much would a bucketful of gold buy?"

"I haven't any idea," returned Al, bewildered at the enchanting prospect. The light in his eyes, as it shone upon her, hurt the old prospector so sharply that he turned away. "Hey, old-timer, what could I buy Ruby with a bucketful of gold?"

"Wal, a heap of things an' that's no lie," replied Jim profoundly. "A house an' lot in town, or a ranch. Hosses, cattle, a wagonload of pretty clothes, an' then have some left for trinkets, not to forget a diamond ring."

Ruby screamed her rapture and swung around Al's neck.

It went on this way until at last the burros were packed and ready. Jim took up his canteen and the long walking stick, and shut the door of the shack with a strange finality.

"Son, I'll go on ahead," he said thickly. "You can catch up. But don't let me get out of sight down the road. Ruby, you have my blessin' an' my prayers. Good bye."

She kissed him, although still clinging to Al, but she could not speak.

"Get up, you burros!" called Jim, and he drove them down the road.

After a while he looked back. The young couple had disappeared and were very likely in the shack, saying good bye all over again. Jim strode on for half a mile before he turned once more. Ruby's white form gleamed on the little porch. Al had started. He was running and looking back. Jim found himself the victim of unaccountable emotions, one of which seemed a mingling of remorse and reproach. Would it have been possible to have done better by Al? He did not see how. After a while he gained confidence again, although the complexity of the situation did not clear. All might yet be well for Al, and Ruby, too, if the goddess who guarded the treasure of gold in the desert smiled quickly.

At the turn of the road Al caught up, panting from his run. "Gosh, but . . . that was . . . tough!"

He did not glance back, and neither did Jim. Soon they turned a bend between the foothills. The sun was still high enough to shed warmth, although the air was cooling. They were leaving the mountains and descending into the desert, glimpses of which could be seen through the passes. Piñons and cedars took the place of pines, and the sage and bleached grama grass thickened.

Al regained his breath and kept pace with Jim, but he did not have anything to say.

Jim wanted to reach Cedar Tanks before dark, a campsite that was well situated for the initiative, for it regulated succeeding stops just about right. This first water was down on the flat still some four or five miles distant. Jim found a spring in his stride that had been missing for months. He was on the heels of the burros, occasionally giving one a slap.

The last foothill, rather more of a mound than a hill, was bare of cedars and had a lone piñon on top, and the sides were flush with a weed that took on a tinge of pink. When this obstruction had been rounded, the desert lay below.

No doubt Al had seen it before from that vantage point, but never with the significance of this moment, which halted him stockstill.

The sun was setting red and gold over the western confines, where the lights were brilliant. Just below the travelers there were flats of grass, and belts of cedars, and, farther on, bare plains of rock, all in the ruddy shadow. Leagues away buttes and mesas stood up, sunset-flushed, and, between them and farther on, wild, broken outlines of desert showed darkly purple. A bold and open space it was, not yet forbidding, but with a hint of obscure and unknown limits.

One long gaze filled Jim Crawford with sustaining strength. His eye swept like that of an eagle. This was a possession of his soul, and whatever it was that had clamped him in perplexity and doubt faded away.

It was dark when they reached Cedar Tanks, which consisted of a water hole at the head of a rocky ravine. Here Al found his tongue. The strain of parting gave precedence to the actuality of adventure. While they unpacked the burros, he volleyed questions, which Jim answered when it was possible. He remembered the stops all the way across the border. Turkey Creek was the next, then Blackstone, then Green Water, Dry Camp, Greasewood, and on to Coyote Wells,

Papago Springs, Mesquite, and then a nameless trail that had as its objective the volcanic peak of Pinacate.

Al packed up water and wood, and built a fire while Jim prepared their first meal, a somewhat elaborate one, he said, to celebrate the start of their expedition. Not in many years had Jim Crawford had a companion in camp. He had been a lone prospector, but he found this change a pleasure. He would not have to talk to the burros or himself. After all, the start had been auspicious.

"Jim, have you ever been to Pinacate?" asked Al.

"Yes. It's an infernal region in midsummer. But I've never been to the place we're headin' for."

"An' where's that?"

"Wal, I know an' I don't know. I call it Three Round Hills. They lay somewhere in from the Gulf of California, a couple of hundred miles below the mouth of the Colorado. It's in Sonora. We get through Yaqui country an' then right into the land of the Seris."

"An' who are the Seris?"

"Wal, they're about the lowest order of humans I know anythin' about. A disappearin' Indian tribe. Cannibals, accordin' to some prospectors I've met. They live in the Gulf durin' the dry season. But when it rains an' the water holes are full, they range far up an' down the coast an' inland. So we've got to dodge them."

"Gosh! You didn't tell mother or Ruby that," remarked Al.

"No, I didn't. An' I reckon I haven't told you a great deal yet."

"Then there's gold in this Seri country," asserted Al, thrilled.

"There sure is. All over Sonora for that matter. But somewhere close under Three Round Hills a wash starts an' runs six miles or so down to the Gulf. I met a prospector who dry-panned gold all along this wash. So rich, he never tried to find the lead from which the gold came. An' he never dug down. Gold settles, you know. He was afraid the Seris would locate him an' poison his water hole. So he didn't stay in long, an' after that he couldn't find the Three Round Hills again."

"An' you're goin' to find them?"

"Reckon we are, son. I feel it in my bones. I believe I can locate them from Pinacate. I brought a powerful field glass, somethin' I never had with me before. If I can locate them, we'll travel across country from Pinacate, instead of workin' down to the Gulf. That would take weeks. We'd have to travel at night along the beach, at low tide, so the water would wash out our tracks. An' then we couldn't find those hills from the shore. I've been savin' this trip for ten years, Al."

"Gosh! An' where does Amber's mirage come in?" went on Al, who had forgotten his supper for the moment.

"Wal, it won't come in at all unless we see it."

"Who was Amber, anyhow?"

"I don't know, except he was a prospector like myself. Queer character. I always wondered if he was right in his mind. But he knew all about the desert."

"Jim, what was the difference between his mirage an' any other?"

"Son, did you ever see a mirage?" asked Jim.

"Sure. Lots of them. All alike, though. Just sheets of blue water on flat ground. Pretty, an' sort of wonderful."

"Wal, you really never saw a mirage, such as I have in mind. The great an' rare mirages are in the sky. Not on the ground. An' mostly they're upside down."

"Jim, I never heard of such a thing."

"Wal, it's true. I've seen some. Beautiful lakes an' white cities. An' once I saw a full-rigged ship."

"No!" exclaimed Al incredulously.

"Sure did. An' they were sights to behold."

"Gosh! Come, old-timer, tell me now about Amber's mirage!" cried the young man impetuously, as if lured on against his will.

The old prospector laid aside his cup, as if likewise impelled, and, wiping his beard, he bent solemn gaze on the young man, and told his story.

Al stared. His square jaw dropped a little, and his eyes reflected the opal lights of the cedar fire.

"An' Amber died after seein' that mirage!" gasped Al.

"Yes, son. There's two men livin' besides me who heard him tell about it an' who saw him die."

"But, old-timer," expostulated Al, sweeping his hand through his yellow locks, "all that might have been his imagination. What's a mirage but an illusion?"

"Sure. Perhaps it's more of a lyin' trick of the mind than a sight. But the strange fact, an' the hard one to get around, is that soon after Amber's death a great gold strike was made there. Right on the spot!"

"Jim, you old prospectors must get superstitious," returned Al.

"Reckon so. But there's no explainin' or understandin' what comes to a man from years on the desert."

"If that's true of the desert, it's true of the mountains, or any other place," argued Al.

"No. The desert is like the earth in the beginnin'," replied the old prospector sagely. "After a while it takes a man back to what he was when he first evolved from some lower organism. He gets closer to the origin of life an' the end of life."

"Gosh, old-timer, you're too deep for me," said Al with a laugh. "But if it's all the same to you, I'd just as lief you didn't see Amber's mirage this trip."

It was June, and Jim Crawford had been lost in the desert for more than a week. At first he had endeavored to conceal the fact from his young companion, but Al had evidently known from the hour of the calamity.

One morning from the black slope of desolate Pinacate the old prospector had located the dim blue Gulf, and the mountain, San Pedro del Martir, and then, away to the southward, three round hills. He had grown tremendously excited, and nothing could have held him back. These colorful hills seemed far away to the younger man, who ventured a suggestion that it might be wise to make for the cool altitudes instead of taking a risk of being caught in that dark and terrific empire of the sun. Even now at midday the naked hand could not bear contact with the hot rocks.

They went on down into the labyrinth of black craters and red cañons, and across fields of cactus, ablaze with their varied and vivid blossoms. The palo verde shone gold in the sun, the ocotillo scarlet, and the dead palo christi like soft clouds of blue smoke in the glaring sand washes. The magnificent luxuriance of the desert growths deceived the eye, but at every end of a maze of verdure there loomed the appalling desolation and decay of the rock fastnesses of the earth.

From time to time the gold seekers caught a glimpse of the three round hills that began to partake of the deceitfulness of desert distance. They grew no closer apparently, but higher, larger, changing as if by magic into mountains. These glimpses spurred Crawford on, and the young prospector, knowing that they were lost, grew indifferent to the peril and gave himself fully to the adventure.

They had been marvelously fortunate about locating water holes. Crawford had all the desert rat's keenness of sight and the judgment of experience. Added to this was the fact that one of his burros, Jenester, could scent water at incredible distances. But one night they had to make dry camp. The next day was hot. It took all of it to find water. And that day Three Round Hills, as they had come to call them, disappeared as if the desert had swallowed them. Cool, sweet desert dawn, with a menacing red in the east, found the adventurers doubly lost, for now they did not even have a landmark to strive for. All points of the compass appeared about the same—barren mountains, dark cones, stark and naked shining ridges, blue ranges in the distance.

But Crawford pushed on south, more bowed every day, and lame. The burros became troublesome to drive. Jenester wanted to turn back, and the others were dominated by her instinct. Crawford, however, was ruthless and unquenchable. Al watched him, no longer with blind faith, but with the perturbation of one who saw a man guided by some sixth sense.

Nevertheless, soon he changed their order of travel, in that they slept in the daytime and went on at night. The early dawns, soft and gray and exquisite, the glorious burst of sunrise, seemed to hold the younger man enthralled, as did the gorgeous sunsets, and the marvelous creeping twilights. As for the other hours, he slept in the shade of an ironwood tree, bathed in sweat and tortured by nightmares, or he stalked silently after the implacable prospector.

They talked but little. Once Crawford asked how many days were left in June, and Al replied that he guessed about half.

"August is the hot month. We can still get out," said the prospector, rolling the pebble in his mouth. And by that he probably meant they could find gold and still escape from the fiery furnace of the desert. But he had ceased to pan sand in the washes or pick at the rocks.

The days multiplied. But try as Crawford might he could not drive the burros in a straight line. Jenester edged away to the east, which fact was not manifest until daylight.

Another dry camp, with the last of the water in their canteens used up, brought the wanderers to extremity. Crawford had pitted his judgment against the instinct of Jenester, and catastrophe faced them.

Darkness brought relief from the sun, if not from overwhelming dread. The moon came up from behind black hills, and the desert became a silvered chaos, silent as death, unreal and enchanting in its beauty.

This night Crawford gave Jenester her head, and with ears up she led to the east. The others followed eagerly. They went so fast that the men had to exert themselves to keep up. At midnight Al was lending a hand to the older man, and, when dawn broke, the young man was half supporting the old prospector. But sight of a jack rabbit and the sound of a mocking bird in melodious song saved him from collapse. Where these living creatures were, it could not be far to water.

Crawford sank less weightily upon Al's strong arm. They climbed, trailing the tracks through the aisles between the cactus thickets, around the corners of cliffs, up a slow rising ridge above the top of which three round peaks peeped, and rose, and loomed. Crawford pointed with a shaking hand and cried out unintelligibly. His spirit was greater than his strength; it was Al's sturdy arm that gained the summit for him.

"Look, old-timer," panted Al hoarsely.

Three symmetrical mountains, singular in their sameness of size and contour and magnifying all the mystery and glory of reflected sunrise, dominated a wild and majestic reach of desert. But the exceeding surprise of this sudden and totally unexpected discovery of the three peaks that had lured and betrayed the prospectors instantly gave way to an infinitely more beautiful sensation—the murmur of running water. A little below them ran a swift, shallow stream.

Crawford staggered to the shade of a shelving rock and fell with a groan that was not all thanksgiving. Al, with a thick whoop, raced down the gentle declivity.

The water was cold and sweet. It flowed out of granite or lava somewhere not far away. Al filled his canteen and hurried back to his comrade, who lay with closed eyes and pallid, moist face.

"Sit up, Jim. Here's water, an' it's good," said Al, kneeling. But he had to lift Jim's head and hold the canteen to his lips. After a long drink the old prospector smiled wanly.

"Reckon . . . we didn't . . . find it any . . . too soon," he said in a weak, but clear, voice. "Another day would have cooked us."

"Old-timer, we're all right now, thanks to Jenester," replied Al heartily. "Even if we are lost."

"We're not lost now, son. We've found our Three Round Hills."

"Is that so? Well, it's sure great to know. But if my eyes aren't deceivin' me, they're sure darned big for hills," rejoined Al, gazing up at the three peaks.

"Make camp here . . . we'll rest," said Crawford.

"You take it easy, Jim. I'll unpack."

The old prospector nodded with the reluctant air of a man who had no alternative.

By stretching a tarpaulin from the shelving rock where Crawford reclined, Al made an admirable shelter. He unrolled his comrade's bed and helped him on it. Then he unpacked utensils and some food supplies, whistling at his work. The whole world bore a changed aspect. What a miracle water could perform!

He built up a stone fireplace, and then, axe on his shoulder, he sallied down in search for wood.

Late in the afternoon, Al discovered his companion wide awake, lying with head propped high.

"Gee, I feel like I'd been beaten!" exclaimed Al. He was wet and hot. "Howdy, Old Rainbow Chaser. Are you hungry?"

"Reckon I am," replied Crawford.

"Gosh, I am too. I'll rustle a meal *pronto*. Whew! Strikes me it's warm here."

"Al, looks like the hot weather is comin' early," rejoined Crawford seriously.

"Comin'? Say, I think it's been with us for days."

"Wal, what I meant was hot."

"Jim, you're a queer one. What's the difference between hot an' hot?"

"Son, when it's hot you can't travel."

Al stared at his old friend. What was he driving at? On the moment the idea of travel apparently refused to stay before Al's consciousness. But a sober cast fell upon his countenance. Without more ado he got up and busied himself around the fireplace.

When the meal was ready, he spread it on a canvas beside Crawford's bed. The old man could not sit up far, and he had to be waited upon, but there was nothing wrong with his appetite. This pleased Al and reacted cheerfully upon him. While they were eating, the burro Jenester approached, her bell tinkling.

"I'll be darned. There's Jen. She's sure well trained," said Al.

"I reckon. But if you'd lived with burros on the desert as long as I have, you'd see more in it."

"Aw, she's only lookin' for some tin cans to lick," replied Al.

Nevertheless, the covert significance Crawford attached to the act of the burro seemed not to be lost upon Al. While doing the camp chores he no longer whistled. The sun grew dusky red and when it sank behind the mountains, it was as if a furnace door had been closed. Presently with the shadows a cool air came across the desert. Then twilight fell. Silence and loneliness seemed accentuated.

The old prospector lay propped up, his bright eyes upon the peaks. Al sat with his back to the rock, gazing out to see the moon come up over the weird formation of desert.

"Jim," said Al suddenly, as if a limit had been passed. "We spent weeks gettin' to your three old hills. Now what're we goin' to do that we are here?"

"Son, we used up our precious time," replied Crawford sadly. "We got lost. We're lucky to be alive."

"Sure, I'm thankful. But I'm hopin' you'll be up tomorrow, so we can look around."

If Crawford nursed a like hope, he did not voice it, which omission drew a long, steady look from the younger man. In the gloaming, however, he could not have gleaned much from his observation.

"Old-timer, I hope, too, that you had more in mind than Amber's mirage when you headed for these triplet hills."

If Al expected his sole reproach to stir Crawford, he reckoned without his host, for the old prospector vouchsafed no word on that score. Al's attempt to foster conversation, to break the oppressive silence, resulted in failure. Crawford was brooding, aloof.

Another day dawned and with it unrest.

After breakfast Crawford called his young companion to his bedside.

"Set down and let's talk," he said.

"Sure, an' I'll be darn' glad to," returned Al cheerfully, although his scrutiny of his friend's face noted a subtle change.

"Son, you've a lot on your mind," began Jim with a

fleeting smile that was like a light on the dark, worn face.

"Uhn-huh, I just found it out," replied Al soberly.

"Worried about bein' lost?"

"Sure. An' a hundred other things."

"Ruby, for one?"

"Well, no, I can't say that. Ruby seems sort of far off . . . an' these close things are botherin' me."

"Wal, we'll dispose of them one at a time. First, then, about bein' lost. We are an' we aren't."

"I don't savvy, old-timer."

"Listen . . . I know where we are now, though I've never been anyways near here. You recall the prospector who told me about these Three Round Hills? Wal, he seen them from a ridge top down near the Gulf. He sure described them to a tee. An' I reckon now he wasn't ten miles from them. The wash he dry-panned so much gold from is almost certainly this one we're on. Water is scarce down here. An' he said water ran down that wash in the flood season. So I reckon we're now less than ten miles from the Gulf. This stream peters out, of course, in the sand below here somewhere. Probably halfway down, I reckon."

"Uhn-huh. An' what of all this?" queried Al suspiciously.

"Wal, a fellow could mosey on down, stoppin' in likely places to shake a pan of gold, an' in a few days reach the Gulf with at least a couple thousand dollars' worth. Then he'd have, I reckon, about six days' travel along the Gulf, bein' careful to go only by night an' at low tide, to the mouth of the Colorado. Then Yuma, where he could cash his gold dust. An' then if he happened to live in Arizona, he could get home *pronto* by stage."

"Sure would be wonderful for that particular fellow," returned Al, almost with sarcasm. "Funny, old-timer, now we're sittin' right under these amazin' Three Rounded Hills, that we don't give a damn much about the gold diggin's they're supposed to mark?"

"Not funny, son," reproved the grave old prospector, "but sure passin' strange. Gold makes men mad, usually. Though I could never see that I was, myself. If we'd only had good luck."

"To my notion we're most darned lucky," declared Al vehemently.

"No. If that were so, we'd've got here six weeks ago, an' I wouldn't be on my back. We'd have had time to fill some sacks an' then get out before the hot weather came."

"Oh, I see, the hot weather."

"It takes a while to heat up this old desert. Then after a while the rock an' sand hold the heat over an' every day grows hotter, until it's a torrid blastin' hell, an' white men don't dare exert themselves."

"Uhn-huh. Then I'd say we haven't many days to waste," said Al significantly.

"*You* haven't, son," replied the other gently.

"Me!"

"Yes, you, Al."

"I don't get your hunch, old-timer. You strike me queer lately."

"Wal, even if I do, I've a clear mind now, an' you may be grateful for it someday. It may have been my dream of gold that made me drag you into this hell hole, but I've got intelligence now to get you out."

"Me! What about yourself?" demanded Al sharply.

"Too late, Al. I will never get out."

The younger man rose with passionate gesture and bent eyes of blue fire down upon his reclining comrade.

"So that's it, old-timer," he asserted fiercely, clenching his fist.

"What's it, son?" queried Crawford.

"You're knocked out an' need days to rest up. But you don't want me to risk waitin', so you'd send me on ahead."

"Al, I meant to lie to you an' tell you that. But I can't do it, now I face you."

"What you mean?" flashed Al suddenly, dropping back on his knees.

"Wal, son, I mean I couldn't follow you out."

"Why couldn't you?"

"Because the rest up I'm to do here will be forever," replied Crawford.

"Jim, you're . . . talkin' queer again," faltered Al, plucking at his friend.

"No, son. I overreached my strength. My body was not up to my spirit. I cracked my heart . . . an' now, Al, pretty soon I'm goin' to die."

"Aw, my God, Jim, you're only out of your mind!" cried Al.

The old prospector shook his shaggy head. He scarcely needed to deny Al's poignant assertion. "Listen," he went on, "you put water beside me here. Then pack Jenester an' one other burro. Pack light. But take both canteens. Start tonight an' keep in the streambed. In the mornin' . . . early . . . pan some gold. But don't let the madness seize on you. It might. That yellow stuff has awful power over men. An' remember when you reach the Gulf to travel at low tide after dark."

"Jim, I couldn't leave you," rejoined Al mournfully, shaking his head.

"But you must. It's your only chance. I'm a tough old bird, an' I may live for days."

"I won't do it, old-timer," returned Al, his voice gaining.

"Son, you'll make my last days ones of grief an' regret."

"Jim, you wouldn't leave me," said Al stubbornly.

"That would be different. You have everythin' to live for, an' I have nothin'."

"I don't care. I won't . . . I can't do it."

"There's your mother to think of."

"She'd be the last to want me to desert my friend."

"An' Ruby. You mustn't forget that little red-headed darlin'."

Al dropped his face into his hands and groaned.

"Perhaps I misjudged Ruby. She really loves you. An' you can't risk losin' her."

"Shut up, Jim!"

"Al, if you don't go now, soon it'll be too late. I won't last long. Then you'll be stuck here. You couldn't stand the torrid months to come. You'll go mad from heat an' loneliness. And if you did survive them an' started out in the rainy season, you'd be killed by the Seris."

"I'll stick," rasped out Al, the big drops of sweat standing on his pallid brow.

"Ruby loves you, but she'll never wait that long," declared Crawford, ruthless in his intent.

Al's gesture was one of supplication.

"Ruby won't wait even as long as she promised," went on Crawford inexorably. "That Joe Raston will get 'round her. He'll persuade her you're lost. An' then he'll marry her."

"Aw, Ruby will wait," rejoined Al, swallowing hard.

"Not very long. She's weak an' vain. She needs you to bring out the good in her. Joe Raston or some other flash cowboy will work on that, if you don't hurry home."

"You're lyin, old-timer," replied Al huskily.

"I saw Raston gettin' her kisses," said Crawford. "That very day before we left."

"Honest, Jim?" whispered Al.

"I give the word of a dyin' man."

Al leaned against the rock and wrestled with his demon. Presently he turned again, haggard and wet of face. "All right," he said. "I always was afraid. But we weren't really engaged till that Saturday night."

"She can't be true to you unless you're there to hold her. Go home now, Al."

"No. I'll stand by you, an' I'll trust Ruby."

"Go, Al. I'm beggin' you."

"No."

"For your mother's sake."

"No!"

"Then for Ruby's. An' for those kisses you'll never . . . never get . . . unless you go . . . now!" shouted Crawford as, spent with passion, he sank back on his pillow.

"No!" yelled Al ringingly, and strode away down into the desert.

At length he came to a wide-spreading palo verde where the shade was dense and had a golden tinge. Half the yellow blossoms of this luxuriant tree lay on the ground, and it was that color rather than the shade that had halted Al. He cast himself down here, sure, indeed, of a mocking loneliness. And in the agony of that hour, when he fought to be true to his passionate denial of Crawford's entreaty, he acted like a man overwhelmed by solitude and catastrophe, yet laboring to victory under the eye of God. It was well, indeed, that the old prospector, who had brought him to this sad pass, could not likewise see him in his extremity. And what would it have meant to the wayward girl, whom he was losing in that bitter hour, to see him ascend the heights?

When it was over, he rose, a man where he had been a boy, and retraced his steps to camp. The sun appeared to burn a hole through his hat. He found Crawford asleep, or at least he lay with closed eyes, a tranquility new to his face transforming it. Al had the first instance of his reward, outside of his conscience.

That very day the hot weather Crawford had predicted set in with a vengeance. Al, awaking out of a torpid slumber, sweltered in his wet clothes. And Al began his watchful vigil. That day dispelled any hope, if one had really existed, of his old friend recovering. Crawford drank water often, but he wanted no more food. Al himself found hunger mitigating.

"Al," said Crawford, breaking his silence at sunset, "you're stuck here . . . till the rains come again."

"Looks like it, old-timer," replied Al cheerfully. "Perhaps that's just as well. Don't you worry."

"*¿Quién sabe?*" replied the prospector, as if he pierced the veil of the future.

At night they conversed more freely, as the effort cost less, but neither again mentioned gold nor Ruby Low. The oppression of heat was on their minds. Crawford had before given stock of his desert wisdom, but he repeated it. Where he had been violently solicitous for Al to go, now he advised against it.

The days passed, wonderful in spite of their terror. And the nights were a relief from them. Al did not leave the old prospector's side except when absolutely necessary. And as Jim imperceptibly faded away, Al made these times more and more infrequent.

One afternoon upon awakening late, Al became at once aware of a change in the sky. Clouds were rare in this section during the hot dry season, yet the sky appeared obscured by pale, green-yellow, mushrooming clouds through which the sun burned a fierce magenta hue.

Al rubbed his eyes, and watched, as had become his habit. A hard hot wind that had blown like a blast from a furnace earlier in the day had gone down with the sinking sun. The

41

yellow, rolling canopy was dust and the green tinge a reflection cast by desert foliage.

"What you make of that sky, old-timer?" asked Al, turning to his companion. But Crawford, who was usually awake at this hour and gazing through the wide opening to the desert, did not make any response. Al bent quickly, as had become his wont lately, to scrutinize the mask-like face.

Getting up, Al set about his few tasks. But the lure of the sky made him desist from camp work and set him out to drive up the burros.

Meanwhile, the singular atmospheric conditions had augmented. The sun, now duskily gold, set behind Three Round Hills. And the canopy of dust, or whatever it was, had begun to lift, so that it left a band of clear dark air along the desert floor, a transparent medium like that visible after a flash of lightning.

The phenomenon was so marvelous and new that Al suffered a break in his idle attention. This stirred his consciousness to awe and conjecture as had no other desert aspect he had watched. Presently he thought to ask the old prospector what caused it and what it signified. To this end he hurried back to camp.

Crawford leaned far forward from his bed, his spare frame strung like a whipcord, his long lean bare arm outstretched. He pointed to the west with quivering hand.

Al wheeled in consternation, and he called in alarm: "Hold on, old-timer."

"Look!" cried Crawford exultantly.

"What do you see, Jim?"

"Amber's mirage!"

Al flashed his gaze from the prospector's transfigured countenance out across the desert to see weird rock and grotesque cacti exquisitely magnified in the trailing veil of luminous gold.

"Jim, it's only the afterglow of sunset," cried Al, as if to try to convince himself.

The old prospector had fallen back on the bed. Al rushed to kneel beside him.

"Oh, God! He's dead! An' I'm left alone!"

Al crouched there a moment, stricken by anguish. To be prepared for calamity was not enduring it. The sudden sense of his terrific loneliness beat him down like a mace. Presently when the salt blindness passed from his sight, he observed that Jim had died with his eyes wide open.

He closed Jim's eyelids, to have them fly open again. Al essayed a gentle force, with like result. Horrified, he shut the pale lids down hard. But they popped up.

"Aw!" he exclaimed, breathing hard.

Al had never seen a dead man, much less a beloved friend, who even in death persisted in a ghastly counterfeit of life. Suddenly Al saw strange shadows in the staring eyes. He bent lower. Did he imagine a perfect reflection of the luminous golden effulgence in the sky, with its drifting magnifying veil? Or were there really images there? He wiped the dimness from his own sight. He was like a man whom shock had gravely afflicted. There was something stamped in Jim's eyes. Perhaps the mirage engraved upon his soul? Or the sensitive iris mirroring, in its last functioning moment, the golden glow of a rare sunset. Al trembled in his uncertainty.

Then he recalled the story of Amber's mirage. And he sustained another shock. According to Jim the miner Amber had died raving about a mirage of gold, with wide-open eyes in which flamed a proof of his illusion and which would not stay shut.

"It's only the mind," muttered Al. A monstrous trick of the imagination, natural to those mad prospectors, a lie as false as any mirage itself. But there shone that beautiful light

43

in Crawford's sightless eyes. And the sky had shaded over. The gold had vanished. The mysterious veil might never have transformed the desert. Al covered the old prospector's face with a blanket.

That night Al Shade kept reverent vigil beside the body of his departed friend. The desert seemed a sepulcher.

With the retreat of the somber shadows came a necessity for practical tasks. He ate a meager breakfast. Then he wrapped Jim in his blankets and tarpaulin, and bound them securely. Whereupon he stalked forth to find a grave.

It would never do to bury Jim in the sand. Of all the desert mediums, sand was the most treacherous. It would blow away, and so he hunted for a niche in the rocks. He found many, some too large and others too small. At last under a cliff he had overlooked he discovered a deep depression, clean and dry, as fine a last resting place as any man could desire. And it would be sweet to the old prospector. It was sheltered from rain and flying sand, yet it looked out upon the desert. If properly filled and sealed it would last there as long as the rocks.

He carried Jim—now how light a burden!—and tenderly deposited him in the hole. Then Al tried to remember a prayer, but as he could not, he made one up.

"To the rocks you loved, old-timer. May God save your soul."

It was going to take considerable time to fill that deep grave. Small stones, such as he could lift, were remarkably scarce, considering it was a region of stone. It would be necessary to fill the grave full or the scavengers of the desert would dig out poor Jim and strew his bones over the sands.

Al went farther afield in search of rocks. Now he would gather a sack of small ones, and then he would stagger back under burden of a heavy one. He performed Herculean labors.

The time came when his task was almost done. Only a few more heavy stones. But where to find them? He had sacked the desert of it loose fragments.

While allaying his thirst at the stream he espied the dull yellow gleam of a rock out in a little pool, rather deep.

Al waded out to secure it. His feet sank in the sand, and, as the water was knee-deep, he had to bend to get the stone. It lifted easily enough, until he heaved it out of the water. Then it felt like lead. All this toil in the hot sun had weakened him or else the stone, which was not large, had exceeding weight; in fact, it was so burdensome that Al floundered with it and at the shore would have fallen if he had not let it drop.

Bare flat rock edged on the stream there, and Al's stone, as it struck, gave forth a curious ring. He gave it a kick with his wet boot, shaking off some of the sand that adhered to it. Dull yellow and white stripes appeared on this queer-looking stone Al had carried out of the stream.

Then he scraped his hob-nailed boot hard on the surface. Bright thread caught the sunlight. Frantically he crawled into the stream and grasped up handfuls of wet sand. He spread them to the sun, gazed with piercing eyes. Specks of gold! They were as many as the grains of sand. Al tore up the bank, his fists tight on his precious discovery.

"Jim! Jim!" he shouted, panting with rapture. "Look a-here! A strike! An' old Three Rounded Hills . . . is her name!" He got no response to his wild outcry. "Jim!"

Silence and loneliness emanated from the camp. They struck at Al's heart with reality. An empty space marked where Jim's bed had lain in the shade.

A second Christmas had come and far gone when Al

Shade set foot in Pine again. It was the last of winter and fine weather for that high country. It was an unusual circumstance for Pine not to have a white winter. The mountain tops were shining, snowy domes, and that pure smooth white extended far down into the timber, but it had not yet encroached upon the lower slopes. A bracing cold wind blew out of the west, whipping dust down the main street of Pine.

The weekly stage had but few passengers that day, and Al was one of them. He wore a new suit and overcoat, and he carried a small satchel. His lean, clean-shaven face was almost as dark as an Indian's. He got out to button his coat and turn up the collar. An icy breath of winter struck through him, coincident with a recurrent and thrilling, yet poignant, emotion that had beset him at times on the long journey up from Yuma.

The hour was still a little short of noonday. Al's first act was to hurry into the bank. He approached the teller's window.

"Hardwick, do you remember me?" he asked.

"Can't say I do," replied the teller, after a close scrutiny. "But your face seems familiar."

"I'm Al Shade. You used to cash my check Saturdays, when I worked for the lumber mill."

"Al Shade? Now I know you. But you've changed . . . grown into a man. Say, didn't you leave Pine with an old prospector a couple of years ago?"

"Yes, but it isn't actually that long," replied Al.

"You were reported lost in the desert."

"It was true enough. But I got out. Hardwick, I want to deposit considerable money."

"Glad to hear it," returned the teller heartily. "Come right into Mister Babbitt's office."

Babbitt did not recall Al, or the circumstance of his departure from Pine.

"Mister Babbitt, just lately I drove two burros into Yuma, packed with gold. I made the exchange there at the assay office, and I have the money with me to deposit."

Al emptied the contents of the satchel on the desk before the bank officials and then he stripped from his waist a thick belt, stuffed all around with greenbacks.

"I'm sure glad to get rid of this," he said. "Count it an' give me a bankbook."

"There's a fortune, young man!" the banker exclaimed, his eyes alight. "I congratulate you. You must have made a rich strike."

"It's little enough for what I went through," Al returned coolly.

"You want this to your credit alone?"

"Yes. My partner, Jim Crawford, died. He is buried on the desert."

"Too bad. I remember the old fellow. Shade, you look as if you'd earned this money. I hope you use it wisely."

"Reckon I will," replied Al, with richer note in his voice. "I promised someone I'd fetch back a bucket of gold."

Al left the bank relieved that this necessary precaution had been fulfilled. For many months the possession of gold, and then for days its equivalent in cash, had been a nuisance and a dread. Soon he would need to consider the possession of much gold—Ruby's. The moment was at hand. No word had he heard of her, of mother, of friends. He felt a total stranger in his hometown. His absence seemed to have been endless. He judged what might have happened to them by the age he had been away, and the tragedy that had chained him to the desert. Yet a fugitive hope always had hung to the fringe of his consciousness. And now it beat at him with tremendous hammer strokes.

All at once he heard the hum of the saw at the lumber mill.

47

It cut into him as if it had actually been at his heart. He saw the blue and yellow smoke rising from the huge stack. He passed on, still some distance from the mill, and turned off the main street into the outskirts of town. Nothing had changed. The boardwalk appeared identically as when he had last trod it that fateful Sunday. Soon he passed by the last several cottages and came to the blacksmith's shop. Ben Wiley, the smith, was busy at his forge. The red sparks flew, and the ring of iron came on the cold air.

Al strode on, past the Mexican gardens, out into the country, to the edge of the pines. The white cone-shaped peak pierced the sky. It looked winter up there, and he had a momentary longing for the hot dry desert.

Then he espied the gray cabin where Ruby lived and beyond it the old shack where Jim Crawford had stayed when he was in from a prospecting trip. Al wondered if he had expected these habitations to be gone.

Blue smoke curled up from the cabin chimney. And, as of old, a saddled horse stood hitched on the porch side. It, as well as the rich trappings on saddle and bridle, gave Al a queer familiar pang. He strode up on the porch noisily, hurriedly, as if to give himself courage. Boldly he knocked. But his knees were shaking.

The door opened to disclose a woman. She had the face, the flaming hair of the girl pictured in Al's mind.

"Al!" she screamed in amazed delight, and rushed out. "Alive? We heard you were dead."

"Ruby!" Al cried, his voice hushed. Certain it was that his arms spread wide to envelop her.

"You desert wanderer!" she exclaimed. "How you've grown . . . changed!"

Al laughed with a happy wildness and was about to kiss her when out of the tail of his eye he espied a figure standing in the open doorway. Releasing Ruby, he faced around squarely, confusion added to his rapture.

A sneering man, fastidiously attired in fancy rider's apparel, stood there, with something familiar about him that stung Al.

"Howdy, Shade. I see your hunt for gold hasn't improved your manners," he said mockingly. "But maybe you didn't know you were hugging a married woman."

"Joe Raston!" Al burst out in an agony of recognition.

"Sure . . . the same," replied Raston, his white teeth gleaming. He had the same red face, the same hard blue eyes, with dark puffs under them. His attire now smacked of the city dandy, instead of the cowboy.

Al wheeled to Ruby. "Is it true . . . you . . . you're . . . ?" he queried hoarsely, breaking off.

"Yes, but. . . ."

Raston stepped down off the threshold, almost between them.

"Married, with a girl baby," Raston interrupted. "Another red-headed girl to make trouble. . . ."

"Hush up, Joe. Let me tell him," Ruby cried, recovering from glad surprise to anger.

"My . . . God," choked Al, with horrified stare. Then he turned and ran.

"Wait, Al . . . !" Ruby screamed after him.

But Al ran on, blindly at first, down the clattering boardwalk, and almost into town before he could check his mad flight. Out of breath he slowed down near Ben Wiley's blacksmith shop. Terror at the thought of being a subject for town gossip and ridicule drove him to swallow his conflicting emotions. What an awful blunder he had made. But had he not expected that very thing? He should have asked questions, have learned something before calling upon Ruby. That sneering devil Raston! Ruby married—a baby girl! Al fought off a deathly sickness, and in sheer desperation turned in to the blacksmith's shop.

"Howdy, Ben," he said, confronting the burly, grizzled giant, who let his hammer fall.

"Jumpin' jack rabbits! It ain't you, Al?" boomed Wiley.

"Sure is, Ben. How are you?"

"Son-of-a-gun, if it ain't Al! Wal, by gum! I am glad to see you," replied the blacksmith, and it was well Al possessed a horny, tough hand. "So that story of you bein' daid on the desert ain't so. You're a healthy-lookin' ghost. An' shore you're a prosperous-lookin' gent."

"Ben, I struck it rich. Jim Crawford took me down into Sonora. We got lost. Jim died, an' afterward I struck gold."

"You don't say! Thet's staggerin' news. Sorry old Jim cashed. He was the salt of the earth."

"Indeed, he was. Ben, I've been down the . . . road," Al said haltingly. "But not home . . . yet. How's my mother?"

"Say, Al, haven't you heerd nothin' all this time?" queried Wiley with concern.

"Not a word."

"Wal, thet's tough. To come home with a stake an' find . . . all changed."

"Ben, I didn't expect anythin' else. Tell me."

"Wal, Al, it's no long story, anyway. After you left, Raston took the farm away from your mother. Mortgage come into his hands through a deal an'. . . ."

"Raston? You mean the cattleman who took over the Bar X an' some of the valley ranches? Not Joe Raston?"

"Joe's father. Thet's the man. Left everythin' to Joe. He's been playin' high jinks here, Al. Owns the lumber mill now an' Halford's store. But nobody has any use for him."

"Go on about . . . Mother," Al returned, fortifying himself.

"Wal, she went to Colorado an' . . . an' died there. Let's see. Must have been in the summer. My wife will know. She read about it in the paper. An' this is the first you've heahed about it, Al?"

"Yes. But I've been afraid," Al replied huskily as he turned away his face.

"It's hard, Al. I'm shore sorry I had to be the one to break it. I reckon you better come to see my wife. She was friendly with your mother."

"Thanks, I will, Ben. An' Ben, can you tell me anythin' about my girl, Ruby Low?"

"That red-head? Wal, I'll be dog-goned! You're in for more bad news, Al."

"Uhn-huh. Come out with it, then."

"Ruby's married."

"Married? Joe Raston?"

"Haw! Haw! Why, Joe Raston wouldn't 'a' married Ruby, as everybody knows. Joe is the high-flier 'round town now. Father left him all his interests."

"But Ben!" Al ejaculated, aghast. "I thought Ruby . . . it must be Joe Raston."

"Wal, like some other folks, an' Ruby herself . . . so they say . . . you figgered wrong. Joe jilted Ruby cold. It went so hard with her thet she up an' married Luke Boyce."

"Luke! Why, he and I went to school together. Luke Boyce! He was a pretty nice boy, if I remember. Younger than me. So it's Luke. An' not Raston."

"Luke's not a bad sort. Used to work for me heah. Things have gone ag'in' him, an' thet's no joke. He was ridin' for the Bar X, an' broke a leg. Raston fired him. After he was able to be about again, he worked heah an' there, at odd jobs. But when winter set in, he was thrown out of work. An' he's hangin' too much around the saloons."

"How long has he been married?"

" 'Most a year. Ruby has a baby."

"Things happen . . . even in a short year," Al rejoined ponderingly. "Well, Ben, good day. Remember me to Missus Wiley. I'll come over some night."

"Do, Al. We'll be plumb glad to see you. An' Ma can tell you all the news."

Returning to town, Al went to the hotel and engaged a room with a fireplace, before which he huddled the rest of the day. When darkness came, he had parted with his mother and the sweet part of the past in which she had figured.

Al had never been given to drink. But now an urge to seek oblivion almost overcame him. It was memory of old Jim Crawford that gave him the final strength to abstain. The sooner he faced the whole fact of his calamity, the sooner he might consider how to meet it. He sensed a vague monstrous obstacle between him and the future. He went out to meet it.

It was in one of the side-street saloons that Al finally encountered Luke Boyce. The recognition was instantaneous on Al's part, but Boyce at first glance failed to see in Al an old schoolmate.

"Howdy, Luke, don't you know me?"

"I don't, but I'll bet you're Al Shade. Everybody's talkin' about you."

They shook hands. Boyce's surprise and pleasure were short-lived, owing, no doubt, to shame at his condition and embarrassment before Ruby Low's old fiancé. Boyce looked like a cowboy long out of a job and verging on the condition of a tramp. He tried to pass off the meeting with a lame remark and to return to his game of pool on the dingy table. But Al would have none of that. "Come on, Luke, let's get out of here. I'm sure glad to meet you, an' I want to talk."

Boyce was not proof against such warmth. He left the saloon with Al, and by the time they arrived at the hotel his constraint had disappeared.

"I reckon you want to talk about Ruby," Boyce queried bluntly.

"Why sure, Luke, but not particular, an' there's no hurry," replied Al frankly. "Naturally I want to hear how things are . . . with my old girl. I want to know a lot else, too."

Boyce laid aside his hat and turned back the collar of his thin coat, and held lean blue hands to the fire. "Let's get it over then," he said with the same bluntness, but devoid of resentment. "I didn't double-cross you with Ruby."

"That never entered my mind, Luke," Al rejoined hastily.

"I was always sweet on Ruby, as you know," went on Boyce. "But I never had a look-in while you an' other fellows were around. When you went away, Ruby quit the boys for a while."

"What?"

"I didn't know it then, Al, but she told me later. After I married her. Ruby didn't go around with anyone for half a year, I guess. You promised you'd be back that Christmas, she said . . . an' she was true to you. But when rumors drifted up from Yuma that you'd been lost on the desert, she took up with Joe Raston again. It didn't last long. Only a few months. Joe wasn't the marryin' kind. He gave Ruby a dirty deal . . . jilted her. That took the starch out of Ruby. I married her in spite of the fact she swore she didn't and couldn't love me. But I loved her. We got along fine, while I was earnin' money. Ruby likes pretty clothes. She was gettin' fond of me. Once she said she liked me better than any beau she ever had, except you. Well, I broke my leg, an' that started us downhill. Joe Raston had me fired. I got well again, but nobody would believe I could ride. An' I had to take odd jobs anywhere. Lately I've been out of work. Then Ruby had a baby, and now I reckon she hates the sight of me. We're poor as dormice. I've borrowed until my old friends dodge a corner when they see me. An' if somethin' doesn't show up this spring, I'll sure lose Ruby an' the baby."

"Somethin' will turn up, Luke," rejoined Al confidently. "Things are never so bad as they seem. Maybe I can help you. Spring will be here before long, an' that's the time to get a job or start somethin'. *¿Quién sabe?* Your luck may change. You might even see Amber's mirage."

"Al, you don't 'pear to have been drinkin'," Boyce said bluntly. "But your talk is plumb good. Sounds like music to me. An' what's Amber's mirage?"

"I never quite satisfied myself about that," Al replied seriously. "Old Jim Crawford used to talk as if Amber's mirage was more than fortune to a man. I took it to be a real mirage or somethin' he imagined. Somethin' close to love an' death . . . somethin' that proved the passion for gold was terrible an' selfish . . . a waste of life, unless the strivin' was for some noble purpose. Anyway, just before Jim died, he saw the mirage. Or he was out of his head an' thought so. But he didn't seem crazy. He looked like the great poet I read about . . . who just before dyin' sat up with wonderful eyes an' said . . . 'More light!' Jim's end was like that."

"Wal!" ejaculated Boyce, deeply stirred. "It shore must have been somethin'. Al, I'll try once more, an' if I can't make a go of it, an' get Ruby back, I'll leave Pine. I've stood a heap, but I couldn't stand to see Raston get Ruby."

"Uhn-huh. So he's after her now . . . since you're married?"

"Sure is. Ruby went back to her mother, an' Raston goes there. Ruby admitted it. But she doesn't trust him."

"Luke, it strikes me you ought to stop Raston."

"How? He's powerful here in Pine. Runs everythin'. If I thrash him, I'll get thrown into jail, where I haven't been yet. What can I do?"

"I'll say a word to him," said Al.

"Shade, am I to understand you . . . you want to be my friend?" Boyce asked incredulously.

"I reckon. What else? But keep your mouth shut about it."

"I think it fine of you," burst out Boyce.

"I've seen Ruby . . . out at her old home. Raston was there. I . . . like a jackass . . . thought he was her husband. But, Luke, I'll stand by you, as you stood by Ruby, an' it's not too late to save her."

Boyce leaped up, radiant, but he could not speak.

"Shake on that. There," added Al.

"Let me get this straight," gasped Boyce.

"Are you in debt?" Al went on imperturbably.

"Yes, an' pretty deep. It was a quarrel over debt that made Ruby leave me. She would run bills, an' I couldn't pay. I tell you, Al, if it wasn't for my hard luck, Ruby would turn out all right."

"How deep are in you in debt, Luke?"

"Somethin' over two hundred," replied Boyce abjectly.

Al laughed. He had long been apart from the struggles and miseries of men. He had no idea of values. He had seen a million dollars in gold in the bed of a stream!

"Come in to see me tomorrow mornin'," Al said. "I want to . . . to lend you the money to pay those debts."

Long after the bewildered Boyce had left, Al sat there watching the fire through dimmed eyes. Then he went out to look for Raston.

The street, the saloons failed to disclose him, but the lobby of the hotel ended his search.

"Raston, I've been lookin' for you," Al said deliberately.

"Yes? About the little joke I had on you?" queried the other maliciously.

"You had no joke on me. My old friend, Luke Boyce, told me you were tryin' to ruin his wife."

"That's his business, not yours," snapped Raston.

"Well, I'm sort of footloose, an' I can make most anythin' my business," went on Al, stepping closer.

"Sure. And now you'll cut me out. You're welcome to the red-head flirt. She'll be easy for you, now you're lousy with gold. I told her so and reminded her. . . ."

Al struck out with all the might of unspent misery and wrath. The blow laid Raston his length upon the lobby floor.

"Hold on," Raston called out.

"Get up, you dog!"

Raston rose shakily, not very much the spectacle of a man. His hand went to a bleeding and puffing lip. "Shade, I had some right to say what I did," he began hurriedly, backing away. Yet he appeared resentful, as if he had been wronged. "I couldn't get Ruby, by hook or crook. She always flirted and let me spend my money on her. But no more. And lately, when I lost patience, she swore there'd never been but one man who could make her disloyal to Boyce. And that man was dead. She meant you, Al Shade."

That staggered Al to an abrupt abandonment of the encounter.

"Raston, you leave Ruby alone now," Al returned passionately, and went his way.

It was afternoon of the next day, somber and still, with storm out in the foothills.

Al, running down the road to catch up with his burros, did not look back, as once he had looked to wave good bye to

Ruby. He had just knocked loudly on the cabin door, thrilling in his cold, sick heart to Ruby's voice: "Come in." But he had needed only the assurance of her presence. Then he had set down a heavy bucket before the door. Ruby's bucketful of gold that he had promised to fetch her from the desert. It was heavier by far than any bucketful of water she had ever lugged so complainingly from the spring. Like a horse freed from a burden he had sped down the road.

A cry pierced his ears—and, as he ran on—again, but fainter. Still he ran, soon crowding his pair of lightly packed burros. As a criminal in flight or a coward at the end of his tether he ran until he turned the bend in the road. Then he strode on, the panting from his breast like hard sobs. Free! The gray hills, the yellow road, the blue haze of desert far on proclaimed it.

Free from that vise-clamp around his heart! The gates of locked, unnatural calm burst at last. It was not so much that he had held in his passion, but that it had been only forming, mounting, damming. He had brooded, planned, talked, while this unknown and terrible choice had taken possession of him.

A storm mourned down from the shrouded peaks and enveloped Al, so black, so furious, that he had to walk beside his burros to keep from losing them.

Al lifted his face to the elements. There was an anguished ecstasy in this kindred spirit, this enveloping and protective storm. It was his gratitude for the return to loneliness. He had escaped from four walls, from streets and houses, from people, from eyes, eyes, eyes—curious, pitying, wondering, ridiculing, hateful eyes that knew his story, yet would never understand. But he was pursued still, down the naked shingle of this winding road, by the tortures he had invited, by the pangs of relinquished love, by the glory of something too great for him to bear.

As he descended toward the desert, he gradually drew out of the storm. Gray space, with a light shining low-down to the west, confronted him. Then Cedar Tanks and night halted him. Habit was stronger than nature. Mechanically he performed the first camp tasks, then sat on a stone, peering into the mocking golden heart of the fire, then crawled like a dog under the cedars, beaten and crushed. Half the night a desert wind wailed the requiem of boyish dreams; half the night he slept. And the dawn broke cold, still, gray.

Al packed and took to the road.

Blackstone, Green Water, Dry Camp, Greasewood—day by day they were reached and passed. Coyote Wells, Papago Springs, Mesquite, and then at last Bitter Seeps, where the seldom-trodden trail headed off the road toward Pinacate.

Bitter Seeps marked another change—the rebellion of physical nature against the havoc of grief. Al Shade lifted his head. There was a ring in his call to his burros. He faced the desert and saw it with clearing eyes. He was entering the empire of the sun. And the desert was abloom with blossoms and sweet with dry wild fragrance.

Slowly the scales of mortal strife fell from Al Shade's eyes. And there came a regurgitation of the dominance of the senses. Far, far behind lay Pine and the past.

Four days' travel brought him to the slope of Pinacate.

Next morning he climbed the black slope to the point where Jim Crawford had made his observation that fatal day long ago. The morning was clear. The heat haze had not come to obscure the wondrous and appalling panorama. Below to the west, seemingly close, lay the blue Gulf, calm and grand, and across it loomed San Pedro del Martir, dim and purple against the sky. But it was the south that held Al Shade's gaze.

The wild desert, like a vivid mosaic, stretched its many

leagues of jagged lava and colored cacti and red stone, down to where three round hills, pale in outline, infinitely strange, appeared to mark its limits.

Only the hard bitter life of that wasteland, only the torment of its heat and thirst, the perils of its labyrinthine confines, only such loneliness and solitude and desolation and death as were manifested there could have brought an exultant, welcoming cry from Al Shade's lips. He would keep lonely vigil by Jim Crawford's grave. He descended to camp, found and packed his burros, and with a trenchant call he drove them south.

There was peace in the desert. The pervading stillness engendered rest in him. He would have liked to dispense with spiritual consciousness, as he had with memory. But it took time for the desert to perform miracles.

At noon he halted to rest the burros in the shade of an ironwood tree on the edge of an elevation. The desert dropped away here. When he gazed out on a level, he encountered sky and mushrooming thunderclouds that were rising above a distant range. It was drowsily warm, and he fell asleep, leaning against the tree. He dreamed of his old friend Jim, and the spell lingered on into his awakening.

Al rubbed his eyes. He could not have slept until approach of sunset, for the sun stood at its zenith. But there appeared to be a clear, dark amber glamour over sand and bush, rock and cactus. Then he gazed straight out from the elevation.

The southern sky had become transfigured by mountains of golden mushrooming clouds. They moved almost imperceptibly, rising, spreading, unfolding. Then they changed until they were no longer clouds. A sharp level line cut across the floor of this golden mass, and under it shone the clear, dark amber desert, weird only in that it had color at noonday.

Above it glimmered a long blue ripple of gentle waves, lapping the line, overcast by golden tinge. Foliage faintly of the same hue bordered shoreline far into the dim verge. And the broad water spread to the marble steps and balustrades and terraces and doors and golden walls of a magnificent city. Empty streets led upward into halls of pearl and chambers of opal and courts of porphyry, all burned through with lucent gold. A lonely city of shining amber! Tiers of walls rose one above the other, towering with a thousand pillared arches and trellises and sculptured images of lifeless gods and wingless eagles, with niche on niche, and window on window of shimmering treasure, all rising to flaming turrets that perished against the pitiless truthful sky.

A mellow drowsy hum of insects seemed to float murmuringly to Al on the dry air. The tinkle of a burro bell further emphasized the silence. Dark veils of heat, like crinkled transparent lace, rose from sand and stone.

Had he really seen the mirage or was that shining city in the clouds the mansion to which the souls of men must climb?

The Kidnapping of Collie Younger

It was Collie Younger who dared the picnic gang to go in swimming. This girl from Texas had been the gayest and the wildest of last June's graduates of Hazelton Normal College, and as on many former occasions her audacity had been infectious. But despite the warm September sun, the water of Cañon Creek would be icy. Frost had long since come to tinge the oaks and aspens of that high Arizona altitude. It was one thing to bask in the golden sunshine and gaze into the amber water, which reflected the red walls, the fringed ledges, the colored sycamore leaves floating down, and quite another to plunge into it.

"You're a lot of dead ones," taunted Collie, with a shake of her bright head. "This picnic is a flop. The boys are playing poker. It's hot down here. Me for a swim!"

"But, Collie, we did not bring any bathing suits," remonstrated Sara Brecken.

"We don't need any."

"You wouldn't. . . ."

"Sure I would . . . if we went up the creek in the shade. But it's nice and sunny here. We can keep something on and dry off *pronto*."

"I'm for it," Helen Bender cried mischievously. "Anything to shock these boys out of their poker game!"

That settled the argument. Sara reluctantly followed her six companions down off the green bench to the huge rocks

61

that lined the shore. Collie was the first to emerge from behind them into the open.

Roddy Brecken, who never had any money to gamble with and no luck besides, sat watching the red-sided trout shining in the crystal water. Espying Collie in her scant attire and slim allurement, he drew up with a start and a sharp breath. He had never seen such an apparition. In town, the couple of times he had encountered her since his return to Hazelton, she had appeared a pretty girl in a crowd of prettier ones. But this was different. Half naked, she was not so small; her form had more roundness than anyone would have guessed; her graceful arms and legs held a warm tint of fading tan; and, as she gingerly stuck a small foot into the water, she leaped up with a shriek and a toss of her shining curls. Then, at the bantering of the girls emerging from behind the rocks, Collie daringly dove into the pool. She bobbed up, splashing and blowing, to call out in a half-strangled voice: "Come . . . on in. . . . Water's . . . great."

Roddy had arisen to make tracks away from there, as soon as he could unrivet his feet. But his retreat was checked by the spectacle of the six girls hurrying over the rocks. It appeared to Roddy that his gaze took in a great deal of uncovered white flesh. The girls made haste to wade in and submerge their charms.

Their squealing, laughing mêlée broke up the poker game. The other six boys came trooping down, headed by Roddy's brother John, upon whose handsome face the expression of amazement was displaced by one of disapproval and annoyance. The other young men did not take the scene amiss.

"I'm a-rarin' to go!" yelled Bruce Jones.

"Let's pile in, fellers, as we are," suggested another.

"Don't be a lot of fools! Not for mine. The sun will soon drop behind the wall."

John Brecken's vigorous opposition to the idea did not deter two of the boys from joining the girls in the water. But the impromptu bathing was obviously destined to a very short duration. John might have spared his peremptory call for his sister Sara to come out. Presently all of them, except Collie, made for the shore, and, if they had looked outrageous before they went in, Roddy wondered what words could be used to describe them now. The boys ran puffing up the rocks. "I'll say . . . it wa . . . was . . . c . . . cold," declared Bruce, making for an isolated place in the sun. The girls, huddling together, slopped out of sight into their retreat. Collie kept swimming and splashing about. Roddy conceived an idea she was doing it to annoy John.

"Collie Younger, you come right out of there!" yelled John. "You'll catch your death."

"Cold water's good for me. Cools me off," replied the girl.

"Yes, and your hair will look fine tonight for the dance."

That clever sally had the desired effect. But Collie did not bother to wade around back of the rocks, like the other girls. She boldly climbed up at the point where she had plunged off.

"You're a sight," declared John, whipping off his coat, and making toward her.

"What for? Sore eyes?"

John's vehement denial was at distinct variance with Roddy's rapt attention. The beauty and the daring of the girl were potent enough to counteract his resentment at her impertinence to John and an underlying disapproval of her lack of modesty.

"Yeah? Well, you don't have to look at me," Collie rejoined flippantly.

"Here. Put this on."

"I don't want your coat."

"Collie! You look . . . like . . . like hell!"

"Jealous, big boy? You would be. I'll bet, if you and I were here alone, you wouldn't register such absurd objection."

"I won't have this," sputtered Brecken.

"*You* won't. Since when were you my boss? Jack, I'm fed up on you. We're not engaged, and even if we were, I'd do as I pleased."

"You bet you would," said John bitterly. "You get a kick out of such indecent display. . . ."

"Who's indecent?" Collie queried hotly. "It's your mind, Jack Brecken. Shut up . . . or I'll drop what I've got on and go in again."

John flung his coat upon her and wheeled in high dudgeon to climb up on the bench, where the boys teased him good-naturedly. Roddy preferred to leave his perch on the rock and saunter up the creek under the trees.

It seemed good to get back to Arizona, to which he had returned only infrequently during the last few years. Cañon Creek had been one of Roddy's haunts as a boy, and the dry smell of pine, the stream rushing here in white wreaths about the mossy rocks, and eddying there in amber pools, where the big trout lay like shadows, brought back memories and dreams that hurt. What days he and John had spent together in these woods. Red squirrels chattered into the still solitude of the forested cañon. He encountered deer tracks in the dust of the trail. What a joy it would be again to take a fall hunt with John. The smoky haze in the glades, the brooding melancholy of the cañon, the plaintive murmur of insects, the intervals of unbroken solemn silence assured Roddy that the hunting season was not many weeks away.

He retraced his steps, sorry to leave the shade of the gray-barked sycamores, reluctant to join the crowd of young people again. The boys were all Arizonians, whom he had always known, but the girls, except Sara, were strangers from beyond Hazelton. Roddy had noted with an unwonted stir of feeling that his bad reputation had in no wise kept them aloof. In fact, it had seemed quite the opposite. The Texas girl, who had made such an exhibition of herself, had cast too many glances in Roddy's direction for him to believe them casual. No doubt she was taking John down the line, and would do the same thing to him if she had the opportunity. He felt sorry for John, who was so obviously in love with her. And to feel sorry for John, to whom he had always looked up, was not a pleasant sensation.

But what eyes that girl had! He had thought they were hazel until he had seen them this day, as she stood bare-headed in the sunlight, and then he decided they were topaz. Their color could not have had anything to do with their tantalizing expression. And he admitted that the rest of her matched her eyes.

Roddy felt ill at ease. He had not wanted to attend this picnic with John, who, however, had insisted until he gave in. Absence and a gradual drifting had not changed his boyhood love for his brother. That, Roddy reflected, had been the only anchor he had known.

When he got back to the others, the sun had gone down behind the fringe of the western rim. Deep shadows showed under the walls. The warm breath moving up the cañon had cooled. Roddy's last glance at the creek took in the green-gold sycamore leaves floating downstream.

The boys were packing baskets and coats to the cars parked some distance away. John, looking somber and with traces of his anger still on his face, stood apart, evidently waiting for Collie. It developed, however, that he was waiting for Roddy. "Collie's riding back with Bruce and Sara," he said. "I'm glad of that, for it'll give me a chance to talk to you. Let's rustle."

Nevertheless, John slowed up as soon as he drew Roddy away from the others. He had something on his mind and apparently found breaching it not so easy.

"Rod, my mind's been simmering ever since you came home," he began presently. "This break of Collie's today brought it to a boil. I told you I was simply nuts over her, didn't I?"

"Yes. But you needn't have told me. Anyone could see that."

"Is that so? Well, she has been playing fast and loose with me. I'm sure Collie cares most for me, else she wouldn't . . . but she plays with the other boys, too, and it's got my goat. I'll simply have to throw a bridle on her. . . . Once my wife, she'd be all right."

"Brother, I reckon what you need on her is a hackamore," Roddy observed with a laugh.

They reached the glade through which the road ran. The cars were leaving. Roddy saw Collie's face flash out of the last one, as she bent a curious glance back at them. On second thought Roddy decided Collie had looked back at him. John might not have been there at all.

"I'll tell the world," admitted John grimly. "I'm at the end of my rope. And if the plan I have fails . . . or if you refuse to do it . . . I'm sunk."

"Me! Refuse?" ejaculated Roddy in amazement. "For Pete's sake, what could *I* do?"

"You can kidnap her, by thunder, and scare her half to death."

For a moment, Roddy stared at his brother, waiting for him to give an indication that he was joking. But John's face remained deadly serious. "Well," John finally remarked impatiently, "did you get what I said?"

"Jack, are you crazy?" Roddy finally stated. "You must

have it bad. Nothing doing!"

"Wait till you hear my proposition," went on John, white and tense. "Listen, Roddy, Dad left all his property to us, fifty-fifty. You hate the store, and you'd never stick there long at a time. I've run the business, improved it, made money. I've given and sent you money every time you asked for it. I didn't begrudge it. I know how you feel about living in town. I've tried to understand you . . . sympathize with you. Some of your scrapes the last two years have been hard for me to swallow and have given you a bad reputation."

"Jack, I haven't been so hot," replied Roddy, dropping his head, ashamed, yet grateful to John for not being harsher.

"Well, I propose to buy you out. Will you sell? It would be better for the business."

"I'd jump at it, Jack."

"Fine. I'll give you five thousand, half down, and my half share in old Middleton's cattle and range. That property has run down. It's not worth much now. But it can be worked into a good-paying business. The old fellow won't last long. That property would eventually be yours. A ranch in the Verde, where there's forest left and game!"

"Right down my alley, Jack," Roddy returned with feeling. "I know the range. Swell! But I'd forgotten you had thrown in with Middleton. What's the string to this proposition?"

"Do you like it?"

"So far, it's great. And darn' fair of you, Jack."

"All right. Here's the string. I've been thinking this over for some time. I want you to kidnap Collie . . . drive her down under the Tonto Rim to that old cabin in Turkey Cañon. Treat her rough. I don't care a damn how mean you are to her. As it turns out, we can easily keep the kidnapping a secret. We'll plan for me to trail you . . . find you on a certain date. Collie will be subdued . . . worn out with mistreatment and hard fare and fright . . . then I'll come along to rescue her."

For a moment Roddy felt an impulse to laugh. This could be nothing but a bad joke of John's. But in John's face was no suggestion of humor, and his voice was anxious and urgent. Almost pityingly, Roddy asked: "Jack Brecken, do you figure she'll fall for you . . . then?"

"I hope she will. If that doesn't fetch her, nothing will . . . the contrary little flirt!"

"But, man alive! She's from Texas. She's a live wire. She'd kill you if she found it out. And I reckon she'd kill me anyhow."

"Yes, Collie will be game. It's a risk. But I've *got* to do it."

"How on earth could I get away with it? She's popular . . . has lots of friends. They'd raise hell."

"Ordinarily, yes. But this deal has been made for me. Listen . . . Collie graduated last spring. But she stayed on all summer, until now. She's leaving for Texas tomorrow. I've offered to drive her over to Colton to catch the main line express. All the girls will be busy or in school when I call for her. She'll say good bye to them at the dance tonight. She intends to stop off at Albuquerque to visit an uncle for two weeks. And she'll not wire him till she gets on the train. I'll send you in my old car, in which you'll pack grub, blankets, *etcetera*. You'll whisk her away . . . and at a time we'll set, I'll drive down to Turkey Cañon to get her."

"Just like that," Roddy commented, snapping his fingers.

"Will you do it?" demanded John tersely.

"I'm afraid I'll have to turn it down. I'd do almost anything for you, Jack. And if that kid has double-crossed you, I could shake the gizzards out of her, but . . . but. . . ."

"Why won't you?"

"Jack, it's so . . . so . . . hell! I don't know what. So ridiculous! And even if we could get away with it, it seems a dirty trick to pull on any girl . . . even if she has played you for a sucker. You can't really love her."

"I'm crazy about Collie. And I tell you again if you fail me, I'll be sunk. And don't forget my offer of the money and ranch." John's tone was verging on despair.

"Money doesn't cut much ice with me. But that Verde ranch . . . I could go for that in a big way," cogitated Roddy.

"Well, here's your chance to get it, along with money to make it a fine thing for you. A place to settle down. You could quit this rolling stone stuff. There'll always be good hunting and fishing in the Verde. Why, that cañon runs down into the Tonto Basin."

"Sounds great, Jack," Roddy said, gripping the car with a strong brown hand. "Only . . . the girl part is the deal that sticks in my craw."

"I don't see why. Listen, Rod! There's something coming to Collie Younger. She needs taming. I should think it'd appeal to you."

"Well, it doesn't," denied Roddy forcibly. But the instant his words were spent, he realized they were false. And that astonished him. The idea intrigued him—took hold of him. Suddenly a picture of Collie flashed into mind—her rebellious face and challenging eyes as she had walked unashamed and free, like a young goddess out of her bath. That picture proved devastating. Then he sensed a resentment toward this high-stepping Texas kid and an urge to avenge her trifling with his blundering brother, who had never had any luck with girls. All the same it looked like a crowning folly for him.

"Sorry, old man. I just can't see it your way," he said, and got into the car.

John violently slammed the door shut and took the wheel. His state of mind might have been judged by his reckless driving up a steep and narrow road to the rim. Roddy gazed across the deep cañon, now full of blue shadows, to the long sweep of the cedared desert toward the west. Purple clouds burned with a ruddy fire, low down along the horizon. To the south, toward the Verde, the cañon wound its snake-like trail of red and gold into the green wilderness. Facing northward, as John headed the car homeward, Roddy viewed the huge bulk of the mountains looming high, crowned with white. How hard to leave this Arizona range again!

John drove like a man possessed of devils and roared past the other cars halfway to Hazelton. Dusk had fallen when he reached home in the outskirts of town. Then he broke the silence. "Rod," he said, "you may have changed. Once you were full of the Old Nick. But if sentiment and romance are dead in you, look at my offer as simply business."

"Jack, I'm no good. All the same I'd hate to pull a low-down stunt like that."

"You're not acquainted with Collie. She'd get a kick out of being kidnapped."

"Why don't you kidnap her yourself?"

"I would. But I figured it wouldn't work. It takes time, and, besides, I haven't an excuse to leave the business just now. The rescue act would be much better, and I'd be more of a hero in her eyes. Collie's a Southerner, brimful of romance. She's crazy over the movies. Goes to every picture. Once she told me she could fall for me much quicker if I did something heroic. That's what gave me this idea."

"That may be OK with you, Jack. But, somehow, it doesn't persuade me. She's spunky, and she won't be bossed. I'd say that was your great fault, Jack."

"I like my own way, and I see that I get it. I've set my heart on Collie, the little fiend."

John's words smacked of arrogance, but Roddy could

sense the panic behind them.

"But this deal of yours isn't on the level," Roddy rejoined curtly.

"Neither is Collie on the level."

"Oh, she isn't!" Roddy stared aghast.

"Not with men, that's a cinch. In the two years she has gone to college here, she has taken every fellow I know down the line. Cowboys are her especial dish. She swears she adores them. But I noticed none of them lasted long."

"Well. It'd depend on how far she. . . ."

"I don't know. But there have been times when I was so jealous and sick I wanted to murder her. Then she'd be sweeter to me than ever."

"Jack, I should think you'd be leery of such a girl . . . for a wife."

John waved that statement aside. "Come to the Normal dance tonight. See for yourself. She'll make a play for you. I got that today. You're husky and handsome. She's heard gossip about you. She's curious."

"But I haven't a decent suit to my back," protested Roddy.

"I'll lend you one. My clothes always fit you."

"If my reputation is so bad, I should think. . . ."

"That will make you all the more interesting." There was a tinge of bitterness in John's voice. "Besides, Normal dances are always short of men. Everybody in town will be invited. All the cowboys on the range. It'll be the first dance of the season and sure a swell affair."

John's importunity weighed powerfully on Roddy. Moreover, he grew conscious of a curious eagerness to see Collie Younger again. He gave in to it. And he had a stubborn conception of his own about that girl—something born from the scornful flash of topaz eyes at his brother.

Roddy accepted John's brand-new dark suit and dressed

himself with a growing amusement and interest. After dinner he walked up to town. The cold night wind whipped down from the black peaks. Roddy wished for a fleece-lined coat, such as he used to wear while riding. For the first time since his arrival home he strolled into poolrooms and hotel lobbies, curious about whom he might meet. No lack of old acquaintances and some sundry drinks of hard liquor warmed Roddy into a heartening mood. He fell in with some cowboys and went to the dance with them.

The Normal College was an institution that had been established since Roddy's school days in Hazelton. He had never been inside the big building, which was situated a little way out of town in a grove of pine trees. The several hundred automobiles parked all around attested to a large attendance at the dance. Reluctant to go in, and thinking it best to walk to and fro a while in the cold air, Roddy gave his eager cowboy comrades the slip.

When he did enter the building, he experienced a pleasant surprise at sight of the many pretty girls in formal gowns and clean-cut Western boys with tanned faces, talking and laughing at the entrance to the colorfully decorated ballroom. A forgotten something stirred in his veins. It swelled with the sudden burst of tantalizing music that drowned the low murmur of voices. Roddy found himself carried along with the crowd into the big hall.

Roddy took to the sidelines, intending to find enjoyment watching the dancers. He quite forgot the reason for coming. But he had scarcely had a moment to himself when a gracious woman, evidently one of the hostesses, swooped down upon him and led him off. To Roddy's dismay he saw a whole contingent of girls in white and pink and blue, all apparently eager-eyed for a partner. Before he realized what it was all about, he found himself on the floor with a dark-haired girl. He was awkward, and he stepped on her feet. Mortified by this, Roddy woke up to exert all his wit and memory to recall a once skillful lightness of foot and accommodations to rhythm. He had begun to dance creditably when the music stopped.

One after another, then, he was given four partners, the last of whom was a decidedly comely girl whose auburn-tinted head came up to his shoulder. With her Roddy started out well. But anyone save a cripple could have danced with this girl, Roddy assured himself.

"Don't you know me, Roddy?" she asked presently, roguishly.

"Indeed, no. I'm sorry. Ought I?"

"Hardly. I've grown up and changed."

"Did I go to school with you?"

"Yes. But I was a kid in the first grade. I'm Jessie Evans."

"Jessie Evans? You couldn't be that long-legged, freckle-faced, red-headed little imp who used to . . . ?"

"You've got my number, Roddy," she replied gaily.

"No? Well, of all things! You, little Jessie, grown into such . . . such a stunning girl?"

"Thanks. It's nice of you to say so."

Roddy got along delightfully with Jessie, and graduated into something of his old ease at dancing. He did not realize at all what a fine time he was having until after that dance, when he encountered his brother and several of the picnic party. Then he remembered, and went to some pains to conceal his self-consciousness.

"Rod, I see you're stepping right out," remarked John amiably. Manifestly he was in good spirits, and looked very handsome with his strong dark face minus its brooding anger. Something had cheered Jack up. No doubt it was the bewitching little girl who clung to his arm.

"Howdy, Jack. Sure, I'm enjoying myself," replied Roddy.

Then he bowed to Collie and the others.

"I'm glad, old man. It's good to see you here," John said, and his heartiness seemed free of any ulterior interest in Roddy's presence. "You must dance with Collie. Here, take her for the next."

"I'd be delighted . . . if she'll risk it."

"Is there any great risk?" drawled the Texas girl, looking up with her penetrating topaz eyes. She wore a gown that matched them and her hair. Her rounded arms and neck, almost as gold of hue as her gown, brought back strikingly to Roddy the picture of her that he could never forget.

"I'm a rotten dancer."

"You can't be any worse than some of these hoofers here," she rejoined, lifting her little hands to him as the music started. In a moment he felt as if he were holding a fairy. He responded to the stimulus by dancing better than he ever had before. When they got halfway around the hall, she said: "Roddy, you're not a rotten dancer. But you'd do better to hold me closer. Not at arms' length!"

"I'm a tenderfoot . . . at dancing," he replied apologetically, but he tightened his clasp.

"Yeah? I hadn't noticed it. But I'd prefer that to these boys who dance so darn' well they can't do anything else."

Collie inspired as well as intoxicated Roddy. It was impossible not to take advantage of her suggestion. Then he felt her as substantial as she had looked that afternoon. Her curly fragrant head rested low upon his shoulder. She clung to him without in the least hampering his step.

"Roddy, you didn't approve of me this afternoon . . . down in the cañon creek?"

"I . . . how . . . what makes you think that?" he stammered.

"The way you looked at me. Maybe I did go too far . . . before a stranger, anyhow. But Jack gives me a pain in the neck."

"You give him a worse pain than that," Roddy said with a laugh. "There! I got out of step. Collie, I can't talk and dance."

"All right. But tell me what you thought . . . about me . . . this afternoon."

"Well, I didn't get beyond how pretty you looked."

"Oh! Not so poor, Roddy." She did not speak again until the dance ended.

"Come, let's beat it outdoors," she commanded, and dragged him from the ballroom. "Pinch somebody's coat or wrap. I'm a Southerner, you know. I love your Arizona, but, oh, it freezes me to death."

They went out under the giant pines. White gowns shone in the moonlight. Other couples passed them going in. It was wonderful outside, despite the cold. Black and star-crowned, the peaks pierced the dark blue sky.

"You're not much of a talker, are you?" inquired Collie.

"Me? Gosh, no. I haven't any line," replied Roddy.

"Not much! You can't fool this girl. I wish you had come back here a year ago."

"Why?"

"Then I could have known you. I leave Hazelton tomorrow, and I won't be back for a while. We might not meet again."

"I reckon you're not missing much."

Collie gave his arm a squeeze. "Don't be so modest, old dear," she replied.

They came to a huge fallen pine that stretched across the campus. "Lift me up," said the girl. Roddy put his hands under her arms and sailed her aloft to a perch on the log.

"How strong you are," she murmured, as she smoothed down her gown. Her head was now on a level with his. The moonlight silvered her hair and worked magic in her eyes and

75

enhanced the charm of her face.

"I've been cowboy, miner, lumberjack," he said lightly. "All professions that require strength."

"I've heard that you were a hard drinker, gambler, fighter . . . in fact, a hard nut."

"I seem to have a good reputation."

"Is it true?"

"True? I reckon so."

"I wonder . . . ? Roddy, you're the best-looking fellow I've met here. And you've a nicer manner than most. You remind me of a Southerner."

"My granddad was from Texas. My mother from Missouri. That's South, you know."

"Are you staying long here?"

"I reckon not. I can't stay any place long. Why do you ask?"

"Oh, I told you I was coming back," she returned with a flash of her eyes.

"But what about John? I gathered you and he had been pretty friendly."

"Oh, John's sort of dotty about me, and I thought I was in love with him. But he's too slow for me and too bossy, so I'm going to give him the gate." There was an insolence in the girl's tone that antagonized Roddy.

"Does Jack suspect that?" he asked, wishing to lead her on.

"Not a chance. He wouldn't believe it. Says I don't know my mind two days' running."

"He appeared happy tonight."

"I made up with him . . . kissed him. If I hadn't done so, this last night here would have flopped. I wanted to enjoy it. I'm enjoying it very much . . . right now."

"Are you going to tell him?"

"Yes, in the morning. Maybe I'll string him along till later. It'd be fun to do it at the train."

Her mocking high-pitched laughter pealed out. Her eyes danced in the moonlight. That was the moment Roddy understood his brother and accepted his offer. To tame this imperious and ruthless young lady appealed to all that was wild and reckless in Roddy. Aligned with his loyalty to John, it set the balance.

"Jack asked me to drive you across to Colton," Roddy said smoothly. "He's a Mason, you know, and has an important conference."

"He did? How jolly. I'm tickled pink," she cried ecstatically.

"When and where shall I call for you?"

"The cottage where I've been living with Helen and Mary is on Oak Street, right next to the women's dormitory. Do you know where that is?"

"Yes. What time?"

"Two o'clock sharp."

"Baggage?"

"Plenty. But no trunks. I'll have the bags taken out."

"OK."

"It's a nice long ride over. I hated the idea of Jack driving me. He's so business-like about everything he does, and he can't enjoy the scenery. If we leave at two, we'll have plenty of time. You don't want to hurry, do you?"

"Reckon I'll creep along, if you like."

"Then we can talk, too, and plan. I'm not saying good bye forever. You'll write to me. . . . Roddy, if I was staying on here, I'd fall for you something awful."

"Oh, yeah? Lucky you're not."

"For me . . . or you, darling?"

"You. I'm a bad *hombre,* Collie."

"So I've heard. Wild guy . . . devil with the women. And you haven't even squeezed my hand. Pooh! That's a lot of baloney."

They walked back to the school building, and sought out John who was standing alone. Roddy gave his brother a significant look.

"I told Collie that you wanted me to drive her over to the main line," he informed John, "and she decided she could trust me."

It was lucky that Collie was looking at Roddy, for such a flood of relief and gratification passed over John's features that Collie would have suspected something had she seen his expression.

Before John could answer, Roddy turned to Collie. "So long, Collie, see you at two tomorrow," he said, and walked off into the moonlight.

He had let himself in for it, he mused rather grimly. But the girl had it coming to her. She was an outrageous flirt, and had tried to do to him as she had done to John, and undoubtedly to numbers of other boys. She needed a lesson, a severe one, and it seemed that he, Roddy, was the one chosen to give it. There was a strange satisfaction in that thought.

Then his doubt set in again. After all, what business was it of his? Why shouldn't John carry out his own crazy plans? What had induced him to give in to his brother's idea? When he came to think of it, no one but the girl herself, with her provocative ways. He was a softy, and she was taking him down the line just as she had taken John. It wasn't a sane thing to do, and he was damned if he'd carry it out. He'd go straight to John and tell him it was impossible.

Roddy turned and started back under the trees. Just as he was about to mount the steps of the school building, a movement in the shrubbery at the side drew his attention. The moonlight flooded down on the tantalizing face of Collie and on the white arms that were creeping around the neck of a cowboy Roddy had never before seen.

Roddy's right-about-face was so swift that he almost lost his balance. "You win, John," he muttered to himself. "I'll go through with it."

II

Next day, the last of Roddy's many errands was to drive to the bank to cash the check for twenty-five hundred dollars that John had forced on him, along with the papers of the transfer of his share in Middleton's ranch. John had not been taking any chances of Roddy's flunking on his part of the bargain.

The teller did not have so large an amount of cash in the cage and had to send to the vault for it. "Can't use checks in the country I'm going to," Roddy explained. "I'm not known, and, anyway, the backwoodsmen don't believe in checks."

"Well, be careful," the teller warned him. "There are always shady characters hanging around."

Roddy laughed and pocketed his bills. "I'll be on the lookout," he assured the man.

It was after two o'clock when Roddy turned in the direction of the women's dormitory. He stepped on the gas to go tearing across the railroad track ahead of a freight train. And in less than two minutes he was passing the noisy sawmill, with its great cloud of creamy smoke rolling aloft, to sight the college building beyond. In another moment he spied Collie at the gate of a small cottage. His heart leaped. All day the adventure had been unreal until he saw her. As he slowed to a stop, he observed there did not appear to be anyone but Collie in sight. She looked very smart in a brown suit and carried a coat under her arm. A pile of suitcases and bags rested on the sidewalk.

"Howdy, Texas. Sorry to be late," said Roddy, as he leaped out. "Hop in the front seat."

"Oh, Roddy, I thought you'd never come," she cried, giving him a radiant smile. "I see stingy Jack gave you his old car. What's all the junk?"

"I reckon I'll need to be alone in the woods for a while . . . after this ride with you. So I'm going camping," replied Roddy, and he began to throw bags into the back of the car. As he slipped behind the wheel, he looked around to see if anyone were observing them. There were no pedestrians, but a car was raising dust at the railroad crossing. Roddy drove rapidly toward the open country. The deed was done.

Collie edged closer to him and hooked a little hand under his arm. Excited and thrilled evidently, she had not noted that they were traveling in the wrong direction.

"Oh, swell!" she ejaculated. "I'm tired. Had only three hours' sleep." And with a sigh she sank against him. But she kept on talking, about the dance, about the girls—about Jack, and how she hated to leave Arizona.

Roddy was too excited to pay much attention to her chatter, but he could not help but be affected by the softness and warmth of her person. At his lack of response Collie presently remarked dryly that she hoped he was going to make the ride interesting.

"I'll tell the world," he assured her. In the little mirror he caught sight of a car gaining from behind. Roddy did not intend to allow anyone to see Collie, let alone pass him, and accordingly he increased his speed.

"Collie, how'd you like to have me drive you clear to Albuquerque?" he queried daringly.

"Wonderful!" she burst out in amaze and delight. "But how long would you take . . . where would we . . . ?"

"A couple of days, loafing along. Chance for us to get acquainted."

"Say, big boy, you're doing pretty well. Where'd we sleep?"

"I'd make a bed for you in the back seat. I have blankets and pillows. I'll sleep on the ground."

"Can we get away with it?"

"Cinch. We'd roll through the few towns there are. Camp in lonesome places. I brought grub, fruit . . . everything . . . and I can cook."

She leaned against him, silent for a long moment. Then she asked: "Can I trust you, Roddy?"

"I reckon it'll be risky," he replied with a laugh.

"Well, I'll take the chance. It'll be a lark . . . my last in Arizona. OK, Roddy."

Roddy was hindered from making a ready response to her immediate acceptance of his proposal. Her tone, when she had asked if she could trust him, scarcely savored of heedlessness—it had contained a note foreign to every other thing she had said to him. It gave him pause.

Roddy happened at the moment to glance into his rearsight mirror, and found that the car behind was coming up fast. Then accelerating his speed, he turned a corner, only to be confronted by a bad stretch of road that would be hazardous to fast travel. He decided to let the car pass, if it caught him before the narrow strip ended.

"Slide down, Collie, so that driver can't see you."

"Gee!" Collie remarked gleefully. "We're starting off well."

The approaching automobile was an old Ford with two occupants. They came on apace and were almost up with Roddy when he reached a wider spot where they might have passed him. They did not, however, make the attempt, until just at the end of the rough stretch, when they astounded Roddy with a honking rush.

It angered him. Instead of swerving, he hit into high speed. And at that instant the front of the Ford shot into sight alongside.

"Stop, that!" came in hoarse bellow. "An' stick 'em up!"

Roddy went cold all over. The rattling car rocked almost abreast of him. A man leaned out behind the windshield, automatic gun extended. His ham-shaped visage, with pointed chin covered by a reddish beard, seemed vaguely familiar. Somewhere, that very day, Roddy had seen it. In a flash Roddy stepped his car to its limit. As he forged ahead, there came a crash of splintered glass accompanied by a gunshot. His left side-shield had been hit by a bullet. A fierce indistinguishable command to stop filled Roddy's ears. He slid down in his seat as far as he dared, yelling to Collie to keep hidden, and drove on, the cold shock to his internals giving way to the heat of anger. A hold-up! Where had he seen that man? Every second he stingingly expected another shot and bullet. But it did not come. This old touring car of John's simply swallowed up the road. Presently Roddy dared to look back. Already he was farther from the pursuing car than he had imagined. Almost out of range! Perhaps the hold-up man had shot to halt him, without murderous intent. Roddy sat up and drove as never before in his life, and presently he had left his pursuers far behind and finally out of sight around a bend.

"Sit up, Collie. We showed them our heels."

She came up as if for air. "Ga . . . gangsters?"

"Search me. But that guy with the gun looked plenty tough. *Where* did I see him?"

"Step on it, Roddy."

"I was doing seventy back a ways. Sixty now. This old bus can go some. Collie, that little play wasn't on the program."

"You ought to pack a gun," declared this young lady from Texas.

"I've got two in the car. But I never thought of them. Where in hell . . . ? By thunder! The bank. It was in the bank where I saw the lantern-jawed *hombre*. I went in to cash Jack's check. He saw me with the money. Well, what do you know about that?"

"They'll trail us. And this country is getting wilder. Oh, I should have made you drive me to the train!"

"Too late now, Collie," he replied grimly, and he meant that in several senses.

Roddy slowed to a reasonable speed. He did not trust the car to hold together. The road was good, and he had no fear of being caught. The fences failed, and gradually the slashed area where the timber had been cut off. Patches of goldenrod blazed among the sagebrush under the pines. Presently he passed the forks of the road, where a signboard marked the branch that turned west down to Cañon Creek.

"Cañon Creek!" exclaimed Collie. "Why, that's the road we took yesterday!"

"You're not liable to forget it . . . or this road, either."

"This road . . . I've been on it. We drove down to the natural bridge a year and more ago. . . . Roddy, it runs to the left of Cañon Creek, and that cañon gets deeper all the way. It's a terribly cut-up country. How'll we ever cross that cañon?"

"We can't."

"But we've got to go east. We'll be farther and farther out of our way."

"Shall I turn back?"

"Oh, no. We can't do that with those bums chasing us."

"There's a road that turns off to the west, down here at Long Valley. It goes to Wilcox. We can take that. But then

83

we'll have to go back through Hazelton."

"No. We'll keep on and drive 'way around somehow. A day or so won't make any great difference. I'm scared yet, but I'll soon get a kick out of it."

Stretches of rocky cedared desert alternated with straggling pine forest. Collie lapsed into thoughtful quiet and again leaned upon Roddy's shoulder. Once he felt her studying his face. Was she beginning to wonder? It was all one to Roddy, for she would soon learn of his nefarious design. They passed a ranch zone, poor range, sparsely grassed, and scarce in cattle. The Depression had hit these ranchers as well as the town folk. Beyond, they climbed into forest country again, passed through bare spots where in spring there were weedy ponds, and so on to the lake and cottages of Hazelton's summer resort. It appeared deserted now. Collie was asleep with heavy head slipping low on Roddy's shoulder when he drove by the lake.

Beyond this point Roddy seldom looked back. He had not thought, however, that the hold-up men would abandon the pursuit. On that dusty road they could trail him as long as he stayed on it. There followed a twenty-five mile stretch that ate up an hour of hard driving. Circling Snow Lake, he passed on through the woods to Crooked Valley.

This was where he had to turn to the left from the main highway into the forest. And he needed to do so without being seen by any of the people who lived there. Moreover, he did not want to leave any tracks into the forester's road that led down to Turkey Cañon. Selecting a grove well carpeted with pine needles, Roddy drove to the right, off under the pines, as far from the highway as level ground permitted.

Darkness was coming on apace. When he stopped, the jolt of the car awakened Collie. She sat bewildered, her curls all awry. "Night! Where the heck am I? Gee, what a lonesome place!"

Roddy explained that he had thought it best to hide here until their pursuers went by. He advised her to get out and stretch her legs while he unpacked something to eat and drink. After that he would make room for her to sleep on the back seat. Here in the woods it was much warmer than out driving on the road. He concluded to get along without a fire, but did not hesitate to use his flashlight.

When presently he was ready to walk back to the road to watch till the Ford went by, Collie said: "Roddy, I'm not stuck on staying here alone. Let me go with you."

"Stay in the car. This is no picnic," he replied, and his tone was gruff.

Collie's eyes flashed, and she retorted spiritedly: "Well, you needn't be so huffy about it."

Before very long Roddy heard the drone of a motorcar, far off in the woods. Reaching the road, he chose a deeply shadowed covert under a pine from which to watch. Soon the drone of the car changed to a hum. Headlights gleamed intermittently through the trees. The car came on, passed by behind its bright yellow lights. And it was not a Ford. This afforded Roddy satisfaction, for that car surely had obliterated his tracks. He settled down to wait patiently. How long since he had been in the forest at night? The wilderness song in the treetops awakened dreamy memory of his hunting days in that country.

In half an hour or less he heard another automobile. At length the lights glimmered under the trees. This car slowed down before it reached him. When it passed, he recognized the Ford. The driver halted some few hundred feet from where Roddy sat. He or his companion got out with a flashlight and appeared to be scrutinizing the ground. Roddy grasped that they were looking for his tracks at the junction of the road to Wilcox. Muttering, impatient voices floated to

Roddy. The waving light went out; a door clicked; the Ford moved on down the road out of sight.

Hurrying back through the woods, Roddy was at some pains to locate his car. He found it, peered in the back to find Collie asleep. Then he got in, switched on the lights, and cautiously drove back to the highway. Reaching it, he crossed to the left side and followed that down to the Wilcox branch on which he turned. Half a mile farther in the woods, he turned off on the rim road.

This was a forest road, seldom traveled by cars. Grass and weeds grew as high as the running board; thick brush lined the sides, with an occasional black-trunked pine rising above. It led down into Jones' Cañon, at the bottom of which ran a creek difficult to ford in spring. But now there was only a dry wash. The slope up the ridge opposite, Roddy remembered, was steep and long. When he at last surmounted it to the ridge top, he felt relieved. All was smooth sailing now.

Collie called out something that sounded like where in the hell was he driving? Manifestly the slow grinding climb and severe jolts had roused her. Roddy told her to shut up and go to sleep. She exclaimed what a sweet boy he was turning out to joy-ride with, and then she subsided.

The forest road took a gradual ascent for twenty miles. Giant pines and silver spruce lined it so high that Roddy could not see their tips. It wound along the crest of the ridge, now through level areas of dense forest and then by heads of ravines that ran down into the cañons on each side. The woods smelled sweet with an odorous tang.

At length, some time late in the night, Roddy reached the rim, where the road ran east and west. As the altitude was over eight thousand feet, the air was bitingly cold. Roddy turned east. At times he passed close to the edge of the rim where it broke abruptly into the great Tonto Basin. In the moonlight it showed its vast gulf, opaque and gray, reaching across to the black Matazels.

Driving became even more difficult owing to potholes, rocky places, sharp bends, hills, and cross-washes. Often Roddy had to get out to drag aside rotten logs and branches that had recently toppled over. Therefore, he had to advance slowly and carefully. The hours passed. He could keep account of his progress and whereabouts by the white signs along the road: **Myrtle Creek, Barbershop Cañon, Quaking Asp, Leonard Cañon, Gentry Cañon, and Turkey Cañon**.

Here he turned away from the rim, straight down into the forest. The road had the same characteristics as the one by which he had reached the rim, only now he was descending the winding crest of a ridge between the cañons. Toward the end, this road became well nigh impassable—full of rocks and gutters and boggy places. When he reached the end of the ridge, where it broke down sharply, the east was lightening and dawn was at hand.

Bright sunlight greeted Roddy as he drove off the ridge into the beautiful park that was his objective. The old brown log cabin, with its mossy shelving roof, appeared as it existed in his memory, although even more weathered and picturesque than before. Here and there in the lonely park stood lofty pines and spruces; silver grass, colorful with autumn asters and daisies, covered the slopes; a wandering line of willow bushes, half bronze, half green, showed the course of the murmuring brook that flowed by the cabin; a grove of aspens, white-trunked and gold-leafed, blazed at the far end of the park.

Roddy's second glance caught the tawny gray coats of great antlered elk disappearing under the trees. He heard the gobble and cluck of wild turkeys. Down the brook two deer stood with long ears erect. And all at once a strange feeling assailed Roddy, something stranger than the joy of solitude and beauty in the wilderness, a wish that he might have come there to stay.

Shutting off the engine, he stepped out. The glistening, frosted grass crackled under his feet. At that moment Collie stuck her tousled bright head out of the car. She looked all around. When her eyes rested upon Roddy, they were wide open, the sleep had vanished, and the topaz hue had darkened wondrously.

"Lovely!" she cried rapturously. "Oh, what a paradise!" And she bounded out to hold up her red lips to him. " 'Morning, Roddy. You may . . . for bringin' me here."

Roddy did not kiss her, he did not want to, but he wondered at himself.

"You'll cuss me *pronto*," he replied grimly.

"Never, darling. I feel like Alice in Wonderland." And she began to run around like a child who could not see all the enchanting things quickly enough.

Roddy unloaded the car of his camp duffle and food supplies. He split dead aspen and kindled a fire. Very shortly he had biscuits browning in a Dutch oven, coffee pot steaming, and he was slicing ham, when Collie returned with her arms full of purple asters, goldenrod, and scarlet maple leaves. Her piquant face, smiling upon him from above this mass of exquisite color, gave him a distinct shock.

"Chuck that stuff and help me rustle breakfast," he said surlily.

"Say, mister, you won't go far with me on such talk as that," she retorted, her smile fading. She laid the flowers carefully aside and warmed her hands over the fire. Evidently they were numb. Then she got a bag out of the car and opened it upon the running board. Presently she went by with a towel and other toilet articles to approach the brook. Suddenly a little shriek reached Roddy's ears. He laughed. She was a tenderfoot, even though she came from Texas. A few moments after that she came back, her face rosy and bright.

"Don't you supply your women with hot water?" she inquired scornfully. "Or didn't they ever wash?" Then she returned to the car to brush her hair and apply her make-up, about which tasks she took her time.

"Come and get it before I throw it out," called Roddy.

She had a ravenous appetite, which might have been responsible for her unusual silence. "I'll say you can cook," she said presently, when she had finished. "I'll help you wash up."

Roddy did not reply. He was revolving in his mind the need to tell her what he had done.

"You drove all night?"

"Yeah."

"You look tired . . . and cross. I'm afraid you're worried about those hold-up men."

"Not any more. I gave them the slip."

"What place is this?"

"Turkey Cañon."

"That doesn't mean anything to me. But I saw turkeys. Oh, so tame and beautiful. Where are we?"

"Over a hundred miles from Hazelton. Half that from the road we drove down on."

"So far!" she exclaimed wonderingly, but perplexed. "Why did you bring me here?"

"I've kidnapped you," he replied with a dark gaze at her.

"You . . . *what?*" Like a bent twig released she sprang up.

"I kidnapped you, Collie Younger."

"Honestly . . . you did?"

"Honest to God."

She sank to her knees in amazement. "Roddy! Have my sins found me out?"

"I reckon they have."

"Oh, I swear I didn't flirt with you. I was thrilled to death to meet a real Westerner, like some of the Texas riders Dad used to tell me about. I . . . I liked you, Roddy Brecken. And because . . . because. . . . You took the chance to fool me . . . get me here in this lonesome place. You fell for me!" Incoherent though her amazement had made her, Collie's last words held a note of triumph, which stung Roddy to immediate denial.

"Miss Younger, it may surprise you further to learn that I did not fall for you . . . at all," he rejoined with sarcasm.

Flaming red burned out the rouge in her cheeks. "Then you kidnapped me for money?"

"I reckon so, partly."

"Who told you I had money?" As he did not vouchsafe any answer to that, she went on, her voice gaining in intensity. "Jack *told* you. I once showed him a letter from my brother about our oil wells in Texas. Jack must have told you."

"No, he never mentioned it."

"Then how did you know?"

"I didn't. You just jumped at conclusions."

"What did you mean by partly?"

"Well, as an after-consideration, some money is OK."

"I don't get you," she returned, shaking her curly head. "Can't you come right out with it? *Why* did you kidnap me?"

"You made a sucker out of my brother," flashed Roddy passionately.

"Oh-h," she breathed softly, with a gasp of realization. "Yes, I did. I suppose the fact that the big conceited stiff deserved it will not get anywhere with you? Well, here we are. What do you think you're going to do with me?"

He regarded her brazenly, hiding in that bravado the conflict he was undergoing. He had not ever seen such a pair of tawny-fired eyes.

"You'll never play fast and loose with another guy."

"Do you intend to . . . to murder me?"

"I reckon I'll shy short of that."

"Then what?"

"You're curious, aren't you?"

"Why wouldn't I be curious? It seems to concern me."

"It'll concern you plenty before I get through with you. You'll be taught a lesson you'll never forget, you damn' cheap little flirt. You'll think twice before you drive men crazy just to satisfy some female love of conquest. I'd think more of you if you'd gone the limit with every fellow you ever knew. Have you done that?"

"Why you . . . you backwoods lout!"

"All right. Call me what you like. The worse you cuss me, the more kick I'll get out of handing you what *I* think you deserve."

"And what's that, Mister Loyal Champion of Brother John?"

"Understand, Collie Younger," his voice rang out, "I don't care a damn for you. Last night you made one of your usual plays for me. It made me sore, instead of soft. All your prettiness, your white and gold skin, your curls, your come-hither eyes . . . don't mean one damn' thing to me."

"Roddy Brecken, you *are* in love with me," she cried triumphantly, and she held out her arms in a gesture that, if it was as deceitful and vile as he believed, merited giving her all that rushed passionately to his mind.

"Yeah, you'll think so. You would! When you slave for me, when I beat you, hog-tie you with a rope, make a rag out of you, till I trade what's left of you for money you're not worth." So convincing did Roddy's fury make his words that

Collie actually took them for truth.

"Jack will . . . kill you," she whispered, ashen white under her rouge.

Roddy dropped his head. To look at her then was insupportable.

"For God's sake . . . Roddy . . . do *I* deserve that? Oh, it's unthinkable. Roddy, I swear I never did a dirty trick in my life . . . one that I *knew* was dirty."

"Well, begin now. Wash up these pans and pots. Use hot water and sand. Then pack your bags inside the cabin and clean it out. I'll go cut some bundles of spruce for beds."

The cold brutality of Roddy's response to her impassioned speech took all the fire out of Collie.

"Beds . . . in there?" she echoed haltingly. "That buggy smelly place! I'd rather sleep outdoors."

"Well, if you'd prefer to freeze . . . but I don't . . . we'll both sleep inside."

"Roddy Brecken, if I sleep with you anywhere . . . I'll be cold plenty. I'll be dead."

"Wait and see. You're a bluff, Collie Younger, and I'm calling you. Once in your life you're going to get the kicks you girls brag you like and never try. You'll show yellow."

"Much *you* know about girls. I won't do one single thing you order."

"You won't, won't you?" Roddy rasped, and, fastening a powerful hand in her blouse, he jerked her off her feet and shook her until her curly head bobbed like a jumping-jack.

"You bum! You bully!" she choked out furiously, when he let her go. And with all her might she slapped him.

Roddy returned the blow in a heat that overcame him, and it was too violent for her slight weight and build. She went down limp as a sack. Rising on one hand, with the other at her red cheek, she glared up with eyes like molten bronze. A fierce animal pain possessed her. As it subsided, she appeared prey to an incredulous awe. Roddy needed no more to see that not only had she never seriously felt pain, but she certainly had never received a blow until that moment.

"Rustle now, before I get mad," he ordered, and, picking up his axe, he stalked off toward the hillside. In all the fights Roddy had ever had, and they had numbered legion, he had never felt the fury this girl had aroused in him. On that score he tried to excuse himself for knocking her down. His threat to beat her had been merely threat. She was as imperious as the savage daughter of a great barbarian chief. She was also the epitome of the female species when infuriated, a cat, a spitfire. Lastly she was intelligent, keen as a whip. Roddy grasped that the one single advantage he had over her, the only thing he could resort to, was physical strength. By being a brute he could cow her. Chafing under this, he chopped down a small spruce tree and trimmed off the boughs. He gathered them into a huge bundle, and, taking this up in his arms, he staggered to the cabin and flung down the odorous mass under the projecting roof that had once covered a board porch.

He noted that Collie had packed all her baggage, and the bedding as well, to the cabin, and was now cleaning out the rubbish. He heard her sobbing before she came to the door with tears streaming down her cheeks. Roddy most decidedly did not undergo the satisfaction that such a sight should have given him. Instead, he felt like a cur. Whereupon he went back after another load of spruce, taking a long time about the task.

Upon returning, he found that Collie had made a pretty good job of cleaning the cabin and had carried in all of the spruce boughs. Peering in, he saw her in the act of spreading the blankets over the branches. She had not ceased crying.

Roddy set to work packing his supplies in under the porch roof, where he intended to build a fireplace of stones and cook the meals. While he was thus busied, Collie came to the door several times. Her expression seemed subdued.

"Stop your sniveling or I'll give you something to snivel about," he said, trying to make his voice as harsh as possible.

She did not reply, but the spirit flared up again in her eyes.

"Take that bag and fetch it back full of pine cones," he ordered brusquely.

After that he kept her at odd jobs until she appeared ready to drop. She was dirty and disheveled. Her brown traveling suit was ruined. A discoloration began to be noticeable on her cheek. But all this did not deceive or placate Roddy. He knew that at any moment he must expect an earthquake or a volcanic eruption. All Collie needed was the spark. He advised her to go into the cabin and change to warmer clothes, outdoor garb, and boots, if she had them. He chopped a pile of firewood, and prepared lunch. When he called her, there was no answer. He went into the cabin to find her lying on the blankets, pale and staring into space with tragic eyes.

"Roddy, I've been pondering," she said without a trace of resentment in her voice. "You know women have a sixth sense. Intuition, clairvoyance, mysticism or what-not. My faith in you has survived that brutal blow. I can't explain it. There seems to be something wrong, unnatural, false in this situation. I don't get it. But despite what you've said and done . . . I don't believe you're rotten."

"Yeah? Well, come out and eat," he replied in self-defense. He would be lost if he tried to bandy words with her or exchange intelligent thoughts or even argue. He feared she would see through him no matter how crude and hateful he could make himself. He was afraid of her in this serious pondering mood. Collie followed him out without further words, but her look was enigmatic.

While Roddy ate, taciturn and silent, he brooded over how to follow up his advantage without sacrificing every vestige of self-respect. He hated her, he believed, yet—he did not finish the thought. He had to carry on. But an almost insuperable obstacle seemed to erect itself on the fact that, flirt though she might be, she was as game as she was pretty, and utterly in his power. This actuality made the pregnant difference.

III

There was a moment that followed—how soon Roddy had no idea—in which he seemed to waver between what Collie had divined he really was and the character he had assumed. For her the situation, all at once raw and ominous, had brought out the graver, more womanly side of her. For Roddy that was harder to withstand than her provocative charms. He had to shock her out of it, kill it quickly, or fail utterly of his part in this impossible travesty. What of John's fatal attachment for this capricious girl, of the deal made and paid for?

With somber eyes upon the appealing pale face, with gaze the passion of which was not pretense, although its reason was his own sick wrath at himself, Roddy deliberately crushed her intuitive faith in him, killed it with profane and coarse speech no man should ever have spoken to a woman. The horror she evinced, he knew, would soon merge into the loathing and fear he wanted her to feel. Then he stalked out of the cabin, despising himself. There was little left, he thought bitterly, but to prove his infamous character in deeds.

Roddy took his rifle and went up the glade to hunt for turkeys. It was necessary to procure meat, although the hunting season was not yet open. Once on the wooded slope, however, he scarcely concentrated his faculties upon the pursuit of game. He sat down on a log to wipe his moist brow. The contending passions within his breast were not harmonious with the serenity, the beauty, the speaking solitude of this colorful forest. He could not sit still for long. He had to move, to walk, to climb. He mounted the ridge that he had descended to get down to the park. He leaned against a huge fallen log, aware of the presence of a frisky red squirrel, the squall of a jay, of the flash of scarlet and orange and silver all around him. His consciousness of these sights and sounds was merely sensorial habit that he could not help. His thoughts and emotions were engaged in a grievous contention against what he knew not, except that it was not concerned with what he had promised to do for his brother. It was deeper than that. For minutes, perhaps hours, he paced the glades, the aisles under the pines, trying to bring to order the havoc in his mind. Then, all at once, he heard a hum foreign to the sounds of the wilderness. Lifting his head, he seemed to suspend all his senses except hearing. The sound was not the drum of a grouse or the whirr of a turkey in flight. It was a motor, and the certainty again sharpened all his faculties. At first he thought the car was coming down the ridge from the rim. But clearer perception proved it was ascending the hill. No car could have gone by, down into the park, without his hearing it.

"By heaven! Collie!" he cried. "She would . . . the game little Texan! And I never thought of it!"

Roddy ran to intercept her, and he ran swiftly, leaping logs, crashing through brush, dodging trees. How far the road? He might be too late. The labor of the engine in low gear filled his beating ears. He rushed harder—burst out into the road.

Not a hundred feet down the grade the car came lurching and roaring up toward him. Roddy caught the gleam of Collie's face, the bright color of her hair.

"Stop!" he yelled, in stentorian voice, leaping to the middle of the road.

But she drove on, bumping to a short level, where the car gathered momentum. It bore down on Roddy. Collie leaned out to scream something indistinguishable. But her white face and piercing eyes needed no accompanying voice. She would run him down. Roddy had to leap to save his life.

Then in a swift dash he caught up with the car and bounded upon the running board. "Stop . . . damn you!" he panted.

"Jump . . . or I'll sideswipe you off!" she cried resolutely.

Holding on, Roddy bent with groping hand for the ignition. He had a glimpse of her face, set and cold, her blazing gaze dead ahead.

"Jump . . . quick!" she warned.

Roddy switched off the engine. But the car kept rolling on a short downgrade.

"Brakes! Look out!" yelled Roddy, frantically grasping the wheel. Collie had swerved toward the bank. He pulled. But she was strong and had a grip of steel. *Crash!* Flying glass stung Roddy as he was thrown off backward. He hit the ground hard. For an instant car and woods vanished in a scintillating burst of stars. Recovering, he sprang up. The car hung precariously over the bank, the left front wheel cramped against a tree.

"Collie, would . . . you . . . kill . . . us?" he panted, his chest lifting.

"I'd kill you damned gladly," she cut out icily. Her eyes shone with an extraordinary sharpness.

"Come out of there," he yelled, seeing the car slip a little. Opening the door, he seized her arm and jerked her out. "You'll take it . . . right now . . . Texas!" he panted grimly, dragging her back to the road. He was vague about all he meant to do, but it included such a spanking as no girl ever got.

"I won't be man-handled, you dirty bum," she spit, struggling to free herself. But failing, she assailed him furiously, beating and scratching at his face, biting the arm that held her. Then she kicked him violently on the shin. Her heavy-soled outing boot struck squarely on the bone that, owing to an injury of long standing, had remained exquisitely sensitive. Roddy let out a yelp and, loosing her, sank down in agony. The forest reeled around him. Hard on that flamed up the fury of a savage. He saw the girl through red-filmed eyes. And utterly beside himself, as she kicked viciously at him again, he seized her leg and upset her. She screeched like a wild creature and, lying on her back, kicked herself free. She sprang up, but did not run. Roddy lurched erect to get his hands upon her. And when, after a moment of blind instinctive violence, he let go his hold, she sank limply on the ground, her face ashen, eyes glazed, with blood running from her lips.

"You Texas . . . wildcat," he panted, gazing down with a sudden reversal to sanity. "Brought that . . . on yourself."

He left her lying there in the middle of the pine-matted road. Out of breath, hot as fire, he limped over to the car. No serious damage had been done, but if it got started down the slope and missed a couple of trees just wide enough to let it through, it would be a lost car. By rocking it, he slipped the front left wheel off the tree. The right front wheel hung six inches above the grade. With stones blocking it up, Roddy thought he might back the car up on the road. He found one of Collie's suitcases on the seat, also a canteen of water and a coat wrapped around a parcel of food. These he removed to the ground, and, cautiously getting in, he left the door open and started the engine. As he backed with full power on, the bank gave away and the car slid over. He lunged out just in the nick of time and, as luck would have it, fell on his bruised leg. Rising on one hand, mad with pain and the miserable circumstance, he watched the car go straight between the two trees and roll down into the brush out of sight, cracking and banging. Then there was a final heavy metallic crash on rocks.

"Uhn-huh, that's that," Roddy muttered, and, laboring to his feet, he limped back up the bank.

Collie lay where he had left her. As he approached, he saw that her eyes were open, distended in dark horror.

"Oh, Roddy . . . I heard it. I . . . I thought you'd . . . gone over . . . ," she gasped huskily. Fury in her, as in him, had evidently weakened at the imminence of death.

"You played hell . . . didn't you?" he queried heavily.

"The car . . . smashed?"

"It pitched over the cliff."

"Then . . . we're stuck here."

"Get up. You're not hurt."

She did not deny that in words, but, observing her closely as she dragged herself to her feet, he began to fear that he might have hurt her seriously. She could hardly stand erect, and her breathing seemed difficult.

"Can you walk?" he queried, conscious of shock.

"I'm all right. After all . . . you're pretty big. . . . I'm only . . . a girl."

Roddy went mute at that. She was not accusing him but excusing herself for having been badly whipped in the fight with him. Was that the Texas of it? She had tried to sideswipe him off the running board, she had tried to kill him, she had fought him tooth and nail, and, having lost, she seemed to be as square as she was game. What a wonderful girl! Roddy saw her in an illuminating light.

"Come on," he said, proceeding to take up her bag and coat and the canteen. Down the road some little distance he found his rifle. Thus encumbered, he could not help Collie. Slowly she followed him, a forlorn little figure now. Measured by his feelings, that descent to the cabin was, indeed, a long and grievous one for Roddy. If the girl had tried her feminine wiles, instead of pulling as nervy a stunt as he had ever heard of, he would have had no compunctions over continuing his program. But a change had begun to work on him, a change of opinion and heart. Still he had to keep up the deception until John came for them.

Arriving at the cabin, Roddy deposited his burdens and waited for Collie. It appeared to him that she would just about make it before collapsing. He had to subdue an impulse to go back and carry her. He judged correctly for, upon reaching the cabin, Collie fell upon the tarpaulin spread under the porch roof, and leaned back against the wall, spent and white.

"I've got to kill some meat," he said. "We can't last here without meat. I'll have to tie you up while I go hunting. If I'd done that. . . ."

"I won't try to beat it again. I couldn't, Roddy. Can't you see when a girl is licked. Please don't tie me."

"I reckon I won't trust you."

"But you can. On my honor."

"On your what?"

Her spirit flared up faintly at that. "Of course, *you* wouldn't."

Without more ado, Roddy bound her ankles securely, cursing inwardly more because his hands shook so than at the heinous act he was performing. Then he slipped a pack strap tight around her waist and arms, and buckled it through the chinks between two logs at her back. All the while he avoided meeting her gaze. But even so the magnificent blaze of her eyes seemed to shrivel him.

"Roddy, you're a lot of things, the least of which is a damn' fool," she said enigmatically, as he picked up his rifle.

Stalking off, he pondered her taunt. But upon reaching the woods at the end of the park, he forcibly dismissed everything from mind except the important issue at hand, which was to procure meat. To that end, he stole into the aspens, on up the narrowing apex of the park, peering all around, and pausing every few paces to listen. He had not proceeded far when he heard turkeys scratching. This was a difficult sound to locate. Apparently it was above him. The afternoon wind was strong from the north. He worked against that. He heard various other noises. Once he stopped short with bated breath at a distant *burr* that he took for a motorcar. He waited long for a repetition. As it did not come, he concluded he had been mistaken. Nerves! He would always be hearing the hum of a car in the forest.

Roddy located the flock of turkeys busily and noisily engaged in scratching for pine nuts. The wind was right, blowing at him, and he kept out of sight while making the stalk. Creeping close, he shot two gobblers before the flock disintegrated in a flapping, thumping escape. Much gratified at his success, Roddy tied the legs of the turkeys together, threw them over his shoulder, and, picking up his rifle, made down the slope for camp. Straightway then his problem with Collie reasserted itself, perceptibly different again and more vexatious.

When he strode out from under the pines, at the foot of the north slope, he saw Collie leaning against the cabin wall where he had tied her. As he approached, Roddy imagined her face even paler. Her eyes resembled black holes in a white blanket. She had watched for his return. Poor kid! Roddy's conscience flayed him. Right there he felt forming in him the nucleus of a revolt against John's preposterous plot.

He crossed the brook. He was within speaking distance and was about to hail Collie when something about her checked the words behind his lips. Her unnatural rigidity, her blanched face—no . . . it was a strained and lightning flash of eyes.

Roddy hurried on. What was wrong with Collie? Even as he interpreted that magic of her eyes as deliberate, a warning of impending peril, a harsh voice rasped out: "Drop that rifle! Stick 'em up!"

Roddy obeyed. A man ran out of the cabin at Roddy. A thin red beard failed to hide his hard lips and narrow chin. He held an automatic gun leveled before him. A second fellow appeared, a gun in one hand, rope in the other.

"Frisk him, Marty," ordered the foremost. In short order Roddy's big roll of bills, his knife and watch, his wallet were tossed upon the grass. The cold gray eyes of the leader snapped as he saw them. Then, in short order, Roddy was bound hand and foot and shoved like a sack of meal to the ground. His head bumped against one of his supply packs.

"Collie?" he burst out, as soon as he could speak.

"OK. They just got here. Can't you use your eyes? A Texas Ranger would have been wise the instant he caught my look."

"I saw . . . I thought . . . but I'm no Texas Ranger," rejoined Roddy heavily.

The man called Marty was a Westerner, unmistakably, but a ragged lout whose sallow visage Roddy had seen on the streets or in the poolrooms of Hazelton. He picked up his gun, that he had laid aside to bind Roddy, and, shoving it back into his hip pocket, he turned to his accomplice. Roddy recognized in this individual the man who had attempted to hold him up on the road the day before. He was under thirty. The singular cold and fanatic expression of his pasty face proclaimed him an addict to drugs. He was counting the many bills in Roddy's roll.

"How much, Gyp?" queried Marty, his bleary eyes rolling eagerly.

"Over two grand. But that's not a patch of what we'll clean up. Marty, you steered me onto something good." Then he turned to Roddy, his scrutiny intense and penetrating.

"John Brecken's brother, eh?"

"Yes."

"Yeah, and John Brecken's best girl," leered the fellow Marty.

"And all tied up tight. That means that she didn't come willing," cogitated the red-bearded one, putting two and two together. "Kidnapped her, eh?" he asked, turning to Roddy.

Roddy made no reply.

"Oh, you won't answer. Well, you don't have to. It's as plain as the nose on your face. If you stole John Brecken's girl, he'll pay to get her back, and he'll pay to get you back just so he can get even with you. Now, ain't that a sweet dish?"

"Yeah," chimed in Marty, "and John Brecken's rich. Owns a store, a garage, and an interest in the sawmill. He ought to come across plenty, Gyp."

"Who's the dame? Does she have any folks that would be happy to have their little tootsie-wootsie safe home again?" inquired Gyp.

"She doesn't live in Hazelton. College girl. Never heard her name."

Gyp approached Collie, got down on one knee before her.

103

"What's your name, sweetness?"

"I guess it's Dennis."

"Say! You're all bunged up besides being tied. Beat you up, did he?"

"No. I tried to escape. Ran the car over a bank."

"I see. That's why we couldn't find the car we tracked down here. Have your folks got any money?"

"My mother works to send me to college."

"Don't try to kid me, sweetheart. Could you get ten thousand dollars for ransom?"

"John Brecken ought to pay that much for me," Collie replied sarcastically.

The gangster arose with a light upon his pale visage.

"Plenty safe, Marty, I'll say. Lovely hide-out to wait, good eats when we were damn' near starved, a pretty little dame to sleep with . . . a swell lay-out! Lemme dope this out while you cook supper. My mouth's watering for turkey."

"I'm shore a no-good cook," replied the lout, too heartily to doubt.

"Little one, you're on the spot," said Gyp to Collie.

"I'm afraid I can't stand on my feet," she replied.

"Hey, girl-snatcher, can you roast a turkey so it'll melt in my mouth?" called the fellow to Roddy.

"I reckon. But hardly while my hands and feet are tied."

"Untie him, Marty. And stand guard over him with a gun while he gets supper."

The instant Roddy was freed and on his feet he began to think of a way to turn the tables on their captors. There would still be several hours of daylight. He must work slowly, watching like a hawk, thinking with all the wit and cunning he could muster. Marty fetched the turkeys to him, and Roddy began to pick off the feathers. Gyp went back to Collie. Roddy saw him sit down to lay a bold hand on her.

Then Roddy, with the blood turning to fire in his veins, dared not look again. He could hear the man talking low, manifestly making love to Collie. While Roddy listened, he thought desperately. How much more than Collie's life had he to save now? That transformed his somber spirit. He recalled then that his gun was in the side pocket of the car. But his rifle lay only a few paces away in the grass under some bushes. Apparently his captors had forgotten that. As a last resort, even with Marty sitting there weapon in hand, Roddy decided he would leap for the rifle. But before being driven to that he must wait and watch for a safe moment.

"You dirty skunk. Take your hands off me!" Collie suddenly cried, her voice rising to a shriek. It had such a withering abhorrence that Roddy marveled how any man could face, let alone touch, any woman who spoke with such passion. The fellow on guard let out a lecherous guffaw. Roddy, acting on a powerful impulse, edged over to kindle a fire. On his knees he split wood to replenish it.

"Need hot fire . . . so it'll burn down . . . bed of coals," he explained huskily. He put his big skillet on the blazing faggots and poured half a can of grease into it, then added a quart of water. He had conceived a cunning though exceedingly dangerous plan.

When Collie broke into hysterical sobs, the gangster got up. "Say, baby," he said caustically, "if I wasn't hard up for a dame, I'd call you a wash-out. You cut that stuff or I'll give you something to squawk about."

Then he took to walking to and fro, apparently in deep thought. Roddy was fearful that he might come across the rifle. But he paced a beat between the cabin and the campfire. His concentration became so great that he forgot the others. No doubt he was working out details of the plot to extort ransom money from John Brecken. That plot no longer concerned Roddy. It would never even get started into action.

Roddy put on the Dutch oven to heat. The greasy water in the skillet had begun to boil. Roddy watched it, listened to it simmer. The last of the water in his bucket he poured into the pan with flour. It was not enough to mix biscuit dough. But he fussed with other utensils and supplies until the grease and water in the skillet threatened to boil over.

The moment had come. Strong and cool, with his passion well under control, Roddy had two arrows to his bow.

"Can I fetch a bucket of water?" he asked.

"No. Stay here," called Gyp, coming to the fire. "Marty, you get it."

Marty took the bucket and slouched toward the brook.

Gyp looked down upon the fire. "Say, it strikes me you're slow."

"Slow . . . but sure," replied Roddy, bending to grasp the skillet.

With an incredibly swift movement he came up with it to fling the scalding contents squarely into Gyp's face. The fellow let out a hideous scream of agony.

Roddy sprang to snatch up his rifle. Wheeling as he cocked it, he saw the blinded man fire from his pocket. Roddy shot him through the heart, and his awful curses ended in a gulp. He was swaying backward when Roddy whirled to look for the other fellow. At that instant he heard a bucket clang on rock and a yell. Marty emerged from the willows with his gun spouting red. Roddy felt something like wind, then a concussion that rocked him to his knees. A white flash burst into a thousand sparks before his sight. But as it cleared, he got a bead on Marty and pulled the trigger.

The fellow bawled with the terror of a man shot through the middle. His arms spread out wide. The gun in his right hand smoked and banged. Roddy, quick as a flash, worked the lever and bored the man again. Blank-visaged and slack, he swayed back to crash through the willows that lined the brook.

Then Roddy, blinded by his own blood, dropped the rifle and bent over, one hand supporting him, the other pulling out his handkerchief. Hot blood poured down his face. He watched it drip on the grass. As fast as he wiped it from his face, it streamed down again.

Collie was calling: "Roddy! Roddy! Oh, my God . . . the blood!"

"I'm shot, Collie, but . . . where are you?"

"Here! Here!"

He crawled on hands and knees, guided by her voice. "Wipe off . . . the blood."

"I can't . . . I can't! Darling, I'm tied!"

"Can you see where I'm shot?"

"Yes. Your head . . . on top . . . all bloody . . . but Roddy, it can't be bad. You've got your senses."

"I feel as if my brains were oozing out."

"Mercy! No! No! That can't be, Roddy . . . cut these ropes."

Roddy felt in his pockets. "They took my knife," he said, and then blindly he began to unbuckle the strap that held her elbows to her sides. It seemed to take long. He reeled dizzily. An icy sickening nausea assailed him.

"Let me get at that rope 'round my feet," Collie said. "Damn, you would tie such a knot!"

He felt her bounce up and heard her swift feet thudding away and back to him. A towel went over his head and face. Ministering hands pressed it down.

"Oh, the blood pours so fast! I can't see," she cried. "I'll feel." And with shaking fingers she felt for the wound. Then Roddy sank under a pain that might have been a red-hot poker searing his bared brain. Collie was crying into his fading consciousness. "Darling! Only a groove! No hole in your skull. Oh, thank God!" Then Roddy lost all sense.

When he came to, his blurred sight seemed to see trees and slopes through a red film. His first clear thought was of the blood that had trickled over his eyes. A splitting pain burned under his skull. But his weak hand felt a dry forehead and then a damp bandage bound around his scalp. The red line then, he grasped, was sunset flooding the park.

"Collie," he called faintly.

She came puttering out of the cabin to thump to her knees. Topaz eyes, glinting softness, searched his face. "Roddy?"

"I'm OK, I guess."

"You came to, twice, out of your head."

"Yeah? Well, I can get it now. My head hurts awful. But I can remember . . . and think. . . . Collie, I reckon I did for those two *hombres*."

"You sure did. That Gyp dog is lying right here by the fire, dead as a doornail, and the other is down by the creek. I screamed like a Comanche when you threw the skillet of scalding water in his eyes. I watched him then. . . . I never batted an eyelash. . . . Saw you kill him! But when the other one shot you, and you went down . . . oh, God, that was terrible. I lost my nerve. And never got it back till you fainted."

"Collie, nerve is your middle name. You're one grand kid. Can you ever forgive me? Oh, you couldn't. I'm a sap to ask."

"Yes, I forgive you. Maybe I deserved it. If only I could get all this straight! But here, let's talk of our predicament. Your wound is not serious. I washed it out with Mercurochrome. Lucky I had some in my bag. No fear of infection. I can keep your fever down with this brook water, which is ice-cold. But you've lost blood. . . . Oh, so much! That frightens me. You can't walk for a long time. Our car is smashed. Of course, those men hid theirs, but maybe we can find it. I wouldn't mind staying here forever. It's so sweet and wild and lovely. I'm a Texas girl, Roddy, and you'd find that I can cook and chop wood and shoot game . . . dress it, too. That'd be swell. But, oh, I'm so worried. You might need a doctor."

"Collie, everything will be all right," replied Roddy, with thought only to relieve her. "Jack will come after us in ten days."

"Here?"

"You see . . . I. . . ." Roddy had betrayed himself and could not retrieve his blunder. He bit his lip.

The girl's face flashed scarlet, then went as white as a sheet. And her eyes transfixed him. "Roddy, you framed me."

He groaned in his abasement, and, try as he might, he could not stand those accusing eyes.

"Why in the world . . . *why?*" she cried poignantly. Then evidently she saw that his physical strength was not equal to his distress. "Never mind, Roddy. Forget it. That's not our immediate problem. There's plenty of work for little Collie, believe me. Now I'll make good my brag."

For moments Roddy lay with closed eyes on the verge of fading away again. But the acute pain held him to sensibility. He heard Collie bustling about the campfire. She roused him presently to give him a hot drink. Dusk had fallen. The red light left the sky. He could not keep his eyes open. Collie covered him with blankets. He felt her making a bed beside him. Then all went black.

In the night he awoke, burning, throbbing, parched with thirst. Collie heard his restless movements. She rose to minister to him. She had placed a bucket of water at hand. She gave him a drink and bathed his face. The air was piercingly cold. Coyotes were howling off in the darkness. While Collie was tucking the blankets around him, Roddy fell asleep. Later he awoke again, but endured his pain and did not rouse her. The pangs, however, could not keep him awake long.

Daylight came, Roddy did not know when. There was ice on the water in the bucket, but he did not feel cold. All day he suffered. All day Collie stayed near to keep a wet towel on his face. He craved only water to drink. That night he slept better. Next morning the excruciating headache had gone. His wound throbbed, but less and less. He was on the mend.

That day Collie half carried, half dragged him into the cabin to the bough bed under the window. She made a bed for herself on the ground close by. She was in and out all day long.

When she had made Roddy comfortable, she brought him his package of money. "Took this out of Gyp's pocket," she explained briefly, with an involuntary shudder.

Roddy thanked her in a weak voice. It was an effort to talk, but his mind grew active once more. He had no appetite, but forced down what food and drink she brought him. As he slowly recovered, it grew harder for him to face her. There must come a reckoning. He divined it. Her care, her kindness, her efficiency added to his shame. Night was a relief.

Next day he struggled to his feet, and walked out, wavering, light-headed, weak as an infant. He noted that Collie had covered the bodies of the dead men with large piles of brush and tarpaulins. In another day or two, Roddy thought, he would be strong enough to bury them. Even now the buzzards were circling around high overhead.

While the warm sun was melting the hoar frost on grass and leaves, Roddy walked and rested and walked again, slowly regaining his strength. All about him were signs that Collie's vaunted efficiency at camp tasks was no vain boast.

The campfire had been moved under the end of the porch where Collie had built up a rude fireplace with stones. She had even strung up a clothesline on which several intimate garments were fluttering with an air of domesticity, and was busy now carrying buckets of water up from the creek. And this was the girl he thought would make such a poor wife for John!

That third day Collie had little to say to Roddy until late in the afternoon, when, as he lay on his bed in the cabin with the gold sunlight flooding in at the window, she entered with an armful of purple asters.

"My favorite wildflowers, Roddy."

"Mine, too. Isn't it funny that we have one thing in common?"

"I could tell you more."

"Yeah."

She knelt beside his bed and leaned close to him. "Roddy, you're doing fine. You'll be well soon. I'm so glad. We can have some walks . . . maybe a hunt . . . before. . . . Tell me now, darling."

Roddy protested and denied and demurred, but in the end, from his procrastination, his lies, his evasions, she pieced together the whole cloth of this miserable travesty.

"You great big sap! Roddy, did you ever read the story of Miles Standish, who got John Alden to do his wooing for him? Do you remember when Priscilla said . . . 'Why don't you speak for yourself, John?' "

"Never was much of a speaker," replied Roddy evasively. His chest seemed to cave in.

She leaned over him with soft look and touch and tone. "That day at Cañon Creek, when I went in swimming in only my brassiere and panties to torment Jack . . . you fell in love with me, didn't you?"

111

"No! I . . . I thought you a little brazen hussy."

"Sure, I was. But that's not the point. You fell for me, didn't you?"

"I did not."

"Roddy! Then at the dance, when I asked you to hold me close?"

"Collie, you're a fiend. You're all . . . almost all, Jack. . . . No, I didn't fall for you then."

"When you kidnapped me?"

"Nor then, either."

"It took you long, didn't it?" she laughed adorably. "Well, then, when you caught me running away in the car . . . and I kicked you . . . here . . . on your shin?" And she laid a tender hand on his leg, moved it gently, caressingly, he imagined in his bewilderment, over the great bruise.

"Collie, don't you kid me," he implored.

"When you beat me half dead . . . was it then, darling?"

"Collie, you win, callous little flirt that you are!" he burst out hoarsely. "It must have been at the creek, when you pulled your shameless stunt . . . and all those other times. But, honest to God, I never knew it till that dizzy Gyp laid hands on you."

"It doesn't make any difference when, so long as you do, Roddy," she said more softly, leaning her face so close that he began to tremble. Could not the insatiate little creature be satisfied without flaying her victim? "Say you love me."

"I reckon."

"More than Jack did?"

"Yes."

"More than any boy ever loved me?" she ended imperiously.

"God help me, Collie, I'm afraid I do," he replied. "Now I'm punished. I'll take my medicine. But don't rub it in. This has been a rotten deal for you. It's proved you to be one grand little Thoroughbred. It'll help me, too, I hope, to make a man out of myself. And when you. . . ."

She was bending to him, her heavy eyelids closed, her expression rapt and dreamy, her sweet lips curved and tremulous with the kiss she meant to bestow, when Roddy saw her start. Her eyes opened wide, dark, flashing, luminous with inquiry.

"Listen," she whispered. "A car."

"You're right. It's coming down the ridge. A forest ranger . . . or hunter. . . . Oh, Collie, it means deliverance for you."

"No, Roddy!" she cried, a note of triumph in her voice. "I've got a hunch it's your brother Jack, showing yellow, jealous, scared, come to square himself with us."

"Jack?" questioned Roddy in astonishment.

From the window they watched the leafy gateway of the road at the foot of the ridge. Collie put a tense arm around Roddy. He felt that if Jack really confronted him there, the world would either come to an end or suddenly be glorious.

A bright car slid out of the foliage.

"Jack and his new car. Look at him, sneaking along so slowly," Collie said gleefully, and, giving Roddy a squeeze, she rolled off the bed. To Roddy's amazement she disarranged her blouse, rumpled her curls, vehemently rubbed the make-up from her face, all in a flash. "Will I hand it to him? I'm telling you, darling. Lie down. Pretend to be dying. Let *me* do the talking." She moved to the wide opening of the cabin, and assumed a tragic pose.

The front of the shining car showed beyond the corner of the wall. It stopped. The click of door and thud of feet brought their visitor to the cabin.

"Collie! Collie?" It was Jack's voice, betraying a decided panic.

"So! You're here ahead of schedule? But too late, Jack Brecken."

"Too late? What do you mean? Collie, what's happened?" he exclaimed fearfully.

"Happened? What usually happens when a man carries a girl off into the woods alone?" Collie's tone held all the drama of a wronged woman.

For a moment Jack was speechless. "Why . . . Collie . . . ," he stammered. Then: "You don't mean that . . . that Roddy . . . ?"

"He's only human, Jack."

"But . . . oh, hell! I didn't dream he'd. . . . Roddy did that?" For a moment his tone was utterly incredulous. Then fury possessed him, and he burst out: "The dirty dog. . . . Where is he?"

Roddy listened, spellbound, half in horror, half in admiration. What an actress she was.

"After all, you can't blame him," retorted Collie accusingly. "This was your scheme. I should think you wouldn't have dared. Roddy loved you, Jack, and that was why he fell for your crazy idea."

Her stinging words had the effect of quelling Jack's rage.

"Collie," he said, and his voice filled with anguish, "after you left, I realized what I had done. That's why I came to confess, to make amends. I. . . ."

"Too late, Jack," cut in Collie in solemn accents. "Your brother lies in here . . . his head shot open."

In the silence that ensued, Roddy heard John's gasping expulsion of breath.

"God Almighty! You killed him!" John's knees shook so that they were incapable of holding him. He sat down on the pile of canvas behind him.

Collie started. For a moment she could not find words, and the pause must have been a lifetime of hell to the stricken man. Then she stuck her head in the door to wink a glowing eye at Roddy.

"Jack Brecken, now that you've realized what could have happened, I'll tell you the truth," she pealed out, her slim form instilled with a liberation of passion. "Roddy is not dead. He's alive . . . and I love him . . . love him . . . love him. . . . Your plot miscarried, you big sap! Roddy kidnapped me all right, but we were both kidnapped by real kidnappers. They planned to make you pay ransom. Oh, that would have been great! But one of them got fresh with me and would have attacked me. Roddy outwitted him . . . killed him . . . and his partner. Jack, I was on the fence about you. I think I would have married you. Thank heaven, I found you out, and at last fell terribly in love with your wicked kidnapping brother."

Relief struggled with anguish in John's pale face. "Roddy . . . not . . . dead?" he gasped, "and . . . and . . . he . . . killed two men?" Then, looking fearfully around. "Where are they?"

Collie's tone was extremely casual. "One of them is over by the creek," she drawled, "and you're sitting on the other."

Call on the County

November had laid its drab hand over the rangeland. The dismal croak of ravens broke the dull soundless day. Clouds hung lowering over the dreary waste of plain and ridge and the dim distant mountains. Purple gloom filled the valleys; somber colors merged on the shaggy slopes; under the gray stone bluffs above the road the vines and sumac showed dull red, faded and sear.

The day, the journey, the desert of ridge and range seemed made for the hard errand that had driven Jane Silver to Hillands.

"Mother, let me down. I can walk some. You must be tired," said the child.

"I'm glad . . . we're up the hill," panted the mother, as she put Lily down.

Low squat houses of mud and stone dotted the slope; gray weather-beaten cottages clustered below them, looking down upon the flat roofs of Hillands. The town had once been prosperous, before the mines in the hill had failed, and when the hordes of cattle roamed the ranges. Up in the notches of the hills black ruins of mills, and along the winding road old taverns with their high-walled bleached fronts, and down along the deserted irrigation canal the patches of weeds and bare dry beds of cracked mud—these were doleful reminders to Jane Silver of the lapse of years.

Yet, after all, it was not so long, judged by actual time.

Her memory in one flash transported her back to the ranch and the range of her girlhood. She saw her father, the prosperous old cattleman, loud-voiced, with slap of hand on knee; her mother, sweet of smile, ever busy at her tasks; brothers and sisters who had teased her, loved her in that swift-fading time of girlhood. School days, vacation days, the long rides with the cowboys! She walked again with lovers under the cottonwoods, not sure even now, in this bitter memory, of the one she had loved best. The smell of cedar smoke came back to her, of burning brush, of the horse corrals, and the corn shocks in the barn. There were faces that shone for her and flashed dark upon one another. She saw the rangeland white with snow. She heard the jingling music of sleigh bells; she felt the smooth rush of the wagon-sled on the way to the dance. The laughter of girls, the banter of boys filled this haunting memory. Always she had slipped a sly hand to a lover on each side, in the darkness, merry in her deceit, yet not unconscious of guile. That had been her undoing.

Gray and grim in contrast returned the world of her womanhood. John Silver had been her father's choice, more than hers; yet John, older, graver than the cowboys, a splendid figure of a man, had appealed to the best in her, had seemed an anchor for her secret and wandering passion for conquest. And she had married him. Bond of marriage with its disillusion! She could not be tamed. Worst of all, she could not endure jealousy and suspicion. Then with these phantoms of her past stood out the great shock, the dividing line, the error of her life. Jim Warner, rider of the ranges, debonair and romantic, a handsome devil, saw her and loved her. Something violent and desperate in the depths of her being had called to its like. After three months of marriage with John Silver, bitterly brought to task for the last time, she had let his jealous rage make of her the madwoman she had never been—and she had eloped with Jim Warner. Then disgrace, slow desertion by friends and family, abandonment, cruel years of want, and now catastrophe.

"Mother, after all . . . you must carry me," said the child.

The appeal brought Jane Silver back to the sudden and most poignant and terrible errand ever undertaken by a mother. She lifted Lily again—how light a burden!—up the worn red stone steps of Judge Silver's house. The sun peeped out of a rift in the clouds and made a warm spot on the judge's porch. Lily, clasping an apple, sat down to rest. She panted a little, and drops of sweat stood upon her blue-veined forehead. Over Lily hovered something shadowy, mystical, spiritual, and it softened the mother's pain.

Jane knocked as one knocked on the door of doom. It opened wide, and a man filled the narrow space. He was lean and dark, vastly changed, yet somehow there was a thrill in her recognition. John Silver had never divorced her, had never loved another woman. For a moment amaze appeared to hold him transfixed.

"Jane?" he ejaculated incredulously, and he took a quick step. Then he seemed to shrink. "So. It's the judge you're here to see," he added bitterly. "Well, come in."

A different kind of past thronged back on Jane. To see the man she had wronged, to realize the havoc she had wrought, hurt more than any memory. Yet if John Silver had suffered the rust of actionless years, if he had shown the corroding lichen of hate, Jane felt she might have borne this ordeal.

"John . . . Judge Silver, I've been driven to come," replied Jane hoarsely. "The doctor said my girl, Lily, is failing. . . . Oh, God, it's hard! I've nothing . . . no people . . . no friends who will help me. . . . And those old women at Turners, where I live . . . they say if there's a call on the county to bury anyone . . . the application must be made to the county magistrate *before*. . . ."

"Well, well, so that's your errand," returned Judge Silver. "Where's your child?"

"She's outside . . . resting," Jane said hurriedly. "You won't need to see her . . . will you?"

"I reckon so. An' why not?" he queried, with the lightning of his gray eyes on her.

"I've no reason . . . no sensible one," went on Jane painfully. "But I hoped it wouldn't be necessary. Lily is such a strange child. Not like other little girls. I never understood her. I'm afraid . . . oh, so terribly afraid . . . she knows what my life has been."

"I reckon I'll have to send for Doctor Bartle an' let him see her," replied the judge.

"Lily was low yesterday. She has queer spells. Today she's bright. Oh, she's uncanny sometimes. It wrings my heart. But she's so sweet, so lovable, so like an angel. Then she was the smartest girl in her class. I had to take her out of school. I've never been sure it was the study that broke down her health."

"Ha! Outcast mother . . . outcast child!" returned Silver tensely. "How old is she now?"

"Nine years . . . nine this month."

"Only nine! Well, well, I reckoned it seemed longer than that, since . . . ," rejoined the judge. "It's too bad. Poor little girl! She wasn't to blame. The sins of the parents are visited upon the children."

"Judge Silver, I'm deathly afraid . . . if she learned why I'm here. . . . Oh, she mustn't know. I beg of you."

"Well, I reckon I've no call to be kind to Jim Warner's child, but I'd never let her know, that's sure. Jane, there's no law about this county buryin' the dead. In fact, the magistrate is the law. If the doctor says your child is dyin', then I'll decide on the case."

Jane could not utter her thanks, or make another appeal on behalf of the errand that had forced her to face him. She sat clasping and unclasping her hands, questioning this lean, austere face with piercing eyes. The woman in her sensed the wrong never forgotten, never avenged; the mother in her feared the righteous wrath of one whose opportunity had come, who must, indeed, be noble to withstand the temptation fate had thrust upon him. Yes, she had it in her power to change his hate, to rob his revenge of its sweetness, although she might not break his will. Locked deep in her heart hid this power, and no scorn, no humiliation, no flaying her could ever bring it to light.

"Here, Jane," he said, "swear on this Bible to tell the truth an' nothin' but the truth."

She heard someone within her, who seemed other than herself, repeating after him the words of the oath. As one fascinated, she watched his slow deliberate movements, turning the leaves of an old ledger, poising his pen as he prepared to question her.

How absurd, aside from the point, these queries as to her people, her birth, age, whether married or single, occupation, and proofs of poverty. Methodically he wrote down answers that he well knew without asking. Then all at once a change came over him. He looked up to face her with eyes she found hard to meet, and began more deliberate questioning, beginning with relation to the present hour and working back toward the past.

He would have the detailed story of her journey from Turners to Hillands. He probed the reason of her errand. He would have knowledge of where she lived and how she lived—for the poverty and sickness of her household. When

Jim Warner had deserted her. What that abandonment had meant. He wanted to know the actions and the gossip of her neighbors. Then the years she had followed Jim Warner from range to range, and so on, endlessly back to the staggering fact of her downfall.

Jane realized now that her appeal to Judge Silver as the dispenser of county charity had been laid aside—that she must face him woman to man and drain this cup of gall to the dregs. Not to answer never occurred to her. She had to speak. She was on trial to bare her soul, to confess that the wrong she had done him had earned its retribution, to feed some abnormal passion of curiosity and agony in him. She saw him slowly transforming under the poignant influence of a love recalled from its grave. His lean face and figure took on the lines of his youth.

No longer did it seem the dry worn judge who arraigned her, but the dishonored and discarded husband, leonine in his wrath, white-faced, strong and terrible. He laid stark and naked the facts of her elopement with Warner. If she had any shame, his fury and his will beat it down, so that she confessed even the miserable kisses she had bestowed upon her lover. The smothered jealousy of the years demanded fuel for its insatiable fire. Jane told him all. Self-abasement and degradation were hers to the fullest.

Then he got no further than the catastrophe of his life. He repeated—you jilted me—dishonored me—abandoned me? Yes!

"You never loved me!" he thundered.

"Ah, John! You cannot make me confess that," she replied softly. "I did love you. But I was a wild thing, hateful of restraint. If you had understood me, I'd never have ruined both our lives. If you had not been jealous . . . not unjustly suspected me of dishonor . . . I'd never have betrayed you."

That stabbed him. The quiver of his intense face told how the truth struck mortally home. Jane had never understood until then the boundlessness of what his love had been. She felt in the presence of an appalling revelation something unquenchable as the fire of the sun, an emotion that made her long-past, wayward infatuation so base and pitiful. If, as a young wife, she could only have gauged the depths of this man's love! What might have been! Across the years now, from her woman's travail, she saw John Silver clearly.

"Woman . . . wife still . . . do you come to me?" he thundered, beating his breast with clenched fist. "Do you come here . . . beggin' me to save your child from the paupers' field?"

"Yes, John, I've come," replied Jane. "What's done is done. God only knows how it happened or why! It can't be undone. But if I had my life to live over, I'd never wrong you."

He towered over her for a silent endless moment, while the white passion of his face gave place to a more normal hue. He changed again, although not back to the Judge Silver he had been. There remained nothing of the old John Silver.

"Well, Jane," he said at last, sighing heavily. "I'll do what you ask. Meanwhile, stay here with my folks . . . you an' Lily, until. . . ."

It was another afternoon, and Jane Silver sat by Lily's bedside, haunted by the shadow in the child's eyes.

A fly buzzed behind the window shade, telling of the autumn sunshine warm upon the pane. Lily lay with wide questioning gaze that seemed to grow wise. The soft lips were locked. After a while she closed her eyelids, dreamy and heavy with mystic thought, and lay as one asleep. Did she really sleep?

Jane Silver was used to long vigils by the bedside. But this one seemed to inaugurate a subtle change. The afternoon faded into twilight and then the gloom of early evening, which was the time when Jane's mind began to awaken and quicken. Soft footfalls sounded through the house. John Silver's old mother and his sister were busy preparing the evening meal. Low voices and faint steps came from the judge's office. Jane's cold heart warmed as she thought of their quiet sympathy and kindness; amaze, too, sometimes filled the brief intervals in which she wandered from the stern grief of the moment.

From outside the house there penetrated sounds somehow full of inscrutable meaning for her. Compared with the hamlet of Turners, this old town of Hillands was bustling with people walking and riding by. Footsteps! *Clip-clop!* Sauntering and hurrying steps passed along the road; the jingle of spurs lent her a thrill. Could she ever hear that musical clink without a strange stir deep in her heart? For years she had listened for that sound, and then for more years she had listened from sad habit, not with hope. Here she was sitting in the first darkness of the November night, by the bedside of her dying child. And from outside came haunting sounds—sounds typical of the rangeland, clinking steps, trotting hoofs, roll of buckboard and freighter, the young fresh drawling voices of cowboys. These passers-by were unknown to Jane, yet seemed to come out of her past life. They had a message, but its meaning was not clear.

Later, when the black lonely night settled down over the house, Jane felt that she would be undisturbed in her vigil. But the wind from the rangeland moaned under the caves; dead cottonwood leaves rustled over the ground, softly brushed the house, whispered of the coming of winter and ice and death, were silent, and then stirred again to a sad rustle. Mice gnawed at the wood in the wall, and squeaked, and ran with tiny thrumming footsteps. The silence of the night hummed noiselessly—the wheels of life whirling and whirring on toward the end.

Through the window Jane watched a pale circle of light grow brighter over the black mountain. At length a white, cold, moving radiance silvered the cedars. Moonlight streamed into the room. On a white patch of floor the shadow of a swinging bough moved regularly, silently, weirdly. It swayed beyond the window to leave clear the moon-blanched square; it returned as steadily. It was a long, dark, moving finger pointing to a fateful hour. Light! Shadow!

Along the floor crept the square of moonlight, as if the time had come for it to sever its relation with the weird shadow of bough. It crept to the bed, slowly up the coverlet, slowly turning to marble Lily's frail hands, at last to illumine her face. How pure and strange and sad! But had Lily's suffering been physical? Whence that look of age, of wisdom, unreal on the beautiful face?

Jane Silver could not bear it. She shut out the moonlight. Yet that helped so little. Always, when Lily slept, there seemed another presence in the room. In slumber she was different from what she was awake. In the change from moonlight to opaque gloom a death-like whiteness hovered on Lily's face. Jane suddenly bent down, closer, straining at the fierce pang in her breast. No—the child still lived. But was that an altered look, a slow, anguished passing from doubt to certainty? What did Lily know? Jane Silver shrank pitifully from the question that now knocked at the gates of her soul. Should she not have told Lily the truth? Then came a whisper out of the night, out of the past, out of the life she had pierced in thought, whence Lily was soon to flee, and it was not a whisper of hope, or of peace, but of endurance.

The blackness paled, the gray light brightened, and Lily's birthday dawned. Jane felt that the gentle life of the child had completed its cycle. Birth to death! Nine years that should have been the fleeting dreamful happy time of childhood! But Jane had begun to be dimly conscious that for Lily these years, almost from babyhood, had been travail. Something had forced the child's mind far beyond her age.

This day then, Jane divined, would bring the rending climax of her sufferings.

She sat between the bed and the window, and, when Lily slept, Jane would gaze down over the quaint old town, out to the dark mountains and the purple rangeland. This day November had gone back to October. Gone were the gray clouds, the gray mists in the valleys, the gray mantle of the peaks, the gray gloom that veiled the distant ranges.

The sky was blue as the sea; great white cumulus clouds rolled over the mountain horizon; the sun shone gloriously, and a fall wind whirled up the golden dust-funnels and swept them pirouetting and expanding, far out on the bleached range.

Time had been when Jane Silver's heart had throbbed with love for this rangeland, so free, so vast, so unbounded. Undulating plain and swelling ridge. How they enfolded with their deceiving distance the many leagues. They seemed the same as in her youth. Red and white cattle dotted the foreground. A long, meandering line of cottonwoods, half bare, and half sear with dead leaves, marked the course of the canal. A patch of trees, a little shack and windmill, scattered here and there, removed this swelling plain from the aspect of a desert. Beyond them it spread and rolled, growing purple in the distance. She felt herself a part of that rangeland, but she had failed it. The glory and freedom and simplicity of the open had been hers all her girlhood, but she had not taken them into her being.

The mountain kingdom Jane had found in her woman-hood to be a better teacher, because it did not haunt her with regret and remorse. All her life the mountains had been distant, an unknown land, barrier from the wilderness beyond. All this day the purple peaks ministered to her. In the clear light she saw the seams and scars of age, the pale cliffs and the dark cañons. She saw the shadows of the cloud-ships sailing along their slopes. These upflung domes of rock were mute monuments to the travail of the earth. They taught endurance. Lift up thine eyes to the mountains whence cometh thy help!

Had they been the secret of John Silver's strength? Jane trembled when she thought of this man. Lover and husband, yet a stranger to her in those wild years of her girlhood! She asked herself why. Only because she had been a shallow, vain, ignorant child whom no one could understand. If she could only have called back the past! Then John Silver had every reason to despise, instead of love, her. Jane remembered his patience, his long talks, his hopes and prayers, entailed in the futile longing to make her a woman.

And now he loomed a strange and vast figure in her anguished mind. His old mother had spared Jane any look or word of reproach. She expressed pity for Jane and love for the child. But with pride, perhaps with purpose, she had talked of her son John. And all the fixed hateful impressions of Jane's memory were suddenly as if they had never been. She had never known John Silver. Now she saw him through the wide-open eyes of womanhood. Then, swiftly, strangely, her abasement flooded out on the tide of passionate exultation—he had loved her greatly—he had never remarried—he had climbed above hate, scorn, revenge. Ah, he might love her still! But that sweet wild thought died at its tumultuous birth. It was the last gasp of the vanity that had been the bane of her life. Jane sighed, poor incomprehensible creature she was.

There came a tap on the door. Jane rose noiselessly, and, opening it, she encountered John Silver on the threshold. His fine dark face showed signs of recent agitation. He entered the room with a strange glance toward the quiet figure on the bed.

"Is she asleep?" he whispered.

"Yes. She's slept on and off all day," replied Jane.

"I've been to Turners," added the judge abruptly.

Jane's lips formed a query she could not speak.

"Jane, I wanted to know about you," he said, answering her look. "So I went. . . . Why didn't you tell me . . . how poor you'd been? I reckoned I'd saved you that. I never knew. No one ever spoke of you to me. Jane, those damned gabby women at Turners. Sure they riled me. Why'd they hate you so? Because you were pretty, I reckon. Well, well, that's no great matter. But what they said about Lily hurt me deep."

"I'm sorry. Tell me . . . what it was," Jane faltered with a numbness creeping over her.

"They say the children taunted Lily," Silver replied darkly. "They say she's known for years . . . she's nameless. Jim Warner's child. That's what ailed her."

"Oh, heaven, of late I feared . . . and now I know," whispered Jane. Her life fell around her in utter ruin. How mocking and terrible the result of her blind pride to hide and spare. Someday, a little later, Lily would be old enough to understand, to pity her mother—that had been the shibboleth. Too late! The innocent child had suffered for the guilty mother.

"Jane . . . ," whispered the judge, leaning down with a strong and beautiful light on his face, "she shall be buried as Lily Silver."

"What do you mean?" gasped Jane.

"I've never divorced you, Jane. You're still my wife. Lily must have my name. You shall stay here. My home is your home, as it would be Lily's if, by the grace of God, she could live."

"You'll take me back? Give my child your name before the world."

"Jane, I reckon so. . . . I love you still."

With bursting heart Jane sought to cry out her agony—to fall before him and clasp his feet—to find utterance for a mighty and mounting storm—to wrench from her depths what now seemed the hate and revenge of a wayward girl.

"John . . . come with me," she whispered. Although she led him, it seemed she needed his support. And he clung to her, as one in a dream. "Look at her . . . now?"

"Is she asleep?" he asked, husky and low. Indeed, he feared she was asleep forever.

The light fell upon a face as white as snow, framed with golden curls. Only the closed mystic eyelids suggested pain. The mouth was sweet, as if about to break into faint smile of relief.

"John, look at her. . . . Lily is your child!"

He uttered a choked cry, gazed with intense fixity at the strangely changing face, turned to Jane with staring eyes of anguished rapture, and back to the child.

"My God! My God! I . . . never . . . dreamed. Oh, Jane . . . I see . . . I believe!" And he fell upon his knees beside the bed.

Suddenly Lily's eyes opened wide. They seemed windows of a soul in transport. "Mother, I wasn't asleep," she said with a smile that seemed not of earth. "I heard you both." And she burst into tears.

Jane bent in fear and trembling over the bed. Not for years had Lily cried. The little white face quivered as she turned to the judge.

"You're my . . . honest father?" she sobbed.

"Yes, dear. But I never knew until now," he replied huskily.

"Everybody will know. I will tell them. . . . My father . . . ! I am not going to die!"

Don

The Story of a Lion Dog

It has taken me years to realize the greatness of a dog; and often as I have told the story of Don—his love of freedom and hatred of men—how I saved his life and how he saved mine—it never was told as I feel it now.

I saw Don first at Flagstaff, Arizona, where arrangements had been made for me to cross the desert with Buffalo Jones and a Mormon caravan *en route* to Lee's Ferry on the Colorado River.

Jones had brought a pack of nondescript dogs. Our purpose was to cross the river and skirt the Vermillion Cliffs, and finally work up through Buckskin Forest to the north rim of the Grand Cañon, where Jones expected to lasso mountain lions, and bring them back alive. The most important part of our outfit, of course, was the pack of hounds. Never had I seen such a motley assembly of canines. They did not even have names. Jones gave me the privilege of finding names for them.

Among them was a hound that seemed out of place because of his superb proportions, his sleek dark smooth skin, his noble head, and great solemn eyes. He had extraordinarily long ears, thick-veined and faintly tinged with brown. Here was a dog that looked to me like a Thoroughbred. My friendly overtures to him were unnoticed. Jones said he was part bloodhound and had belonged to an old Mexican don in southern California. So I named him Don.

We were ten days crossing the Painted Desert, and protracted horseback riding was then so new and hard for me that I had no enthusiasm left to scrape acquaintance with the dogs. Still I did not forget and often felt sorry for them as they limped along, clinking their chains under the wagons. Even then I divined that horses and dogs were going to play a great part in my Western experience.

At Lee's Ferry we crossed the Colorado, and I was introduced to the weird and wild cañon country, with its golden-red walls and purple depths. Here we parted with the caravan and went on with Jones's rangers, Jim and Emmet, who led our outfit into such a wonderful region as I had never dreamed of.

We camped several days on a vast range where Jones let his buffalo herd run wild. One day the Arizonians put me astride a white mustang that apparently delighted in carrying a tenderfoot. I did not know then what I was soon to learn—that the buffalo always chased this mustang off the range. When I rode up on the herd, to my utter amaze and terror, they took after me and—but I am digressing, and this is a dog story.

Once across the river, Jones had unchained the dogs and let them run on ahead or lag behind. Most of them lagged. Don for one, however, did not get sore feet.

Beyond the buffalo range we entered the sage, and here Jones began to train the dogs in earnest. He carried on his saddle on old blunderbuss of a shotgun, about which I had wondered curiously. I had supposed he meant to use it to shoot small game.

Moze, our black-and-white dog, and the ugliest of the

lot, gave chase to a jack rabbit.

"Hyar, you Moze, come back!" bawled Jones in stentorian tones.

But Moze paid no attention. Jones whipped out the old shotgun, and before I could utter a protest, he had fired. The distance was pretty far—seventy yards or more—but Moze howled piercingly and came sneaking and limping back. It was remarkable to see him almost crawl to Jones's feet.

"Thar! That'll teach you not to chase rabbits. You're a lion dog!" shouted the old plainsman as if he were talking to a human.

At first I was so astounded and furious that I could not speak. But presently I voiced my feeling.

"Wal, it looks worse than it is," he said, with his keen gray-blue eyes on me. "I'm usin' fine birdshot, an' it can't do any more than sting. You see, I've no time to train these dogs. It's necessary to make them see quick that they're not to trail or chase any varmints but lions."

There was nothing for me to do but hold my tongue, although my resentment appeared to be shared by Jim and Emmet. They made excuses for the old plainsman.

"He shore can make animals do what he wants," Jim said. "But I never seen the dog or hoss that cared two bits for him."

We rode on through the beautiful purple sageland, gradually uphill, toward a black-fringed horizon that was Buckskin Forest. Jack rabbits, cottontails, coyotes and foxes, prairie dogs and pack rats infested the sage and engaged the attention of our assorted pack of hounds.

All the dogs except Don fell victim to Jones's old blunderbuss; and surely stubborn Moze received a second peppering, this time at closer range. I spied drops of blood upon his dirty white skin. After this it relieved me greatly to see that not even Moze transgressed again.

Jones's method was cruel, but effective. He had captured and subdued wild animals since his boyhood. In fact, that had been the driving passion of his life, but no sentiment entered into it.

"Reckon Don is too smart to let you ketch him," Jim once remarked to our leader.

"Wal, I don't know," responded Jones dubiously. "Mebbe he just wouldn't chase this sage trash. But wait till we jump some deer. Then we'll see. He's got bloodhound in him, and I'll bet he'll run deer. All hounds will, even the best ones trained on bear an' lion."

Not long after, we entered the wonderful pine forest and the reckoning of Don came as Jones had predicted. Several deer bounded out of a thicket and crossed ahead of us, soon disappearing in the green blur.

"Uhn-huh! Now we'll see," ejaculated Jones, deliberately pulling out the old shotgun.

The hounds trotted along beside our horses, unaware of the danger ahead. Soon we reached the deer tracks. All the hounds showed excitement. Don let out a sharp yelp and shot away like a streak on the trail.

"Don, come hyar!" yelled Jones, at the same time extending his gun.

Dan gave no sign he had heard. Then Jones pulled the trigger and shot him. I saw the scattering of dust and pine needles all around Don. He doubled up and rolled. I feared he might be injured badly. But he got up and turned back. It seemed strange that he did not howl.

Jones drew his plunging horse to a halt and bade us all stop.

"Don, come back hyar," he called in a loud, harsh, commanding voice.

The hound obeyed, not sneakingly or cringingly. He did

not put his tail between his legs. But he was frightened and no doubt pretty badly hurt. When he reached us, I saw that he was trembling all over and that drops of blood dripped from his long ears. What a somber sullen gaze in his eyes.

"See hyar," bellowed Jones, "I knowed you was a deer chaser! Wal, now you're a lion dog."

Later that day, when I had recovered sufficiently from my disapproval, I took Jones to task about this matter of shooting the dogs. I wanted to know how he expected the hounds to learn what he required of them.

"Wal, that's easy," he replied curtly. "When we strike a lion trail, I'll put them on it . . . let them go. They'll soon learn."

It seemed plausible, but I was so incensed that I doubted the hounds would chase anything, and I resolved that, if Jones shot Don again, I would force the issue and end the hunt unless assured there would be no more of such training methods.

Soon after this incident we made camp on the edge of a beautiful glade where a snow bank still lingered and a stream of water trickled down into a green swale. Before we got camp pitched, a band of wild horses thudded by, thrilling me deeply. My first sight of wild horses! I knew I should never forget that splendid stallion, the leader, racing on under the trees, looking back at us over his shoulder.

At this camp I renewed by attempts to make friends with Don. He had been chained apart from the other dogs. He ate what I fetched him, but remained aloof. His dignity and distrust were such that I did not risk laying a hand on him then. But I resolved to win him if it were possible. His tragic eyes haunted me. There was a story in them I could not read. He always seemed to be looking afar. On this occasion I came to the conclusion that he hated Jones.

Buckskin Forest was well named. It appeared to be full of deer, the large black-tailed species known as mule deer. This species must be related to the elk. The size and beauty of them, the way they watched with long ears erect and then bounded off as if on springs, never failed to thrill me with delight.

As we traveled on, the forest grew wilder and more beautiful. In the park-like glades a bleached white grass waved in the wind and bluebells smiled wanly. Wild horses outnumbered the deer, and that meant there were some always in sight. A large gray grouse flew up now and then; most striking of the forest creatures to fascinate me was a magnificently black squirrel, with long, bushy, white tail, and tufted ears, and a red stripe down its glossy sides.

We rode for several days through this enchanting wilderness, gradually ascending, and one afternoon we came abruptly to a break in the forest. It was the north rim of the Grand Cañon. My astounded gaze tried to grasp an appalling abyss of purple and gold and red, a chasm too terrible to understand all at once. The effect of that moment must have been tremendous, for I have never recovered from it. To this day the thing that fascinates me most is to stand upon a great height—cañon wall, or promontory, or peak—and gaze down into the mysterious colorful depths.

Our destination was Powell's Plateau, an isolated cape jutting out into the cañon void. Jones showed it to me—a distant, gold-rimmed, black-fringed promontory, seemingly inaccessible and unscalable. The only trail leading to it was a wild horse hunter's trail, seldom used, exceedingly dangerous. It took two days over this cañon trail to reach the Saddle—a narrow strip of land dipping down from the plateau and reaching up to the main rim. We camped under a vast, looming, golden wall, so wonderful that it kept me from sleeping.

That night lions visited out camp. The hounds barked for hours. This was the first chance I had to hear Don. What a voice he had! Deep, ringing, wild, like the bay of a wolf!

Next morning we ascended the Saddle, from the notch of which I looked down into the chasm still asleep in purple shadows; then we climbed a narrow deer trail to the summit of the plateau. Here, indeed, was the grand wild isolated spot of my dreams. Indeed, I was in an all-satisfying trance of adventure.

I wanted to make camp on the rim, but Jones laughed at me. We rode through the level stately forest of pines until we came to a ravine on the north side of which lay a heavy bank of snow. This was very necessary, for there was no water in the plateau. Jones rode off to scout while the rest of us pitched camp.

Before we had completed our tasks, a troop of deer appeared across the ravine, and motionless they stood, watching us. There were big and little deer, blue-gray in color, sleek and graceful, so tame that to me it seemed brutal to shoot at them.

Don was the only one of the dogs that espied the deer. He stood up to gaze hard at them, but did not bark or show any desire to chase them. Yet there seemed to be a strange yearning light in his dark eyes. I had never failed to approach Don, whenever opportunity afforded, to continue my overtures of friendship. But now, as always, Don turned away from me. He was cold and somber. I had never seen him wag his tail or whine eagerly, as was common with most hounds.

Jones returned to camp jubilant and excited, as far as it was possible for the old plainsman to be. He had found lion trails and lion tracks, and he predicted a great hunt for us.

The plateau resembled in shape the ace of clubs. It was

perhaps six miles long and three or four wide. The body of it was covered with a heavy growth of pine, and the capes that sloped somewhat toward the cañon were thick with sage and cedar. This lower part, with its numerous swales and ravines and gorges, all leading down into the jungle of splintered crags and thicketed slopes of the Grand Cañon, turned out to be a paradise for deer and lion.

We found many lion trails leading down from the cedared broken rim to the slopes of yellow and red. These slopes really constituted a big country, and finally led to the sheer perpendicular precipices, three thousand feet lower.

Deer were numerous and as tame as cattle on a range. They grazed with our horses. Herds of a dozen or more were common. Once we saw a very large band. Down in the sage and under the cedars and in ravines we found many remains of deer. Jones called these lion-kills. And he frankly stated that the number of deer killed yearly upon the plateau would be incredible to anyone who had not seen the actual signs.

In two days we had three captive lions tied to pine saplings near camp. They were two-year-olds. Don and I had treed the first lion; I had taken pictures of Jones lassoing him; I had jumped off a ledge into a cedar to escape another; I had helped Jones hold a third; I had scratches from lion claws on my chaps, and—but I keep forgetting that this is not a story about lions. Always before when I have told it, I have slighted Don.

One night, a week or more after we had settled in camp, we sat around a blazing red fire and talked over the hunt of the day. We all had our part to tell. Jones and I had found where a lioness had jumped a deer. He showed me where the lioness had crouched upon a little brushy knoll, and how she had leaped thirty feet to the back of the deer.

He showed me the tracks the deer had made—bounding, running, staggering with the lioness upon its back—and where, fully a hundred paces beyond, the big cat had downed prey and killed it. There had been a fierce struggle. Then the lioness had dragged the carcass down the slope, through the sage, to the cedar tree where her four two-year-old cubs waited. All that we found of the deer were the ragged hide, some patches of hair, cracked bones, and two long ears. There were still warm.

Eventually we got the hounds on this trail and soon put up the lions. I found a craggy cliff under the rim and sat there, watching and listening for hours. Jones rode to and fro above me, and at last dismounted to go down to join the other men.

The hounds treed one of the lions. How that wild cañon slope rang with the barks and bays and yells! Jones tied up his lion. Then the hounds worked up the ragged slope toward me, much to my gratification and excitement. Somewhere near me the lions had taken to cedars or crags, and I strained my eyes searching for them.

At last I located a lion on top of an isolated crag right beneath me. The hounds, with Don and Ranger leading, had been on the right track. My lusty yells brought the men. Then the lion stood up—a long, slender, yellowish cat—and spat at me. Next it leaped off that crag, fully fifty feet to the slope below, and bounded down, taking the direction from which the men had come. The hounds gave chase, yelping and baying. Jones bawled at them, trying to call them off, for what reason I could not guess. But I was soon to learn. They found the lion Jones had captured and left lying tied under a cedar, and they killed it, then took the trail of the other. They treed it far down in the rough jumble of rocks and cedars.

One by one we had ridden back to camp that night, tired out. Jim was the last in, and he told his story last. And what was my amazement and fright to learn that all the three hours I had sat upon the edge of the caverned wall, the lioness had crouched on a bench above me.

Jim on his way up had seen her, and then located her tracks in the dust back of my position. When this fact burst upon me, I remembered how I had at first imagined I heard faint panting breaths near me somewhere. I had been too excited to trust my ears.

"Wal," said Jones, standing with the palms of his hands to the fire, "we had a poor day. If we had stuck to Don, there'd have been a different story. I haven't trusted him. But now, I reckon, I'll have to. He'll make the greatest lion dog I ever had. Strikes me queer, too, for I never guessed it was in him. He has faults, though. He's too fast. He outruns the other hounds, and he's goin' to be killed because of that. Someday he'll beat the pack to a mean old Tom or a lioness with cubs, and he'll get his everlastin'.

"Another fault is, he doesn't bark often. That's bad, too. You can't stick to him. He's got a grand bay, shore, but he saves his breath. Don wants to run an' trail an' fight alone. He's got more nerve than any hound I ever trained. He's too good for his own sake . . . an' it'll be his death."

Naturally I absorbed all that Buffalo Jones said about dogs, horses, lions, everything pertaining to the West, and I believed it as if it had been gospel. But I observed that the others, especially Jim, did not always agree with our chief in regard to the hounds. A little later, when Jones had left the fire, Jim spoke up with his slow Texas drawl: "Wal, what does he know about dawgs? I'll tell you right heah, if he hadn't shot Don, we'd had the best hound that ever put his nose to a track. Don is a wild strange hound, shore enough. Mebbe he's like a lone wolf. But it's plain he's been mistreated by men. An' Jones has just made him wuss."

Emmet inclined to Jim's point of view. And I respected this giant Mormon who was famous on the desert for his kindness to men and animals. His ranch at Lee's Ferry was overrun with dogs, cats, mustangs, burros, sheep, and tamed wild animals that he had succored.

"Yes, Don hates Jones and, I reckon, all of us," said Emmet. "Don's not old, but he's too old to change. Still, you can never tell what kindness will do to animals. I'd like to take Don home with me and see. But Jones is right. That hound will be killed."

"Now I wonder why Don doesn't run off from us?" inquired Jim.

"Perhaps he thinks he'll get shot again," I ventured.

"If he ever runs away, it'll not be here in the wilds," replied Emmet. "I take Don to be about as smart as any dog ever gets. And that's pretty close to human intelligence. People have to live lonely lives with dogs before they understand them. I reckon I understand Don. He's either loved one master once and lost him, or else he has always hated all men."

"*Humph!* That's shore an idee," ejaculated Jim dubiously. "Do you think a dog can feel like that?"

"Jim, I once saw a little Indian shepherd dog lie down on its master's grave and die," returned the Mormon sonorously.

"Wal, dog-gone me!" exclaimed Jim in mild surprise.

One morning Jim galloped in, driving the horses pell-mell into camp. Any deviation from the Texan's usual leisurely manner of doing things always brought us up short with keen expectation.

"Saddle up!" called Jim. "Shore that's a chase on. I seen a big red lioness up heah. She must have come down out of the tree whar I hang my meat. Last night I had a haunch of venison. It's gone. Say, she was a beauty! Red as a red fox."

In a very few moments we were mounted and riding up the ravine, with the eager hounds sniffing the air. Always over-anxious in my excitement, I rode ahead of my comrades. The hounds trotted with me. The distance to Jim's meat tree was a short quarter of a mile. I knew well where it was, and, as of course the lion trail would be fresh, I anticipated a fine oppor-tunity to watch Don. The other hounds had come to regard him as their leader. When we neared the meat tree that was a low-branched oak shaded by thick silver spruce, Don ele-vated his nose high in the air. He had caught a scent, even at a distance. Jones had said more than once that Don had a won-derful nose. The other hounds, excited by Don, began to whine and yelp and run around with noses to the ground.

I had eyes only for Don. How instinct he was with life and fire! The hair on his neck stood up like bristles. Suddenly he let out a wild bark and bolted. He sped away from the pack and like a flash passed that oak tree, running his head high. The hounds strung out after him, and soon the woods seemed full of a baying chorus. My horse, Black Bolly, well knew the meaning of that medley and did not need to be urged. He broke into a run and swiftly carried me up out of the hollow and through a brown-aisled, pine-scented strip of forest to the cañon.

I rode along the edge of one of the deep indentations on the main rim. The hounds were bawling right under me at the base of a low cliff. They had jumped the lioness. I could not see them, but that was not necessary. They were running fast toward the head of this cove, and I had hard work to hold Black Bolly to a safe gait along that tricky rim. Suddenly she shied, and then reared, so that I fell out of the saddle as much as I dismounted. But I held the bridle, and then jerked my rifle from the saddle sheath. As I ran toward the rim, I heard the yells of the men coming up behind.

At the same instant I was startled and halted by sight of something red and furry flashing up into a tree right in front of me. It was the red lioness. The dogs had chased her into a pine, the middle branches of which were on a level with the rim.

My skin went tight and cold, and my heart fluttered. The lioness looked enormous, but that was because she was so close. I could have touched her with a long fishing pole. I stood motionless for an instant, thrilling in every nerve, reveling in the beauty and wildness of that great cat.

She did not see me. The hounds below engaged all her attention. But when I let out a yell that I could not stifle, she jerked spasmodically to face me. Then I froze again. What a tigerish yellow flash of eyes and fangs. She hissed. She could have sprung from the tree to the rim and upon me in two bounds. But she leaped to a ledge below the rim, glided along that, and disappeared.

I ran ahead and with haste and violence clambered out upon a jutting point of the rim, from which I could command the situation. Jones and the others were riding and yelling back where I had left my horse. I called for them to come.

The hounds were baying along the base of the low cliff. No doubt they had seen the lioness leap out of the tree. My eyes roved everywhere. This cove was a shallow V-shaped gorge, a few hundred yards deep and as many across. Its slopes were steep with patches of brush and rock.

All at once my quick eye caught a glimpse of something moving up the opposite slope. It was a long, red, pantherish shape. The lioness! I yelled with all my might. She ran up the slope, and at the base of the low wall she turned to the right. At that moment Jones strode heavily over the rough loose rocks of the promontory toward me.

"Where's the cat?" he boomed, his gray eyes flashing. In a moment more I had pointed her out. "Ha! I see . . . don't like that place. The cañon boxes. She can't get out. She'll turn back."

The old hunter had been quick to grasp what had escaped me. The lioness could not find any break in the wall, and manifestly she would not go down into the gorge. She wheeled back along the base of this yellow cliff. There appeared to be a strip of bare clay or shale rock against which background her red shape stood out clearly. She glided along, slowing her pace, and she turned her gaze across the gorge.

Then Don's deep bay rang out from the slope to our left. He had struck the trail of the lioness. I saw him running down. He leaped in long bounds. The other hounds heard him and broke for the brushy slope. In a moment they had struck the scent of their quarry and given tongue. As they started down, Don burst out of the willow thicket at the bottom of the gorge and bounded up the opposite slope. He was five hundred yards ahead of the pack. He was swiftly climbing. He would run into the lioness.

Jones gripped my arm in his powerful hand. "Look!" he shouted. "Look at that fool hound! Runnin' uphill to get that lioness. She won't run. She's cornered. She'll meet him. She'll kill him. . . . Shoot her! Shoot her!"

I scarcely needed Jones's command to stir me to save Don, but it was certain that the old plainsman's piercing voice made me tremble. I knelt and leveled my rifle. The lioness showed red against the gray—a fine target. She was gliding more and more slowly. She saw or heard Don. The gun sight wavered. I could not hold steady. But I had to hurry. My first bullet struck two yards below the beast, puffing the dust. She kept on. My second bullet hit behind her. Jones was yelling in my ear. I could see Don out of the tail of my eye. Again I shot.

Too high! But the lioness jumped and halted. She lashed with her tail. What a wild picture! I strained—clamped every muscle, and pulled the trigger. My bullet struck under the lioness, scattering a great puff of dust and gravel in her face. She bounded ahead a few yards and up into a cedar tree.

An instant later Don flashed over the bare spot where she had waited to kill him, and in another his deep bay rang out under the cedar.

"Treed, by gosh!" yelled Jones, joyfully pounding me on the back with his huge fist. "You saved that fool dog's life. She'd have killed him shore. . . . Wal, the pack will be here *pronto,* and all we've got to do is go over and tie her up. But it was a close shave for Don."

That night in camp Don was not in the least different from his usual somber self. He took no note of my proud proprietorship or my hovering near him while he ate the supper I provided, part of which came from my own plate. My interest and sympathy had augmented to love.

Don's attitude toward the captured and chained lions never ceased to be a source of delight and wonder to me. All the other hounds were upset by the presence of the big cats. Moze, Sounder, Tige, Ranger would have fought these collared lions. Not so Don! For him they had ceased to exist. He would walk within ten feet of a hissing lioness without the slightest sign of having seen or heard her. He never joined in the howling chorus of the dogs. He would go to sleep close to where the lions clanked their chains, clawed the trees, whined and spat and squalled.

Several days after that incident of the red lioness we had a long and severe chase through the brushy cedar forest on the left wing of the plateau. I did well to keep the hounds within earshot. When I arrived at the end of that run, I was torn and blackened by the brush, wet with sweat, and hot as fire. Jones, lasso in hand, was walking around a large cedar tree under which the pack of hounds was clamoring. Jim and Emmet were seated on a stone, wiping their red faces.

"Wal, I'll rope him before he rests up," declared Jones.

"Wait till . . . I get . . . my breath," panted Emmet.

"We shore oozed along this mawnin'," drawled Jim.

Dismounting, I untied my camera from the saddle, and then began to peer up into the bushy cedar.

"It's a Tom lion," declared Jones. "Not very big, but he looks mean. I reckon he'll mess us up some."

"Haw! Haw!" shouted Jim sarcastically. The old plainsman's imperturbability sometimes wore on our nerves.

I climbed a cedar next to the one in which the lion had taken refuge. From a topmost fork, swaying to and fro, I stood up to photograph our quarry. He was a good-size animal, tawny in hue, rather gray of face, and a fierce-looking brute. As the distance between us was not far, my situation was as uncomfortable as thrilling. He snarled at me and spat viciously. I was about to abandon my swinging limb when the lion turned away from me to peer down through the branches.

Jones was climbing into the cedar. Low and deep the lion growled. Jones held in one hand a long pole with a small fork at the end, upon which hung the noose of his lasso. Presently he got up far enough to reach the lion. Usually he climbed close enough to throw the rope, but evidently he regarded this beast as dangerous. He tried to slip the noose over the head of the lion. One sweep of a big paw sent pole and noose flying. Patiently Jones made ready and tried again, with similar result. Many times he tried. His patience and perseverance seemed incredible. One attribute of his great power to capture and train wild animals here asserted itself. Finally the lion grew careless or tired, at which instant Jones slipped the noose over its head. Drawing the lasso tight, he threw his end over a thick branch and let it trail down to the men below.

"Wait now!" he yelled, and quickly backed down out of the cedar. The hounds were leaping eagerly.

"Pull him off that fork and let him down easy so I can rope one of his paws."

It turned out, however, that the lion was hard to dislodge. I could see his muscles ridge and bulge. Dead branches cracked, the treetop waved. Jones began to roar in anger. The men replied with strained hoarse voices. I saw the lion drawn from his perch, and, clawing the branches, springing convulsively, he disappeared from my sight.

Then followed a crash. The branch over which Jones was lowering the beast had broken. Wild yells greeted my startled ears and a perfect din of yelps and howls. Pandemonium had broken loose down there. I fell more than I descended from that tree.

As I bounded erect, I espied the men scrambling out of the way of a huge furry wheel. Then hounds and one lion comprised that brown whirling ball. Suddenly out of it a dog came hurtling. He rolled to my feet, staggered up.

It was Don. Blood was streaming from him. Swiftly I dragged him aside, out of harm's way. And I forgot the fight. My hands came away from Don wet and dripping with hot blood. It shocked me. Then I saw that his throat had been terribly torn. I thought his jugular vein had been severed.

Don lay down and stretched out. He looked at me with those great somber eyes. Never would I forget! He was going to die right there before my eyes.

"Oh, Don! Don! What can I do?" I cried in horror.

As I sank beside Don, one of my hands came in contact with snow. It had snowed that morning, and there were still white patches of it in shady places. Like a flash I ripped off my scarf and bound it around Don's neck. Then I scraped up a double handful of snow and placed that in my bandanna handkerchief. This also I bound tightly around his neck. I could do no more. My hope left me then, and I had not the courage to sit there beside him until he died.

All the while I had been unaware of a bedlam near at hand. When I looked, I saw a spectacle for a hunter. Jones, yelling at the top of his stentorian voice, seized one hound after the other by the hind legs and, jerking him from the lion, threw him down the steep slope.

Jim and Emmet were trying to help while at the same time they avoided close quarters with that threshing beast. At last they got the dogs off and the lion stretched out. Jones got up, shaking his shaggy head. Then he espied me, and his hard face took on a look of alarm.

"Hyar . . . you're all . . . bloody," he panted plaintively, as if I had been exceedingly remiss.

Whereupon I told him briefly about Don. Then Jim and Emmet approached, and we all stood looking down on the quiet dog and the patch of bloody snow.

"Wal, I reckon he's a goner," said Jones, breathing hard. "Shore I knew he'd get his everlastin'."

"Looks powerful like the lion has about got his, too," added Jim.

Emmet knelt by Don and examined the bandage round his neck. "Bleeding yet," he muttered thoughtfully. "You did all that was possible. Too bad! The kindest thing we can do is leave him here."

I did not question this, but I hated to consent. Still, to move him would only bring on more hemorrhage and to put him out of his agony would have been impossible for me. Moreover, while there was life, there was hope! Scraping up a goodly ball of snow, I rolled it close to Don so that he could lick it if he chose. Then I turned aside and could not look again. But I knew that tomorrow or the following day I would find my way back to this wild spot.

The accident to Don and what seemed the inevitable issue weighed heavily upon my mind. Don's eyes haunted me. I very much feared that the hunt had reached an unhappy ending for me.

Next day the weather was threatening, and, as the hounds were pretty tired, we rested in camp, devoting ourselves to needful tasks. A hundred times I thought of Don, alone out there in the wild brakes. Perhaps merciful death had relieved him of suffering. I would surely find out on the morrow.

But the indefatigable Jones desired to hunt in another direction next day, and, as I was by no means sure I could find the place where Don had been left, I had to defer that trip. We had a thrilling hazardous luckless chase, and I for one gave up before it ended.

Weary and dejected I rode back. I could not get Don off my conscience. The pleasant woodland camp did not seem the same place. For the first time the hissing, spitting, chain-clinking, tail-lashing lions caused me irritation and resentment. I would have none of them. What was the capture of a lot of spiteful vicious cats to the life of a noble dog? Slipping my saddle off, I turned Black Bolly loose.

Then I imagined I saw a beautiful black long-eared hound enter the glade. I rubbed my eyes. Indeed, there was a dog coming. "Don!" I shouted my joy and awe. Running like a boy, I knelt by him, saying I knew not what. Don wagged his tail. He licked my hand! These actions seemed as marvelous as his return.

He looked sick and weak, but he was all right. The hand-kerchief was gone from his neck, but the scarf remained, and it was stuck tight where his throat had been lacerated.

Later Emmet examined Don and said we had made a mistake about the jugular vein being severed. Don's injury had been serious, however, and without the prompt aid I had so fortunately given he would soon have bled to death.

Jones shook his gray old locks and said: "Reckon Don's time hadn't come. Hope that will teach him sense."

In a couple of days Don had recovered, and on the next he was back leading the pack.

A subtle change had come over Don in his relation to me. I did not grasp it so clearly then. Thought and memory afterward brought the realization to me. But there was a light in his eyes for me that had never been there before.

One day Jones and I treed three lions. The largest leaped and ran down into the cañon. The hounds followed. Jones strode after them, leaving me alone with nothing but a camera to keep those two lions up that tree. I had left horse and gun far up the slope.

I protested. I yelled after him: "What'll I do if they start down?"

Jones turned to gaze up at me. His grim face flashed in the sunlight. "Grab a club and chase them back," he replied.

Then I was left alone with two ferocious-looking lions in a piñon tree scarcely thirty feet high. While they heard the baying of the hounds, they paid no attention to me, but after that ceased they got ugly. Then I hid behind a bush and barked like a dog. It worked beautifully. The lions grew quiet. I barked and yelped and bayed until I lost my voice. Then they got ugly again. They started down. With stones and clubs I kept them up there, while all the time I was wearing to collapse.

When at last I was about to give up in terror and despair, I

149

heard Don's bay, faint and far away. The lions had heard it before I had. How they strained! I could see the beating of their hearts through their lean sides. My own heart leaped. Don's bay floated up, wild and mournful. He was coming. Jones had put him on the back trail of the lion that had leaped from the tree.

Deeper and clearer came the bays. How strange that Don should vary from his habit of seldom baying. There was something uncanny in this change. Soon I saw him far down the rocky slope. He was climbing fast. It seemed I had long to wait, yet my fear left me. On and up he came, ringing out that wild bay. It must have curdled the blood of those palpitating lions. It seemed the herald of that bawling pack of hounds.

Don espied me before he reached the piñon in which were the lions. He bounded right past it and up to me with the wildest demeanor. He leaped up and placed his forepaws on my breast. And as I leaned down, excited and amazed, he licked my face. Then he whirled back to the tree, where he stood up and fiercely bayed the lions.

When I sank down to rest, overcome, the familiar baying chorus of the hounds floated up from below. As usual they were behind the fleet Don, but they were coming as fast as they could.

Another day I found myself alone on the edge of the huge cove that opened down into the main cañon. We were always getting lost from one another. And so were the hounds. There were so many lion trails that the pack would split, some going one way, some another, until it appeared each dog finally had a lion to himself.

Then as I sat there, absorbed and chained, the spell of enchantment was broken by Don. He had come to me. His mouth was covered with froth. I knew what that meant.

Rising, I got my canteen from the saddle and poured water into the crown of my sombrero. Don lapped it. As he drank so thirstily, I espied a bloody scratch on his nose.

"Aha! A lion has batted you one, this very morning!" I cried. "Don . . . I fear for you."

He rested while I once more was lost in contemplation of the glory of the cañon. What significant hours these on the lonely heights! But then I only saw and felt.

Presently I mounted my horse and headed for camp, with Don trotting behind. When we reached the notch of the cove, the hound let out his deep bay and bounded down a break in the low wall. I dismounted and called. Only another deep bay answered me. Don had scented a lion or crossed one's trail. Suddenly several sharp deep yelps came from below, a crashing of brush, a rattling of stones. Don had jumped another lion.

Quickly I threw off sombrero and coat and chaps. I retained my left glove. Then, with camera over my shoulder and revolver in my belt, I plunged down the break in the crag. My boots were heavy soled and studded with hobnails. The weeks on these rocky slopes had trained me to fleetness and sure-footedness. I plunged down the sliding slant of weathered stone, crashed through the brush, dodged under the cedars, leaped from boulder to ledge and down from ledge to bench.

Reaching a dry streambed, I espied in the sand the tracks of a big lion, and beside them smaller tracks that were Don's. As I ran, I yelled at the top of my lungs, hoping to help Don tree the lion. What I was afraid of was that the beast might wait for Don and kill him.

Such strenuous exertion required a moment's rest now and then, during which I listened for Don. Twice I heard his bay, and the last one sounded as if he had treed the lion. Again I took to my plunging, jumping, sliding descent, and I was not long in reaching the bottom of that gorge.

Ear and eye had guided me unerringly, for I came to an open space near the main jump-off into the cañon, and here I saw a tawny shape in a cedar tree. It belonged to a big Tom lion. He swayed the branch and leaped to a ledge, and from that down to another, and then vanished around a corner of wall.

Don could not follow down those high steps. Neither could I. We worked along the ledge, under cedars, and over huge slabs of rock toward the corner where our quarry had disappeared. We were close to the great abyss. I could almost feel it. Then the glaring light of a void struck my eyes like some tangible thing. At last I worked out from the shade of rocks and trees, and, turning the abrupt jut of wall, I found a few feet of stone ledge between me and the appalling chasm. How blue, how fathomless! Despite my pursuit of a lion I was suddenly shocked into awe and fear.

Then Don returned to me. The hair on his neck was bristling. He had come from the right, from around the corner of wall where the ledge ran, and where surely the lion had gone. My blood was up, and I meant to track that beast to his lair, photograph him, if possible, and kill him.

So I strode onto the ledge and around the point of wall. Soon I espied huge cat tracks in the dust, close to the base. A well-defined lion trail showed there. And ahead I saw the ledge—widening somewhat and far from level—stretch before me to another corner.

Don acted queerly. He followed me, close at my heels. He whined. He growled. I did not stop to think then what he wanted me to do. But it must have been that he wanted to go back. The heat of youth and the wildness of adventure had gripped me, and fear and caution were not in me.

Nevertheless, my sensibilities were remarkably acute.

When Don got in front of me, there was something that compelled me to go slowly. Soon, in any event, I should have been forced to that. The ledge narrowed. Then it widened again to a large bench with cavernous walls overhanging it.

I passed this safe zone to turn onto a narrowing edge of rock that disappeared around another corner. When I came to this point, I must have been possessed, for I flattened myself against the wall and worked around it.

Again the way appeared easier. But what made Don go so cautiously? I heard his growls; still, no longer did I look at him. I felt this pursuit was nearing an end. At the next turn I halted short, suddenly quivering. The ledge ended—and there lay the lion, licking a bloody paw.

Tumultuous, indeed, were my emotions, yet on that instant I did not seem conscious of fear. Jones had told me never, in close quarters, to take my eyes off a lion. I forgot. In the wild excitement of a chance for an incomparable picture I forgot. A few precious seconds were wasted over the attempt to focus my camera.

Then I heard quick thuds. Don growled. With a start I jerked up to see the lion had leaped or run half the distance. He was coming. His eyes blazed purple fire. They seemed to paralyze me, yet I began to back along the ledge. Whipping out my revolver, I tried to aim. But my nerves had undergone such a shock that I could not aim. The gun wobbled. I dared not risk shooting. If I wounded the lion, it was certain he would knock me off that narrow ledge.

So I kept on backing, step by step. Don did likewise. He stayed between me and the lion. Therein lay the greatness of that hound. He easily could have dodged by me to escape along that ledge!

A precious opportunity presented when I reached the widest part of the bench. Here I had a chance, and I recognized it.

Then, when the overhanging wall bumped my shoulder, I realized too late. I had come to the narrowing part of the ledge. Not reason but fright kept me from turning to run. Perhaps that would have been the best way out of the predicament. I backed along the strip of stone that was only a foot wide. A few more blind steps meant death. My nerve was gone. Collapse seemed inevitable. I had a camera in one hand and a revolver in the other.

That purple-eyed beast did not halt. My distorted imagination gave him a thousand shapes and actions. Bitter, despairing thoughts flashed through my mind. Jones had said mountain lions were cowards, but not when cornered—never when there was no avenue of escape!

Then Don's haunches backed into my knees. I dared not look down, but I felt the hound against me. He was shaking, yet he snarled fiercely. The feel of Don there, the sense of his courage caused my cold thick blood to burst into hot gushes. In another second he would be pawed off the ledge or he would grapple with this hissing lion. That meant destruction for both, for they would roll off the ledge.

I had to save Don. That mounting thought was my salvation. Physically he could not have saved me or himself, but this grand spirit somehow pierced to my manhood. Leaning against the wall, I lifted the revolver and steadied my arm with my left hand, which still held the camera. I aimed between the purple eyes. That second was an eternity. The gun crashed. The blaze of one of those terrible eyes went out.

Up leaped the lion, beating the wall with heavy, thudding paws. Then he seemed to propel himself outward, off the ledge into space—a tawny figure that careened majestically over and over, down—down—down to vanish in the blue depths.

Don whined. I stared at the abyss, slowly becoming unlocked from the grip of terror. I staggered a few steps forward to a wider part of the ledge, and there I sank down, unable to stand longer. Don crept to me, put his head in my lap.

I listened. I strained my ears. How endlessly long seemed that lion in falling! But all was magnified. At last puffed up a sliding roar, swelling and dying until again the terrific silence of the cañon enfolded me.

Presently Don sat up and gazed into the depths. How strange to see him peer down! Then he turned his sleek dark head to look at me. What did I see through the somber sadness of his eyes? He whined and licked my hand. It seemed to me Don and I were more than man and dog. He moved away then around the narrow ledge, and I had to summon energy to follow.

Shuddering, I turned my back on that awful chasm and held my breath while I slipped around the perilous place. Don waited there for me, then trotted on. Not until I had gotten safely off that ledge did I draw a full breath. Then I toiled up the steep, rough slope to the rim. Don was waiting beside my horse. Between us we drank the rest of the water in my canteen, and, when we reached camp, night had fallen. A bright fire and a good supper broke the gloom of my mind.

My story held those rugged Westerners spellbound. Don stayed close to me, followed me of his own accord, and slept beside me in my tent.

There came a frosty morning when the sun rose over the ramparts of colored rock. We had a lion running before the misty shadows dispersed from the cañon depths. The hounds chased him through the sage and cedar into the wild brakes of the north wing of the plateau. This lion must have been a mean old Tom, for he did not soon go down the slopes.

The particular section he at last took refuge in was impassable for man. The hounds gave him a grueling chase, then one by one they crawled up, sore and thirsty. All returned but Don. He did not come home.

Buffalo Jones rolled out his mighty voice that pealed back in mocking hollow tones. Don did not come. At noonday Jones and the men left for camp with the hounds.

I remained. I had a vigil there on the lofty rim, alone, where I could peer down the yellow-green slope and beyond to the sinister depths. It was a still day. The silence was overpowering. When Don's haunting bay floated up, it shocked me. At long intervals I heard it, fainter and fainter. Then no more!

Still I waited and watched and listened. Afternoon waned. My horse neighed piercingly from the cedars. The sinking sun began to fire the Pink Cliffs of Utah, and then the hundred miles of immense chasm over which my charmed gaze held dominion. How lonely, how terrifying that stupendous rent in the earth!

Lion and hound had no fear. But the thinking, feeling man was afraid. What did they mean—this exquisitely hued and monstrous cañon—the setting sun—the wildness of a lion, the grand spirit of a dog—and the wondering sadness of man?

I rode home without Don. Half the night I lay awake waiting, hoping. But he did not return by dawn nor through that day. He never came back.

Rangle River

It was the glaring coral shore, the whispering palms, the blue lagoon, and the crawling line of white reef far out that brought an intense and fixed realization to Marian Hastings's troubled mind. These, added to the dry heat of the Australian town, the flying dust, the blaze of the tropics, all so vastly different from cold foggy London, from which she had fled, constituted the last straw of weight under which she succumbed.

Marian had just arrived at Coombs, a town far up on the Queensland coast, and after the endless ride from Sydney in the stifling train she wanted a little breathing spell before making inquiry about the property she had inherited from an uncle, Dan Hastings. Leaving her hand luggage with the station agent, she had headed down a dusty street toward the green and blue that beckoned welcomingly, and she was attacked by a stormy she knew not what.

It passed after a little while, as she sat in the shade, leaving her with a gradually dawning consciousness of gladness and relief. Pleasant sensations began to wear away the intolerable discomfort that had been hers for days. At home in London Marian had often worried that, if she ever got where it was warm and dry and bright, she would stay there. And, lo, here she was, as if by magic, fourteen thousand miles from home, north of Sydney, at a sleepy town on the edge of the vast Queensland desert. The fact became terribly real, and she felt a strange exultation creeping over her.

She was twenty-two now, and for more years than she could remember she had cherished a secret longing for adventure, for a new and fuller life, to get far away from the conventionality which wealth and social position demanded. Since her brother had been lost in the war there had been no strong family ties. So, when Marian fell heir to a cattle station belonging to an uncle of whom she had dim loving memories, she leaped at this opportunity to be free. At that time she had been harassed by a fear she might fall in love with an idle and charming man she could not respect, and by a futile disgust for another man who had made his persistent courtship, fostered and aided by her relatives, something well-nigh intolerable. Half across the Atlantic had been enough to prove but groundless her fear of giving away her heart. But wireless news that Mannister, the other man, had boarded a ship for Australia, was not readily dispelled. It would not be easy for him to locate her in the hinterland of this large country, but if he did so, and persisted further in his unwelcome attentions she would be at a loss to know what to do. She had an idea Mannister was unscrupulous. But in that lovely but hard country how would the effete man about town conduct himself? He would not measure up. He would not stay. Anyway, sufficient unto the day!

I think I will love it here, mused Marian. *No one here, or passing by this out of the way place, could know me, or anything about me. But I'll be careful. I must plan . . . how to proceed . . . what to do. . . . Oh, wonderful!*

Rested and keen at the prospect of she knew not what, Marian arose and turned from the murmuring beach, with its lonely seagulls and swishing palms. Half a block from the shore the heat settled down on her like a blanket. Returning to the station, she got her hand-luggage, and, saying she would send for her remaining luggage later, she took a taxi to a hotel. The streets, the buildings, the vehicles were so different from any Marian had ever seen before that she had no comparison at hand. Despite the heat and dust this town of Coombs appeared to be alive. The hotel lobby was thronged with countless men, weather-beaten and dusty-booted. A polite and smiling boy carried Marian's baggage to her room. It was such that brought back to her mind her oft-asserted belief that she could live without luxury.

"Boy, it's a very hot day," she said, as she removed her hat.

"No, ma'am, begging your pardon. Cool today. Only ninety-eight," he replied cheerfully.

"Only! What do you call a hot day?"

"It was a hundred and eighteen out at Rangle River yesterday."

The name gave Marian a slight wink. Don Hastings's cattle station incorporated that river. She asked where it was.

"Sixty odd miles out back. Dick Drake came in last night with his racehorse. He's going to run in the races today."

There was a decided thrill for Marian in the boy's information. Her uncle had mentioned his foreman, a lad named Drake, who took care of his horses. It seemed that her long unsatisfied love for horses might find its fulfillment here. Marian asked for ice water, which the boy fetched promptly.

"Excuse me, lady, but aren't you going out to the Melvilles?" asked the boy brightly.

"No. Why do you ask?"

"Well, if you was, you should have got off the train a hundred miles down . . . at Melville Station."

"Who are the Melvilles?" asked Marian.

"They own the biggest cattle station in Australia. Millions of acres. Nobody knows how big it is."

"How very interesting! I'll ask you to tell me more later. I'd like to know now where to find your courthouse, or whatever you call your place for legal matters."

"One block down, on the corner. You can't miss it. But you'd better hurry. This is Saturday, and they close at noon."

Marian took her bag that contained her papers, letters of credit, and identification and rallied forth with her zest quickening. It afforded her real pleasure to see what little attention she appeared to draw from the men in the lobby. She was used to being noticed. This was an agreeable contrast. Perhaps out here what counted was what you were, what you could do, and not your looks. She found the building on the corner, a gray structure, secure and forbidding, and upon questioning at several offices finally found the record department for that district. The clerk appeared to be a pale, stoop-shouldered man of middle age, obsequious and kindly.

"Have you record here of the property of one Daniel Hastings?" she asked.

"Hastings? Hastings . . . ? That'd be old Dan of Rangle River. Yes, miss, the record is here."

"I am his niece, Marian Hastings, from London. Uncle Dan bequeathed the ranch to me. Here are all the necessary papers. Will you please look them over, and make what necessary record of transaction, or formalities, whatever they are. I have letters of credit and identification."

The official appeared delighted to serve Marian, and presently returned her papers with a serious air. "Miss Hastings, you came, of course, just to see the old man's place? You can hardly have any intention of living there?"

"That's just what I intend to do."

"Gracious! Didn't old Dan . . . excuse me, your uncle . . . tell you about the . . . his place?"

"No. Years ago he used to write about it . . . his herds of cattle . . . droves of horses, *etcetera*. But nothing of late."

"I'm sorry to inform you that Rangle River is no place for a girl," he said gravely.

"You mean it is a wild out back place, without conveniences or comforts, terribly run down . . . and all that?"

"All that certainly. But worse. There is really no place a young woman of . . . like you . . . could live in. No water. No green."

"Oh!" Marian cried in dismay. "No grass? No trees?"

"Grass in patches. And there are trees . . . great eucalyptus four hundred feet high, some of them. Grand trees . . . but it's a ghastly range."

"Have you seen it lately?" asked Marian faintly.

"I never saw it. Only hearsay. But it's generally known around Coombs."

"Are there any encumbrances?"

"No mortgage or debts, except what old Dan owed Drake and Jim Bates. He could not pay them wages, but they refused to leave him. Just carried on somehow. Bates had seen gold digging days with Dan, a long time ago. They were done. Drake drifted in there a few years ago and stayed."

"Do you know these men?"

"I know Jim Bates fairly well. But have only a speaking acquaintance with Drake. He is . . . er . . . well . . . rather an odd one, Miss Hastings, but these men are in town today. You will meet them, of course, and form your own conclusions. I'm sure they will strongly advise you against your going to Rangle Rim."

Marian thanked him and headed toward the hotel, revolving in mind a rather thought-provoking interview. It enhanced, rather than discouraged, interest in her Australian property, and she was curious to meet these men who had been loyal to Dan Hastings. Marian visited some of the stores, to be agreeably surprised. Coombs appeared to be quite a town and a center for a large buying district. She learned that this was the beginning of the hurricane season, during which period tourists from the south did not come. Returning to the hotel, she asked the boy to page Mr. Jim Bates, and then went into the dining room. It was crowded and noisy. She spied a few women amidst the many men. There were seven men at the table where she was seated. And Marian's advent changed her opinion about the little notice accorded a young woman. In fact, the attention she received somewhat tested her indifference. The truth was she was not indifferent. She wanted to talk to these men.

The luncheon was generous and wholesome, if not perfectly served. Upon her return to the lobby the bellboy had in tow a stalwart rugged man whose seamed countenance was brick red. He had keen gray-blue eyes that must have peered long over dusty ranges. Marian liked his look.

"You are Mister Jim Bates?" she inquired.

"Yes, ma'am, at your service," he replied, his interest only outdone by his credulity.

"You have recently been associated with Dan Hastings, at Rangle River?"

His start appeared slight, but did not escape Marian's keen eyes. "I have, indeed, ma'am."

"He was my uncle. I am Marian Hastings. He left the station to me, and I have come out to take possession."

"Lord Almighty's sake!" he exclaimed. "So you're the little Marian old Dan used to talk about . . . ? Well, you've got the Hastings' good looks. Never saw a handsomer man than Dan in his day."

"Let's get out of the lobby where we can talk," suggested Marian, and, when they had found seats in an adjoining room, she went on. "I have been to the courthouse to have my deed recorded. I was not able to get much information there."

"I reckon not," returned Bates dryly. "Nobody knows anything about Rangle River."

"It is my business to find out all about Rangle River," said Marian deliberately. "Mister Bates, if you have been friend and companion to my uncle for so many years, surely you are the one to help me."

Bates regarded her with a friendly yet unfavorable air. He was not yet over his astonishment. "I reckon I am, Miss Hastings," he rejoined presently. "And the first thing I say to you is, give up any idea of going to Rangle River, let alone live there."

"Why?"

"It's a ghastly place."

"So the courthouse man said. But . . . is the property worth anything?"

"No."

"How big is it?"

"Pretty big, even for North Australia, ma'am. Hundred miles along each of three sides. The south line, adjoining the Melvilles' station, has always been in dispute. That is, they disputed it. And for some queer reason old Dan and I could never figure out why they wanted to buy the land. Offered nothing much, but still it was an offer. And I advise you to sell out, Miss Marian."

"No. I'll keep it . . . run it. I want to live there."

"But, my God, lady, it's no place for the likes of you," protested Bates.

"But I'm a Hastings as well as Uncle Dan was. Please do not waste more words over that, Mister Bates. I'll stay."

"By God, I admire your spunk," Bates declared with fire in his eye. "Old Dan and I always swore Rangle River would make a magnificent range if we had the money to develop it. But we hadn't, and now . . . it's yours to waste."

"Sad. All the same I'll have a go at it."

"You will? You can't be turned back?"

"No."

"Very good. That's settled, then. Have you any money?"

"Not much, judged by station-developing standards in Australia."

"Well, how much, if you'll excuse me being blunt?"

"Enough perhaps to pay back-wages to you and your man. . . ."

"You can't pay me any back-wages. Or Drake, either. We've lived off the land," interrupted Bates, his red visage growing ruddier.

"No? Well, we won't quarrel over that now. . . . Let's see, I can buy a car . . . a stock of supplies and . . . what kind of a house have I to live in?"

"Live, do you mean it? You're going out there to live?"

"Yes, I mean it. I'm thrilled to death."

"Drake won't see it. He'll think you're mad. You are, a little. Old Dan was."

"Drake will see my venture my way . . . or he'll have to go. Is there a house fit for me to live in?"

"Lord, no. But I reckon old Dan's could be cleaned out and made to shelter you from heat and sand."

"That's fine. You will help me make out a list of things . . . and supplies, too. How do you get from Rangle Rim to Coombs? A car, of course."

"We've got an old truck. How Dick makes it go I can't understand. But he does. That reminds me, Miss Marian. There's a horse race today."

"Grand! Who is Dick?"

"Drake's name is Richard . . . he trucked Blue in yesterday, and we'll bet every last farthing. . . ."

"Blue? That's Drake's horse?"

"Yes. As a matter of fact Blue is *your* horse, Miss Marian. He's a three-year-old and the prettiest, fastest piece of horseflesh we've ever seen in this country. Drake trained him. Old Dan was keen on horses. Rangle River was originally a cattle station. But often our cattle went wild or was drove off by thieves who bred horses. We've got a few left."

"Oh, why didn't you tell me that at once?" exclaimed Marian, unable to repress something glad that burst within her. "Will you take me to the race?"

"I will that. And be proud. We must be going, though."

"Give me a moment. I must get a veil and a linen coat. That dust is terrible." Marian flew to her room, and actually danced a moment before her mirror. When had she seen her eyes dark and shining like this? She hurried down to rejoin Bates, who led her out. A stream of people was passing down the street, and excitement was in the air. Stores were being closed.

"Every last soul in this town will be there," averred Bates, with pride. "We're Australians, Miss Marian."

"You haven't anything on me. Bates, does Drake ride Blue in the race?"

"Lord, no. Dick is a grand horseman. Drake's too big for Blue in this race."

"Will we see him before . . . ?"

"Like as not. And if we do, Miss Marian, let's keep the news from him till afterward. It's bound to upset him."

"That'll be fine. Blue will win, of course, and then Dick will be a right mind to meet his new boss. Oh, this dust! Is it far to go?"

"Just outside town. We'll get a ride there from the garage."

In due time Marian was free of the dust and heat, with a good seat down in front of a grandstand, eagerly viewing a racecourse that would have been a joy to any horseman.

"I'll be back in a few minutes, Miss Marian," said Bates.

"Don't tell our secret," she returned brightly. "Let me tell it. And, oh, I almost forgot. Here . . . bet this on Blue for me."

Bates took the money, which was a crisp new hundred pound banknote Marian had gotten in Sydney. The old man's eyes widened. "My God . . . when have I seen one of these? But, too much, Miss Marian. Give me a quid. That'll be plenty."

"I'll risk that on Blue."

"But it's no sense. If you have only a little money. . . . Dick would be angry . . . if you lost."

"He won't lose. Blue will win this race. I feel it. Go . . . place my bet . . . and come back soon."

The big open grandstand was rapidly filling; a babble of voices assailed Marian's ears from all sides; town and country people mingled with the eager banter of the racetrack; a band was filing in at the upper end; and between the stands and the track fence a milling crowd momentarily augmented.

Marian experienced more of an approach to comfort than at any time since she had arrived at Coombs. A breeze blew through the stand. Evidently the racetrack was situated near the sea.

Presently Bates rejoined her, broadly smiling, waving a program. "Your money's on and you're getting odds. Eight to five. It seems there's a Melville colt in the last race, favorite in the betting. Some big Melville money forced up those odds. Blue will run rings around their horse."

"Fine!" Marian exclaimed happily. "Let's put up more money on Blue."

"Dick and I have plunged on the roan. Every pound we had and could borrow. We'll be ruined if he loses."

"I'll take a chance. Here's another fifty."

"Say, lady, you said you were poor."

"Certainly. I am. But only relatively so. I have a little money. It must go for Rangle River. Only a trifle more or less on Blue. . . ."

"No, Miss Hastings. I feel awful guilty now. But you are sure sporting. This will tickle Dick."

"Have you seen him?"

"For a moment. He rushed off to the stalls. Ah, here come the ponies. They'll be off in a jiffy."

Marian gave over herself whole-heartedly to the excitement and enthusiasm of the crowd. The very atmosphere of that place seemed charged with the potentialities for what she yearned. Something new, far-flung, liberating! She picked a horse in the first race and offered to bet Bates on her choice. The clean-limbed racers lined up, the prancing and jockeying, the bell and the flag—they were off! And Marian was just one of thousands who loved to see a horse run. Judging from the approval of the crowd, the favorite won. Thereafter, the races followed one another in rapid succession, each adding to the fervor, and, when the final and big race was called, she felt with the onlookers, even though she did not manifest it openly.

"There's Blue," Bates said, pointing. "Number four."

"Oh! Blue. I never saw a horse of that color. What a beauty! And the boy up? Can he ride?"

"Ha! That he can. Dick has been training this lad as well as the horse. Look, lady. Number six is the Melville colt. Classy, isn't he?"

"That sorrel? Pooh! He'll just be one that races. No high and mighty, Bates."

"Maybe you know horses. I hope on high you do. But I'm scared bad. Dick's heart is so set on this race. How he loves that pony! Why, Blue has kept him at Rangle River for three years. There . . . at the post, Marian! Did I tell you Blue's sire was old Dan's best-loved horse? Off!"

The crowd roared. Marian heard her cry pealing out into the clamor. Blue had taken the lead at the jump and was off like a blue streak. At the quarter he was lengths ahead of two horses that ran neck and neck, the outside one number six, the Melville colt. Bates boomed into Marian's ear: "Don't worry. Blue hasn't started to run. He's a finisher."

"Then the race is won!" cried Marian. Her feelings were stirred. Was this a happy augury of her future adventure? Blue was running away from the field. Straight across the oval he appeared a most beautiful, gliding, running machine. The others were so far behind that Marian could see them only out of the corner of her eye. In the stretch Blue came in with the speed of the wind, and there were few in that crowd who did not hail him as a grand colt. He ran under the wire a dozen lengths ahead.

Marian found herself standing on the bench, clinging to Bates's arm. The old cattleman was roaring. It took a moment or two for the crowd to roar itself out, and for the majority to return to sanity.

"Marian, what do you think of Blue? Your colt!" yelled Bates.

"Why, he's great!"

"He sure is. I wonder now. Drake will enter Blue for the Melbourne Summer Sweepstakes if he has to. Lady, you wait here for me. I'll cash our tickets. You won a tidy sum."

"I told you I'd bring luck."

"Bless your heart. You did. When the crowd breaks up a little, I'll take you down to see Blue and Dick. Lady, this bids fair to be interesting."

"To me it surely will be, Bates," Marian replied with a bright smile.

Marian watched the people slowly file out of the stands.

She noticed the heat again, during an interval when the breeze lulled. It seemed rather a long wait for Bates. But he came presently, and forced upon her a packet of money that stuffed her bag nearly to bursting.

" 'Most everybody happy," Bates was confiding, as he led her down the steps. "You see it was the Melville money that made those odds. Coombs folk all got some of it, too."

It was dusty below and noisy. Lines of people were heading out of the grounds, and cars sent up clouds of dust. Marian was glad to get out of that into the open. But still there were knots of men together here and there. They came to the stalls, in the first of which a groom was rubbing down the Melville colt. Marian liked his looks, and wanted to linger.

"Come, Miss Hastings, or you'll miss something," he said with humor. "If I don't miss my guess, here's an argument. Drake and Melville!"

Marian's quick glance took in a group surrounding a blanketed horse. In the fore stood two men, the first of whom, a tall, coatless fellow, wide of shoulders, with tanned lean profile, rather hard and bitter, she took to be Drake. The other was an Englishman such as Marian was used to seeing at races. Only in this instance this young man's face appeared full of heat and vexation. He wore riding breeches and boots and carried a crop. His eyes were light gray.

"Drake, I'll give you a thousand pounds for the colt," he bit out arrogantly.

"Won't sell at any price," replied Drake coolly.

"But why not, man?"

"Melville, in the first place, Blue is not mine to sell."

"You raised him, trained him, they say."

"That's true. But I don't regard him as my property. And what's more, if he was mine, no money could buy him."

"I should think it a chance you'd jump at. It's a beggar's

life you lead at Rangle Rim. A run-down station with a shady reputation. You should get out before you are thrown out."

"Yes, and who's going to do that?" demanded Drake.

"I will. We have a lien on Rangle Rim, and, when we locate the new owner, we'll. . . ."

"Aye, you're a liar, Melville," interrupted Drake tersely. "No one had a lien on Dan Hasting's land. You always disputed that south boundary for reason of your own. But we know Rangle Rim is free."

"Drake, you know something more . . . something that won't stand the light of day."

"I do? Well, what is it?" snapped Drake, and he took a long threatening stride toward Melville.

"You know Black and his gang of thieves have holed up on Rangle River for years," rang out Melville.

"Yes. 'Most everybody knows that," returned Drake harshly. "What of it? Rangle River is a hundred miles square. There are cañons and holes all through the northern half. Robbers have always hid out there. Dan Hastings knew that. He could do nothing. What could Bates and I do, even if we wanted to?"

"There are dark hints you. . . ."

Drake slapped the speaker smartly across the mouth, checking his utterance and making him stagger back.

"Sure, but don't you throw that in my face," flashed Drake.

Here Bates stepped between the men. "That'll do, Dick. Don't lose your temper."

Marian took advantage of the moment to slip around the cluster of men, up to the colt. At the moment no one appeared to think of Blue. Marian found him sensitive, but not unapproachable, and she was making overtures to him when the jockey intervened.

"Miss, you must keep your hands off him. Drake's orders."

Marian laughed, and, finding a five pound note, she transferred it to the boy.

"Here, lad. You rode a great race."

"Did you bet on us, miss?"

"You bet I did."

She was caressing Blue when Bates and Drake came up to them. She grasped at once that Bates had made no mention of her. His eyes were twinkling. But Drake's, falling full upon her, still had fire in their tawny depths. Marian mustered an odd little thrill throughout her being.

"Jimmy, I told you not to let anyone touch Blue," Drake said severely.

"But it didn't work with this girl. Besides, she gave me five quid."

"I'll take it away from you, rascal," retorted Drake, and without humor.

"Blue won a lot of money for me," interrupted Marian, smiling up at Drake.

He appeared to notice her then and ran keen eyes over her person. His look was a compliment, but evidently he hardly approved of her. Bates stepped up beside him with a grin on his red face.

"How much?" asked Drake bluntly.

"I bet one hundred pounds on Blue, at five to eight."

Drake whistled. "Well, miss, you are a sport. Thanks a lot. Blue can run, can't he?"

"He's fast, Mister Drake."

The way Marian said that, and the embrace she had on the sleek blue neck of the racer, must have been significant to Drake.

"It's not hard to see you fell in love with Blue."

"Indeed, I did. I heard Melville trying to buy him from you. That pleased me. But I think I'll have to take Blue away from you."

"Take! Say, Bates, listen to this girl." He laughed, not unpleased, and his manner, as he turned to Marian again, was less brusque. "Miss, I know how you feel. I can make allowances. But to take Blue away from me you'd have to be a horse thief."

"That doesn't scare me. I could."

"But I'm easily scared, miss," he returned darkly. "Pardon me, but who are you? I never saw you before."

"I just arrived. It's my lucky day."

"That's fine. Mine, too . . . but please, let Blue go now. He must be looked after."

"No, I won't let him go!" exclaimed Marian.

Drake appeared at a loss for words. He was kindly, understanding, yet irritated. Traces of his temper still lingered.

"Can't I hug my own property?" Marian went on demurely. The excitement Blue had roused in her communicated itself to the presence of this striking young man, ill-clad and rough as he appeared.

"What?" he burst out, nonplussed. It helped but little to turn to Bates. That worthy appeared amused like all the others in the little group. Drake was impatient. He took hold of Blue's bridle. "Let go, miss. You've had your hug."

"Drake, if you take Blue from me right this minute," declared Marian, cool and sweet, "I'll . . . I'll, what is it they say in America . . . I'll fire you."

"Fire me!" echoed Drake, aghast, and suddenly his tan visage went fiery red.

"I'd hate to, but I shall," continued Marian.

"Who the devil . . . ? Bates, what is this? You look guilty, you old duffer. Who is this exceedingly willful person?"

"Ask her yourself, Dick," replied Bates.

Drake was pale when he faced Marian again. Suddenly he suspected something incredible. "Miss, this is not funny at all . . . to me. Please explain. Who . . . ?"

"I am your new boss," said Marian, and her tone and look should have made amends for much.

"Boss!" he gasped.

"I'm sorry if that upsets you. Bates and I thought it'd be fun. I'm Marian Hastings. My Uncle Dan left me Rangle Rim, and I have come out to take possession."

Drake was astounded, staggered, unable to speak. Marian turned to the jockey. "Come, Jimmy, let me go with you to his stall." And she walked beside Blue as the lad led him away. In a few paces they came to a stall. Marian stepped up on a fence bar and looked on. She had enjoyed the situation hugely until the climax. Then she had felt rather nonplussed and sorry. How repugnantly Drake had taken the joke. He must love Rangle River—and a child could have seen how he worshipped Blue. Marian wanted to give him a little time before she went back.

"Was all that true, miss?" asked Jimmy eagerly. "You being our new boss . . . and that?"

"Yes, Jimmy. I'm afraid it was bad news for Mister Drake."

"Aw, he was just bowled over. Dick is the finest man in the world. He'll be glad when he comes to."

Upon returning, Marian found the crowd dispersed and Bates talking earnestly to Drake. At her step Drake turned, quite a different man.

"Miss Hastings, before I welcome you to Australia and Rangle River, let me make one honest attempt to turn you back," he said gallantly.

"By all means, Mister Drake. But you cannot turn me back."

"Rangle River is no place for you."

"So Bates told me. Because it's desert, ghastly, hot, barren, sordid?"

"No. English women before have stood privation to the making of a country."

"Well, then what?"

"It is not safe for you."

"Safe? From what?"

"From the desperate characters who have found refuge upon your wild range."

"Badmen? Bates never mentioned them. But I am not afraid. . . . Cannot you protect me, Drake?"

"I can try," he said in sober simplicity.

"What else, then?"

"The Hastings name here has gathered an evil shadow."

"Oh! My Uncle Dan. . . . Drake, I've more reason to stay on. I shall do so. Will you help me to dispel that shadow?"

"I will, indeed," he promised somberly, and Marian felt the obligation was not slight. "That's the spiritual side, Miss Hastings. The physical ordeal . . . that is vastly different. Bates says you have no money."

"Very little, besides what I won today."

"That was a lucky run for Blue. Very well, the die is cast, *if* you say."

"It is, Mister Drake," replied Marian gravely, and she offered her hand. His clasp was hard, like steel, and shot a current through her. Then she shook hands with Bates. "Let's go back to the hotel and talk. When had you planned to return?"

"Tonight, taking Blue in a truck."

"We must stay over until tomorrow. There will be endless things to buy."

Drake appeared to be unable to shake off some dominating thought. "Did Bates tell you we have no drinking water at Rangle River?" he queried, as they started toward town.

This information, at the particular moment when Marian was parched with dust and heat, was most discomforting.

"No, he did not. What do you drink?"

"There's water. But you couldn't swallow it. Full of wigglers. There's fine water to be had at Rangle, if we could drill for it."

"Let's hope we may be able to."

Bates interposed, saying they could pack some cases of bottled water out to the station. He and Drake talked in an undertone. Then Drake supposed to Marian that like all English girls she was used to baths, with hot and cold water. Marian replied enthusiastically that she adored bathing, and quite often. Drake threw up his hands.

"Jim, I tell you it's hopeless," he said. "We mustn't let her come out there."

"Say, how are we going to prevent it?"

Arriving at the hotel Marian was about suffocated with heat and dust. If never before, she could appreciate ice and water then. Marian asked for paper and pencils, and cheerfully faced her perplexed and dubious men at a table.

"You gentlemen make out a list of supplies, and whatever is most needed out there," she said. "And I'll make out one for what I'll need. You say there's nothing . . . in the way of comforts?"

"Miss Hastings, comforts have not been for Rangle River. There are not even bare necessities. It's not possibly livable for you out there."

"Well, let's make it so," replied Marian, and she set to work on her list. It was so thrilling to make out, and so long that she quite forgot the time. But her men were waiting expectantly, and Drake took the sheets of paper she proffered with much concern. He hardly scanned the first one.

"Good heavens, girl!" he ejaculated.

Marian instructed Bates to get her prices on a strong towing automobile.

"Gee, ma'am. Used car, or new?"

"New, of course. I wouldn't use anything second-hand."

Bates stamped away, plainly energized, while Drake frowned at Marian.

"I'm not so sure about you," he said darkly.

"Sure? Of what?" asked Marian lightly.

"That you're what you pretend to be?"

"My dear sir, I'm not pretending."

"Bates says you're English, like we are, or were. Good old English middle class. You must have been a clerk or in some business, and, when this property fell to you, why you had a crazy idea to come out and make your fortune."

"Drake, I didn't tell Bates that, but he's not so far off."

"Well, the crazy part of it I'll stand. But you're no poor clerk or stenographer or. . . ."

"I didn't say I was," interrupted Marian. "All I said was that I had a little money. We're going to spend it. And when it's gone, well. . . ."

"You're game. Oh, it'd be fine to have you go out there if. . . . I forget myself. But I'll bet you're a swell having a lark . . . masquerading . . . or just run off."

"Wrong again. Drake, don't be so concerned about me. I'm not crazy. I want to see this thing through. Tell me something about yourself. You're from England. You were in the war."

"Yes. I came of age the last year," he rejoined rather briefly, and he arose. "I've an hour or more before closing time. I'll see about buying all this stuff and having it packed. We can't get away till tomorrow afternoon, that means Rangle River late."

"But it's only sixty odd miles, someone said."

"Wait until you see the road. I'll include a tent in this list and a cot for you. I wouldn't care to see you in Dan's house for a while."

"A tent and cot? Quite intriguing! Oh, here are my baggage checks. These trunks and bags should go with us tomorrow."

Drake counted the checks. "Sixteen!" he ejaculated, "and you say you're not lying to me?"

"Mister Drake, I'm not saying anything. My trunks contain all my worldly possessions. You see, I've come to stay."

He shook his head over her, but warmed to her smile and gladness. As he went out, Marian conceived the idea that his gravity indicated he had something to hide, which forced itself upon him now and then. Marian went upstairs, deep in thought. A bath refreshed her, and, upon going downstairs again to find Drake and Bates had not returned, she went out on the street and headed for the sea.

The sunset was gold and red through the palms. The dust had settled. On the beach it was pleasant, although still warm. Marian sat down to watch the colorful and moving scene. She probed her feelings. Her adventure had assumed enthralling proportions.

How much had it to do with this rolling stone, Drake? She knew that he had thrilled her at the very onset, but it took introspection to find that already she liked him more than any man she had ever met. She let that be enough to learn on the moment, and she also put out of her mind the vague, disturbing sense of something wrong about Drake. When after a little rest there she retraced her steps uptown, it was with a conviction that something definite had been decided for her.

She found the men waiting anxiously. Drake appeared clean-shaven and quite handsome for a change. Bates was beaming. They took her into the dining room and ordered dinner. That hour and another afterward flew by in the interest of their project, which had manifestly grown upon Drake and Bates, as they had plunged into actualities. They had not purchased half of Marian's lists.

"I'll help tomorrow," she said. "I'm tired now, and think I'll get some sleep. Good night."

Marian rested so well that she slept late, and was somewhat mortified to be called by Bates. But she arose with alacrity and was now at breakfast. Drake had long been out on the job, Bates said. He had a first-rate car to show her. "Dick said he'd need an extra truck to pack all this stuff. You see Blue takes up a good deal of room in our truck."

"How about Jimmy? Can we take him along to work?"

"He's already asked me to ask you. Wages no object. He's a good kid."

"One thing more, Bates. I want a woman. A good cook and housekeeper. Nationality no object."

"That should be easy. Miss, who's to drive the new car? I'm not so good."

"Why, I can drive, if necessary."

"That's well. Jimmy said he was one swell driver. But it's a bad road."

"I'm thrilled to death. Now I'll be off to do my shopping. I'll have my purchases sent here to be packed. You see to that, Bates. And when I come back, have all the bills ready for me."

"That worries me, miss. But not so much as it does Dick."

The morning flew by for Marian. When her work was done, she thought of going to the bank with her letter of credit. But she thought better of that. She had already established connection with the Bank of Australia in Sydney, and she did not want to have it found out here that she was very far removed, indeed, from a poor girl.

At the hotel, Bates informed her that Drake had gone ahead with the two trucks. Her car was ready. Jimmy was packing her many parcels.

"Let's have lunch and then . . . ho for Rangle River! I hope the Lord will forgive me for my part in this."

"I feel a little thoughtful myself," declared Marian tremulously. But it was the poignancy and sweetness of the situation, not any real fear or discouraging doubts.

At last they were out of town, heading west on a dusty, uneven road that appeared to end in purple infinity. Trees and brush lined the road. With the car gliding along, the heat was not noticeable. Marian relaxed.

"Oh, it's lovely," she murmured as she lay back in the front seat.

"What is, miss?" asked the bright-eyed Jimmy, as he bent over the wheel.

"This gray sandy lonely country. Already we are away from civilization."

"Houses few and far betweens, miss. And none after we cross Aroombi."

"What is that?"

"A big dry wash."

Marian asked questions with avidity, and few there were that Jimmy could not answer. Birds and small animals, snakes and brush and trees were all interesting to Marian. Presently a queer gray beast bounded away from the roadside in a jerky, ludicrous manner.

"What on earth was that?" she cried.

"Only a kangaroo, miss."

"Kangaroo? Oh, of course, of course. How perfectly thrilling! Oh, he was big and wild-looking. Wonderful! Are there any on my place?"

"Any? Say, miss, Bates says they overrun the land."

"That'll be great. What else?"

"You'll sure like the laughing jackasses, miss."

"Laughing jackasses! Well, they are new to me. What are they?"

"I reckon it'd be more fun for you to see for yourself."

They talked, and the car made on over what appeared a safe, if jolting, road. But after they crossed Aroombi, good time could not be made. The road had ruts, and climbed rocky ridges, and turned corners where Bates cautioned Jimmy to be careful. But the lad could drive. Trees and rough going increased with the miles. The eucalyptus trees began to grow pretentious in size and stately in appearance. Bates kept telling Marian to withhold her enthusiasm until she saw the Rangle River country from a high plateau they were slowly ascending. That long awaited time came at last.

They came out on the crest of the large rock-rimmed plateau, from which an unobstructed view could be had for two hundred miles. Marian was stunned. The vast, gray, uneven expanse appeared mild, lovely, and grand in the extreme. Lines of ridges showed rising one above another, and, as the land dropped away to the south, a dim, boundless abyss appeared to yawn.

"That's Rangle River, Miss Marian," said Bates, pointing downward. "Ninety miles yet, and the worst going. Take your look or you won't see any more of it."

"I never dreamed of such . . . such a country," murmured Marian. "Terrible . . . appalling. Yet . . . oh, so beautiful! I understand Drake now. Drive on."

But at length slow progress through a swale where view was restricted and dust and heat magnified wore Marian out, and she succumbed to weariness. She did not sleep, although she might as well have done so for all she saw of the country.

Toward sunset the road climbed out of the depression into a level country. Marian was brought to grateful awareness by Bates's hearty call to her.

"Rangle River. All out."

Marian discerned that the car was coming to a halt in what appeared to be a park covered with gigantic trees, wide apart. Dusk had fallen—a strange luminous dusk, pointed by bright lights. When the car finally stopped, she made out a long, low building, melancholy and deserted, on her side of the car. Lights and voices directed her attention to the other side. Marian leaped out despite cramped muscles. The air seemed cool. She felt a soft wind fan her hot cheek.

"Welcome to Rangle River, Miss Hastings," Drake said from behind her. "How'd you like the ride?"

"Wonderful, until I gave out. Oh, this is not what I expected."

"Supper is about ready. It appears Bates dug up a very capable woman. Here's your tent, Miss Hastings. Canvas floor, cot, netting, vermin-proof . . . all the luxuries. . . . Here's your wash basin, on this box." Drake flashed a light on the several things he mentioned. "Your luggage is all stacked on the porch. Any particular piece you want, we'll get."

"Where's Blue?" asked Marian, as she removed her hat and veil.

"He's in the pasture. Glad to get back. He's a range horse, all right. Here, use this flashlight. I've a lantern for you that I'll get presently."

While refreshing herself, Marian gazed about her, wonderingly, awed. What gigantic trees! She could not see the tops. A weird place, fascinating, almost frightful.

In a few moments she was called to supper, which appeared to be laid on a table set under a canvas fly.

"Lucky there's no wind, or you'd be eating wood," said

Drake, holding a canvas chair for her. "Strikes me you're lucky all around."

"I told Bates I brought luck to Rangle River."

"Let us hope that you do," he replied fervently.

Marian did not eat heartily, but that certainly was no fault of the wholesome food and clean service. She saw that the dark-faced woman, intently Scotch, whom Bates called Kate, would fill a very much needed place. Drake appeared tired and disinclined for conversation. He had a dark, haunted look. If Marian would have allowed anything to dismay her at that moment, this would have done so. After the meal Marian asked Bates if she could walk around a little, to stretch her legs.

"Sure. But don't go far. And look out for Daddy."

"Who's Daddy?"

"Didn't Drake tell you? Oh, of course, he had no chance."

Bates did not tell her, either. Marian supposed Daddy was an aborigine. She strolled about in the strange shadows. The fragrance of eucalyptus was almost overpowering. But it was sweet, dry, invigorating. The long gloomy house intrigued her, but she took care to stay away from the sandy ground that was difficult to walk upon with her high heels. She was afraid of snakes and some other crawling things. Still she bravely persisted in her walk, going a little way along the pale road. Rustling of leaves and brush sent her back to her tent. There was not a bright light. Marian identified some bags that Jimmy carried for her, and presently she was on her knees in her tent, unpacking. Jimmy showed her how to turn out the lantern.

"I'll fasten the flaps down, so nothing can get in," he concluded.

"Goodness! Jimmy, are there things that'd try to get in?"

Presently Marian went to bed, so tired she could only stretch out, and despite the strangeness, the mournful wind, the soft noises outside, she fell asleep at once, and did not awaken until daylight. Then she lay there thinking, until the sun cast gold and black shadows on her tent. Then she arose, put on her slippers, and, slipping into a dressing gown over her pajamas, she unfastened the tent flap, and stepped out into what appeared the most golden and marvelous place in the world. Huge, pale-barked trees soared aloft; the ground was golden sand; a tumble-down picturesque old house seemed to greet her. Marian had hardly straightened up to draw a full breath of joy when a clarion voice burst out: "Haw! Haw! Haw, Hawahals!" She was startled out of herself, and resentful. Some Australian laughing at her costume. And she turned to look for him, when a huge grotesque gray shape hopped right at her. Marian screamed in fright and fled. She heard the thing thumping at her. With her heart in her throat she ran, losing her slippers. Again that hoarse bellow of a laugh sounded, more derisive than before. Suddenly Marian came upon Drake, into whose arms she ran like a frightened child. Shaking, convulsed, breathless, she clung to him a moment.

"Why, Miss Hastings!" exclaimed Drake. "What is it?"

"Oh . . . some terrible . . . beast chased . . . me," she panted.

"Ha! Ha! It's only Daddy. Here, you rascal, clear out."

"Daddy?" faltered Marian.

"Yes, our tame kangaroo. He was your uncle's favorite. He won't hurt you. He's a pet."

"Yes? Daddy was a little . . . precipitate." Then Marian realized that Drake was still holding her, throbbing, and Marian, in his arms, hurriedly disengaged herself, conscious of more than the embarrassment of the moment. "Men . . . there was someone laughing at me . . . my appearance in these things . . . a horrid loud brazen haw, haw,

haw! I shall most certainly fire that person."

"That was Jack. He's sitting just over your tent."

Marian looked up to see a ludicrous dark bird, apparently all head and bill, and at the moment it let out that raucous laugh.

"Australian kookaburra, our laughing jackass," said Drake, smiling at her.

"So this is my introduction to Rangle River," murmured Marian, as she gazed through the wide portal of the grove, out into the open. "Mister Drake, either your appreciation of beauty has been atrophied . . . or else you are a monumental liar."

A first check in the extraordinary favorable impression Marian was getting of Drake succeeded only in disappointing her and not alienating her. She divined he had some personal reason for wanting to prejudice her against Rangle River, probably to precipitate her abandoning it. Marian hurried through breakfast and then went over the place. The old structure, half barn, half house, possessed a huge porch, a living room, and another room that could be made most comfortable. Bates, who accompanied her, was instructed to clean, scrub, paint, and put in window screens. Marian elected to live outdoors until the work was done and furniture installed. She visited the outbuildings, advised the demolishing of most of them, the leveling of old fences, and elimination of the heaps of rubbish.

"And this squalid hole . . . what is this?" she demanded, indicating a puddle of muddy water surrounding plank walks, leading to a shaft from which a pipe projected.

"We've got fine water here, if we can only raise it. Costs money."

"How much?"

"Matter of a hundred pounds, including pipe and labor."

"Have that truck driver fetch out what is necessary, and some workmen. Is Drake a carpenter?"

"No, ma'am, but I'm pretty fair."

"All right, Bates. Get things started. I want this place cleaned up. Kate and Jimmy and I will tackle the barn kitchen first. Where's Drake?"

"He rode off somewhere," replied Bates uneasily. Marian did not like the cloud of boding glow on his brow. Again she sensed something wrong in this situation.

Marian was strong, athletic, and work was no stranger. She set in to help, and that day flew by. She had not even time to walk out to the open from which she could gaze down into the great yellow and gray break in the upland. Sundown was a blessed relief. While she lay in her hammock, waiting for supper call, she heard horses, and she hurried out toward the corrals, hoping to see Drake, who had been absent all day. In the sand Marian's light step made no sound. She came upon Drake and Bates who did not see her. Drake was dust-laden, his visage dark and grim.

"Black was there, Jim," Drake said with an oath. "At Stony Way. Had six men, two of them new. Bad cases." And Drake shook his lean head gloomily, as he lifted off the red saddle.

"Stony Way! That close?" ejaculated Bates. "Dick, some of them will find out Miss Hastings is here. What'll we *do?*"

"Of course, they'll find out. We *can't* help it."

"Rangle Rim won't be safe for Marian."

"Hell, no!"

"It didn't take long to fall on us. And Dick, I like this girl. She's a real Thoroughbred."

"I'll say. Good as she is beautiful. Jim, I can't run off and leave her here to the mercy of Black and his thieves. And if I stay . . . I . . . I'll go mad over her."

"Fine. Go mad. It'll be good for you. But if you even think of deserting her, I'll take a pot shot at you."

"I'll stay. But this is tough. Black is after me hot. He's going to raid the Melville north herd, now on water, near the line."

"Hell he is! That's *our* water."

"Yes. Black reminded me of that. He wants me in with him. I turned him down cold. He said I'd better think it over a few days, while he sent some men to Coombs for supplies."

"Dick, they'll find out about Marian."

Drake agreed in gloomy silence. He turned the horse loose in the corral. Then he spoke. "Bates, that can't be helped, and it's no matter. What scares me sick is a fear that girl will find out about *me*."

At this juncture Marian tore herself from the spot, and ran along the fence to the sheds, arriving breathless at her tent and not sure she had not been seen.

Lying on her cot she was quick to realize two devastating facts—that she had fallen in love with Drake, and that he was somehow connected with this robber, Black. The shock dismayed Marian. But in the succeeding few minutes of strife she could not wholly lose faith in Drake. It was something she felt but could not explain. And she decided to carry on her own deception, while she undertook to solve this mystery of Rangle River. Presently a call for supper moved her to freshen up a bit and go to table as if nothing had upset her.

"Drake," she said easily, as she took her seat and looked directly at him, "do you expect to take orders from me, or come and go as you please?"

"I'm sorry. I should have awakened you. I left before sunrise," he replied hastily.

"I'd like to have ridden with you. I want to see my land. By the way, neither you nor Bates have told me how much stock I own."

"We don't know. I think there are upwards of two hundred head of horses, ranging free, of course. And cattle scattered all over the station."

"Two hundred horses? Oh, splendid. Isn't there danger of their being stolen?"

Drake bent his dark face over his plate while Bates replied: "They *are* stolen, ma'am, whenever any of them gangs want some more mounts."

"That will never do."

"It can't be stopped. Even if we had more riders while we scouted one section of the range, these thieves would ride another."

"Will I ever be able to make a living here?" queried Marian earnestly.

"No," interrupted Drake.

"Aw, Dick, I wouldn't say that. It can be done, and we will do it. Big herds of cattle and droves of horses aren't necessary. In fact, they make it harder."

Later, when alone, Marian discounted the various unfavorable aspects of the case to dwell upon the intimate and romantic issues. She could not forget Drake's face, when he told Bates he would go mad over her. That haunted Marian. But she fought it, resisted it with all her might. From the stress of Drake's emotion, she had grasped that he craved her respect, that he wanted to protect her, that no matter what he had ever done that was bad, he hated it now, and would not descend to it again. She conceived the idea that, if she could save Drake from ruin, she would go to great lengths to attain more land. Yet her good sense kept her from combating this insidious, imperious love. Despite all the consternation and doubt she went to sleep happy.

Next day she proved to be a capricious and exacting mistress. She drove Bates at his manifold tasks. She attempted things she should not have. Drake quarreled with her, swore and raged, but all to no avail. Marian felt secretly gleeful.

In the succeeding days, after the other laborers had come, she led Drake a merry dance around the place. Jimmy was easily persuaded to be her ally, and, with his help, she rode horses she should not have ridden. She went off alone on long rides, but she knew what she was doing and kept sharp watch. She was falling desperately in love despite herself. Once she got caught in a sandstorm, but she happened to be close to the house. She took refuge in a cave and stayed there for hours until the storm subsided. Drake returned from endless search to find her unsaddling her horse and gaily describing her adventures to Jimmy. Drake came up, and then they had it hot and heavy. He had been horribly frightened for her, so there was excuse for his anger. Marian wanted to run into his arms, and perhaps that made her willful.

"Who's boss around here?" she demanded. "Can't I ride when and where I like? What's a little sandstorm?"

"If you do that again, I'll quit you," Drake declared, pale, with pleading eyes.

Marian was careful about storms after that. But one afternoon her horse stepped in a hole and threw her over his head. She hurt her leg or sprained her ankle so badly she could not get back into the saddle. And her horse headed for home. In half an hour Drake came riding down upon her. The situation intrigued her, and she meant to play up to it.

He dismounted beside her, anxious and chafed. What a worry she must be, Marian thought. But he did not seem to be even a little mad over her yet.

"Are you hurt?" he asked sharply.

"I'm nearly killed," moaned Marian.

"Let me see. . . . Move it, girl, move your leg. God, I hope it's not broken. Let me straighten it."

"*Oww!*" burst out Marian. "You horse doctor! There's nothing broken. I hurt my knee, and I guess sprained this ankle. Help me on your horse. You can lead him."

"No. This horse is mean. I can't trust him." Drake leaped astride the skittish beast, and reached for her. "Come. Put your good foot in the stirrup and. . . ."

"I can't stand on the other," protested Marian.

But he lifted her up in front of him and held her in the hollow of his left arm. Marian closed her eyes as he started to ride home. He carried her easily, and she felt thrillingly aware of his strength, and the closeness of him. Her head lay right on his shoulder. Marian opened her eyes presently to look up at him. Their glances locked. No doubt the glamour of the moment communicated itself to them both simultaneously. Suddenly Drake bent down to kiss her. His kisses stifled her faint utterances, and presently it was not embarrassment or pretense that made Marian lie back spent and pale, with eyes closed.

Soon they arrived at the house and Marian's tent. Bates and Kate came running. Marian was helped down, into her rocker.

"What happened?" shouted Bates.

"A little sprain, I reckon."

"Say! You look like she might be dead. Kate, take her boots and stockings. I'll fetch hot water."

Drake stalked off, leading his horse, and a side view of his face gave the perfidious Marian a pang. Presently she was resting comfortably in her hammock, and she sent Jimmy for Drake. He came at once, as if he had expected the summons and was ready and glad to be executed. For all Marian's spirit she could not at first meet the fire and hopeless gloom of his eyes. She sent Jimmy away.

"Drake. I . . . you . . . please explain your conduct."

"Didn't it explain itself?" he asked uneasily.

"No. How did you come to . . . to insult me so outrageously?" she asked, low-voiced.

"Insult? Good heaven! It wasn't. . . . I just looked down. There you lay in . . . my arms. It . . . it happened."

"Indeed, it did happen. But how . . . why?"

"How? Why? I don't know. I suppose a man just gives in to such an impulse. But this was no insult. You lay there, looking up at me . . . so lovely. And I just did it."

"Aren't you going to ask my pardon?"

"No. I don't merit that. And I wouldn't ask. Besides, I'm not sorry."

"Not sorry! Mister Drake!"

"Oh, I'm sorry to distress you. Sorry that I've ruined myself. But I'm really glad. I think that moment was the only sweet one . . . the only fulfilled one I've had since long before the war."

"Still, if you don't tell me why . . . and apologize, I will . . . you must. . . ."

"You needn't say more. I'll leave in the morning. I've already told Bates, and he cursed me for a mad man . . . you see, Miss Hastings, I fell in love with you at first sight. You seemed to come to me like a dream from home . . . from long ago. My life here has been hard . . . and *bad,* too, though I never knew that until too late. You are really being my salvation . . . in that I must leave Rangle River." His lean, hawklike head was lowered, so that he could not see Marian as she spoke. She overcame much in that moment.

"Drake, I won't send you away from Rangle River," she said hurriedly. "I forgive you. It's not so . . . so terrible, after all. I only thought. . . ."

"But I must go."

"You promised to protect me?"

"Yes, I did. Lord help me . . . I never guessed you'd need protection *from* me."

"Drake, you wouldn't transgress that way again?"

"I swear not. But I might. I might feel that love. It has been so lonely here . . . so ghastly. And once I knew sweet pretty girls like you. . . . You'd better let me go."

"No. I ask you to stay . . . at any risk," she murmured. "I begin to feel what it might be here. . . . Leave me now, please. I'm tired."

He appeared overcome with shame and gratitude and some wandering emotion she could not define, and with a bow and incoherent word he left her. In the first flush of the succeeding moments, so full and tumultuous, Marian felt that she could not have yearned for more. She reveled in her dream and wanted it to last.

Next day she was able to go about, walking with a stick. Drake, with his laborers, struck a goodly vein of water that gushed out like a brook. Bates was exuberant. He had always claimed a stream of water had run underground there, and had been choked or clogged to prevent it surfacing. If they had struck gold, Drake could not have been more intense and exultant. From the conversation of the men Marian gathered that, if this water were permanent, it would make Rangle River the best station in that region.

"I tell you, it's Rangle River itself," declared Bates.

"Mebbe. But it'll ruin us anyway. What made this place possible for us was its worthlessness. Black will run us off or the Melvilles will take it away from us."

"Dick, you didn't used to be so pessimistic," growled Bates. But he, too, was concerned.

Before the day was done, the débris had been cleared out of the water hole, leaving a fine big pool that poured down into the rocky cut below. Birds and cattle and horses lined up along its course.

At supper Drake had relapsed into his taciturn self. Marian had to make a direct question to get a word out of him. Bates had told him they expected Black's men back from town, and awaited them with apprehension. It added to Marian's fears to make an observation—Drake had a big gun in his belt. Jimmy told her presently that Drake had been keeping Blue tied up out in a thick grove, and it had been Jimmy's job to watch him.

Another day came, with most of the workmen gone. The house would soon be ready for Marian to go into. She looked forward with keen interest to fixing up her two rooms and porch, after her own idea of comfort.

Her kookaburra, that she had re-christened Jack, still regarded all her ventures with his raucous guffaw, if not actual unfriendliness. But Daddy was friendliness itself. In fact, he was still too abrupt for Marian's nerves. However, she played with him.

That morning, when Bates announced the living room was ready for furnishing, Marian went in to see. It still smelled of fresh paint. She decided to go on with the furnishing, but to sleep out yet a little while. She had grown to like the tent under the big trees.

At the outside wall of this room ran a log the whole length and evidently served as a foundation. While chasing a lizard with her broom, Marian accidentally knocked against the log. To her surprise a piece of it fell out, like a lid sliding off. It disclosed a long hollow under the log, filled with little canvas sacks. "Well! What are these?" soliloquized Marian, puzzled, and she knelt down to feel of one. It was full of something hard. She opened it. Gold dust! In a flash Marian divined that these bags were full of gold. With hands so shaky she could scarcely use them she put the lid back. It fitted perfectly. She could not see the crevice. Then she gazed furtively about. No one had been near at the moment. Bates and Jimmy were uncovering things out on the porch. Marian went out, and she divined with her quick intuitiveness that Bates could not have known the gold was there and have concealed his knowledge from her. That gold had been Dan Hastings's fortune, packed from the gold fields. Marian had heard of such a romance when she was a girl.

It so happened that the corner where this gold was hidden was the one where Marian intended to put her bed. She had Jimmy carry the several pieces in, and she, very carefully, helped him put it up. Then the mattress went on. After that she breathed freer. She instructed them to carry the heavy pieces of furniture in and put them anywhere. The rugs they could spread on the floor. After that she went out to lie in the hammock and think. She could scarcely believe her senses. But there the gold was, dull, glittering, heavy grains.

She had come straight to the pot of gold at the foot of the rainbow, and she was so exultant that she could not think at all. Bates came out, mopping his brow. "It's all inside, now, ma'am, ready for you."

"Call me Marian. Am I an old lady to be spoken to as ma'am?"

"Excuse me, Marian . . . and thanks. Well, with the workmen all gone, it feels like home again."

"Bates, I never asked you about it, though I often wondered. Did Uncle Dan buy this property?"

"He did that. And got it for nothing. But that was twenty years ago."

"Has it ever been surveyed?"

"It was blazed. I can show you the line any day."

"One hundred miles square! Incredible. Ten thousand square miles."

"Nothing to wonder at here in Australia. Why, the Melville Station is half again as large. Our place, however, is mostly rough country. The timber will be worth a pretty good sum, if ever the time comes when it can be marketed. But I'll tell you, Marian, this spring of fine water makes Rangle a different proposition."

"I should think so. Oh, the luck we have. Tell me, Bates, did Uncle Dan come here without money?"

"Say, I'll let you in on a secret that even Drake doesn't know," interrupted Bates, bending low. "Old Dan buried a fortune in gold on this place. He never told me where. When he lay dying, he tried to, but too late. I've hunted for that gold ever since."

"Did this outlaw, Black, ever suspect it?"

"I've often thought he did, and been afraid he might have found the gold. Black always has money. He goes to Sydney and Melbourne to play the races. Did I ever tell you that Dan lived down in Stony Way before he built this house? But the water went dry, and he moved up here. Then this water failed, too. Strange. Well, Black lived in Stony Way a long while. Dan couldn't drive him out."

"It's a wonderful story."

"Hello. Horses! By gum, I'll bet that's the crew Drake has been expecting. Better get out of sight, ma' . . . Marian."

But Marian lay still, listening to the thud of hoofs on the soft sand. Presently she heard hard cries, then a long rolling yell. Drake appeared striding up from the corrals. He waved Bates on and made for Marian. His tawny hair stood up like a mane; his eyes flared. His dark skin was actually pale.

"Get in your tent," he ordered peremptorily.

"I'll not do anything of the kind."

"Yes, you will."

"I want to see this Black."

"Must I pack you into your tent?" he demanded grimly, gazing down at her.

Marian trembled, she knew not from what. "Don't you touch me!"

But he lifted her, as if she had been a sack, and carried her into her tent to drop her ungently upon her cot. Marian was so furious and scared that she could not speak. She kicked at him viciously.

"You stay in here till I let you out," he concluded, and went out to tie the flaps tight. And at the moment Jack burst out uproariously: *"Haw! Haw! Haw!"*

Marian lay back to relax, thinking that Drake must know what was best for her. There was no doubt about his force. Her arm and leg ached where he had grasped them to carry her in. And Marian had almost broken her toe kicking him.

"The man is iron," she said darkly. "I should have been reasonable. He's frightened for me . . . for my safety."

And that conviction held the restless girl quiet for a while. At length, however, her curiosity and resentment got the best of her, and she arose to peer out the screened window of her tent, and then through the front flap. She could not see anyone. The place appeared deserted. But there were sounds to prove the contrary. If not sounds of revelry, they were close to it. Pondering the situation, Marian concluded that no matter how irksome, she should stay in her tent until Drake came to reassure her.

He did not come, and the hours wore away. Sometime in the afternoon she heard soft footfalls and then a low voice calling at her door.

"Yes, I'm here. Is that you, Jimmy?"

He unfastened the lower strings and crawled in. Marian sat up with a start. "Drake sent me to tell you to have patience," the boy whispered. "He reckons they'll leave soon."

"Who are they . . . and what's been going on?"

"A lot, ma'am. But I couldn't see or hear it all. Nine men in all. Black wasn't with them. I've seen him. Big hard-faced man, black as his name. They ate this morning, and then some of them slept, then they gambled. More than one of the gang sort of started over this way, but this Spencer called them back. He had the gang under him."

"What was he like?" queried Marian.

"Young, snappy kind of man. Like a wolf. And cold. He didn't drink. It was plain he was set to get something out of Drake. And just now it come about that I found out. Spencer drew Drake aside, over by the big woodpile, on top of which I was hidden. And I heard something like this talk.

" 'Drake, we've got over a hundred head of Rangle horns corralled down at Stony,' Spencer said. 'We're to drive them off this station. That's a deal for us men. But Black wants your blue roan. He's gone to Sydney. Expects to be back in two weeks. He aims to train Blue and enter him in the sweepstakes at Sydney.'

" 'I can't let Black have the colt,' Drake replied. 'He's not mine to sell or give.'

" 'Black doesn't count on that. He said to tell you he'd let you out of the Melville raid, and that you'd be getting off cheap.'

" 'I told him I'd not consider any of his demands.'

" 'He admits that. But he's allowing you time to consider. Give me the colt, or else take the consequences.'

" 'And what are they?'

" 'My orders are to drive the herd of horses up here and wait for Black.'

" 'Here!'

" 'Yes. We're to make ourselves at home. Black wasn't curious about Miss Hastings. But I am, and I'd like to have a go at her.'

"Drake walked up and down, his head bent. Finally he said . . . 'What guarantee have I you'll not do that if I give up Blue?'

"Spencer laughed kind of hard and said Drake would have to take a chance on that.

" 'You'll steal half the Rangle horses, and Black forces me to let Blue go?'

" 'Drake, I don't mind helping you out. Black is almost through with this Rangle hide-out. He can't find the gold. . . .'

" 'What gold?'

" 'The gold old Hastings buried somewhere at Stony Gap. Hadn't you heard of it?'

" 'No. Does Bates have any knowledge of it?'

" 'Black says Jim has been hunting that gold for years. Anyway, Black is about done here. He will be . . . after the big Melville raid. My tip to you is this. Give Blue up. Come in on the Melville raid, and then shake this Rangle country.'

" 'Give me an hour to think it over,' said Drake.

"They left then, and pretty soon I heard Drake calling me. I slipped down without him seeing me. Then he told me to tell you to have patience . . . that they'd be gone soon."

"Jimmy! He's going to give in?" cried Marian.

"Ma'am, I don't know. He appeared pretty white and quiet. I don't believe he's the kind of a man to give in."

"Is _he_ a . . . a horse thief?" whispered Marian.

"I don't believe it," declared Jimmy stoutly.

"Oh, I'm afraid . . . there's something _wrong_ here."

Jimmy hung his head in silence. He knew that, too. And into that distant silence rang a heavy gunshot. Jimmy leaped off the tent floor, his eyes big and startled. "Dick shot him. I knew that's what he was thinking about."

"But, it might be that Dick . . . ," faltered Marian, with a pang in her breast. "Run . . . run out . . . and see, Jimmy."

The lad bolted, and Marian fell back upon her cot, a prey to fear and anguish. She knew then that she loved Drake. Her ears stirred to a medley of shouts pierced by a stentorian voice in command. She recognized that voice, and her heart lifted with a wild leap. These sounds ceased, only to be followed by a thud of hoofs. Trembling, Marian lay there, trying to piece out of what she had heard some fragment of fact. Then it seemed that voices rose again, and a concerted movement of hoofs. From the tent window Marian saw pack horses, hastily packed, bobbing away under the trees, driven by dark riders in a hurry. Still she could not be certain about the shooting. But hardened characters like these would not be liable to depart hastily after shooting a man. They had been driven. Then Jimmy's flying footsteps roused Marian. The lad stuck a pale little face between the flaps.

"You're not supposed . . . to know," he panted. "Dick'd beat me . . . if he found . . . out. . . . Dick shot that . . . horse thief, Miss Marian . . . killed him dead. Bates and Dick are digging his grave right now. They were quarreling. Bates excited and hot . . . Dick cool and grim. I heard enough. I figured it out when Jim said . . . 'Good job, Dick, but why the hell did it take you so long?' and Dick said . . . 'Save your breath. Let's get *this* job over.' Then Jim said . . . 'By God. You withheld your hand when that thief Spencer tried to rob us blind. But when he jeered at you . . . said you were in love with your boss . . . and that he'd come back to beat you to her . . . then you knocked him down. And when he reached for a gun, you shot him!'

" 'Will you shut up!' cracked out Drake. 'Do you have to blab like an old woman? We don't want her to find it out. Jimmy, I'll skin you alive if you tell!' Well, miss, you bet I promised I wouldn't. Don't you give me away."

With that he bobbed out and ran away. This time, when

Marian fell back upon her cot, it was with conflicting emotions. The period however was scarcely long enough for her to compose herself before Drake arrived at the tent.

"Marian," he called. His voice had a cool ring.

"Yes, I'm here."

"Wonderful to see. I didn't expect to find you," he said, and swept open the flap with a strong hand. He gazed down upon her. Marian had a sense of something surprisingly comforting in his presence.

"What are you so white about?" he demanded.

"Am I . . . white?" she faltered, with a little laugh.

"You are. Has Jimmy been here?"

"Once. He told me you said they'd be gone presently."

"Then what were you frightened about?" he queried.

"I guess . . . I haven't gotten over the rough way you treated me. And then I heard voices. The suspense was great. And that shot."

"Oh, that? Just a gunshot. Nobody hurt. You may come out now. I'm sorry you've been confined so long. I guess we can feel safe for a while. I drove those fellows away. But Black will bother us when he comes back."

With that Drake left Marian. It was growing late in the afternoon. She busied herself about her tent until called to supper. Drake was conspicuous by his absence. Bates did not seem natural. But Jimmy was lively and vivacious, still under a spell of excitement. Marian did not sleep well that night.

Next day she moved into the house, and that task took most of the day. Drake was about, the same as usual, except more solicitous for her. Marian found that the comfort of her rooms, with all her possessions at hand, her desk, books, and neglected correspondence to attend to, gave her a feel of home she had not felt there before.

One morning she heard a car droning up the sandy road. She ran out on the porch. Drake was off somewhere with Jimmy. But Bates met the car in the yard. The young placid man who stepped out Marian recognized as the Melville she had seen Drake encountering at the race. There was another man in the car, and Bates addressed him in a manner far from welcoming.

"Bates," called Marian, "who are those men and what do they want?"

Then Melville wheeled to see her. Certain it was that he appeared greatly astonished. "Who is that?" he asked Bates.

"It's Miss Hastings."

"But they told me she was . . . was . . . well certainly not what I see." And with that he approached Marian with a quick eager step. She answered his greeting politely and coldly.

"You know me?" he queried in astonishment.

"No. I merely recognized you. I was present at the race-track that day you tried to buy Blue from Drake."

That visibly annoyed Melville. But he threw it off, evidently determined to make friends with her. "Aren't you going to ask me in?"

"I'm quite busy. Bates will talk to you."

"But I want to talk to *you*." He sat down on the steps. "What an improvement you've made in this tumble-down place. I was here once. It's really most attractive. And your porch . . . very comfortable, indeed. Evidently you've spent a bit of money?"

"Not very much," she replied, and did not give him much satisfaction for his keen queries. Marian noted that the possibility of her possessing means had interested him as much as her youth and comeliness.

"Don't I hear running water?" he asked suddenly.

Marian pointed through the trees to the shining fountainhead.

"What? Rangle Rim burst out again?" he cried, and rushed off toward the great spring. Marian watched him, wondering at his excitement. She rather hoped Drake would return. She was curious about Melville's visit. The large man talking to Bates bent curious eyes after her. Presently Melville returned to the porch.

"Magnificent! That water changes the status of Rangle River."

"Yes. We have grasped that."

"Miss Hastings, our station is holding eight hundred thousand head of stock. But water is scarce. Would you consider joining with us . . . on equal shares?"

"No, thanks. I prefer to go it alone."

"But you have no stock. Only some wild herds of cattle and horses. If you are poor, you can't run this place. With us you'd be half owner of the finest station in Australia."

"I'll have a go at running my place, in a modest way."

"This water will stir up complications. Your line is in doubt. There are other reasons, too, why it'd be wise for you to come in with us."

"For instance?"

"This man Drake. . . ."

"Mister Melville, I am not interested in range gossip. Please excuse me."

"It's not gossip. Drake is a horse thief."

"I wouldn't advise you to tell *him* that to his face."

"I came out here. . . . But, Miss Hastings, I'll let this go this time. You will listen to reason. I must consult my brother. I'll go to Sydney and fetch him here. This is a serious situation, as well as a marvelous opportunity. Pray forgive my intrusion."

He bowed and left her. Entering the car he drove away.

Then Bates plodded slowly up to where Marian stood, watching the car disappear.

"Bates, that man had something in his mind when he came here, and he changed it."

"Yes, Marian. After seeing you. He was flabbergasted. Well, you do look uncommon pretty today."

"What'd he come for?"

"I think he had an idea he could arrest Drake. But he couldn't . . . not out here . . . with no constable."

"He said Drake is a horse thief."

"That's a lie, Marian."

"But what's all this mystery? Is Dick guilty of any . . . anything?"

"Marian, he's guilty in a way, but absolutely innocent."

"Thank heaven for that last. But how can that be?"

"I wanted to tell you. But he wouldn't let me. You get it out of him."

"Melville was dazzled by our water. He offered to throw the Melville Station in with mine, share and share alike."

"A big offer, Marian," said Bates, impressed. "With our water and their stock . . . and their riders to drive out these robbers . . . we'd have a proposition second to none in Australia."

"I refused him."

"Well, he'll be back. And like as not he'll want to throw himself in the bargain."

Days passed. Drake appeared to avoid Marian after the Melville incident. And he looked dark and sad. Marian waited for she knew not what, unless it was to give in to her heart.

About a week later Drake and Jimmy returned from a ride down the river way. They not only did not get to the end of the flat, but could not even see it. Dusk had fallen. There were no lights from the buildings. Drake called. The housekeeper, Kate, answered from a shed, where she had been barred in. Black, with some of his men, had come along. The woman was terribly frightened. She did not know what had happened to Bates and Marian. Jimmy's shrill yell proclaimed some discovery. Drake ran to find Bates tied to a post. He choked with rage when Drake cut him free.

"Black, with four men. They ransacked the house . . . carried Marian off."

"How long ago?"

"Not half an hour. Going to Stony Way, where Black expects Spencer's gang with a raid of stock from Melville's."

"Jimmy, get fresh horses," ordered Drake. "Bates, get the rifles . . . plenty of shells, water bags. We'll beat Black to Stony Way."

In short order the three were mounted and riding down the river. Drake led over a devious and rough trail until late in the night. Above Stony Way they tied their horses and glided down to the gray stone house. No lights, no horses, no camp. Neither Black nor Spencer's gang had arrived. Drake and his allies went into the stone house and hid until daylight.

Shortly after that a line of horses bobbed down out of the trees. The pack animals were in the fore.

"They'll unpack there by the water," whispered Drake. "But Black will drag Marian in here. Spread out now. Don't shoot till I've got her safe. You might hit her."

Presently Black could be heard cursing Spencer for not being there. His men were quiet. They halted to get off. Daylight had come. Black approached the open door, dragging Marian. She was white and weak, her flimsy summer dress torn and disordered. Her arms were tied behind her back. Black had hold of her, one arm around her shoulders, and he half carried her in.

"I'll break you, my lady, before. . . ."

Drake did not dare shoot. He leaped up to strike at Black's shaggy head. The blow glanced, felling Black, who dragged Marian down with him. Drake pulled her loose, which effort helped Black upon his feet. And he swiftly closed with Drake. In that first violent wrench Drake's gun was knocked from his hand.

A terrific struggle ensued. Drake heard Bates shooting rapidly with his rifle, while Jimmy darted screaming around the wrestlers, trying to find a chance to shoot. Black was far heavier than Drake and more powerful. At length he came up on top of Drake and was jerking a hand for a weapon when Jimmy shot him in the head. Black fell over upon Drake, who had to wriggle to get out from under. Marian had fainted. Bates came in with smoking rifle, and hard, compressed lips.

"One got away crippled . . . on his horse."

"Good. It worked," panted Drake. "Jimmy, run for water."

They brought Marian to. She sat up wild-eyed and disheveled, clinging to Drake.

"Is he . . . dead?"

"Rather. And three more. Only one got away."

"Dick . . . did you kill him?"

"Sorry. I tried to. But Jimmy gets that credit. Marian, are you . . . did he . . . ?"

"I'm unharmed. But he was brutal. About tore me to pieces. Look at that bruise . . . and that. . . . *Ughh!*"

"Don't look at him."

"Boss," interrupted Jimmy, "when I ran after the water, I saw cattle way down the creek. Driven, sir. It's the raid comin'."

"So!" exclaimed Drake, helping Marian up. "Bates, search Black. You and Jimmy follow me up to the horses. We'll hide and have a go at Spencer's gang. Marian, I'll carry you."

"But I can walk."

"Come, then."

He helped her climb the bank to the line of trees. There, under cover, they saw a herd of cattle straggling up the wide creekbed driven by riders on each side and behind.

"A thousand head," whispered Drake. "The nerve of these thieves! We'll make it hot for them."

"Dick, this looks like the end of Black's gang."

"Well, it's the end of Black, anyway."

In due course the thieves, nine in number, rode unsuspectingly into range. After the first shots that accounted for two of the gang, there ensued a short, sharp conflict, wholly in favor of the hidden attackers. It was over almost as soon as it had begun.

"Poor shooting," complained Bates bitterly. "I saw three of them ride away."

"Now what'll we do?" asked Jimmy fiercely.

"We won't risk any shots from those fellows who escaped."

"I reckon they'll ride off the station."

"We can come back tomorrow. Let's go. My horse will carry double. Come on, Marian. It's over, except the hard ride back."

Drake led off, carrying Marion as he had once before. Only this time her eyes were on him, with a look he could not need twice.

"Dick, I'm grateful. You saved me," she murmured. "And *this* isn't such a . . . a hard ride."

They reached home, and by dinnertime Marian, except for sundry bruises and a queer, suspended, exalted mood, was herself again.

On the following day Drake sent Jimmy to Coombs in the

car to report the happening and to have some official come out to verify. Jimmy was back before nightfall, accompanied by two cars full of men. Next day Drake led them down to Stony Way.

When in another day their visitors had departed, and with every reason for Drake to feel happy, he appeared darker and sterner than ever. Marian at length approached him, after a short satisfactory word with Bates.

"Dick, why so strange . . . so hard?" she asked. "I think we are fortunate. You saved me, Dick . . . and doesn't this clear away that shadow?"

"I guess so, *that* one. But there's a worse one."

"Nonsense. We have Kate, and Bates, besides Jimmy."

"No matter. It mustn't go on. I suspect Melville."

"If it doesn't worry me, why should it you?"

"Listen, darling," he said, and the tender epithet, the look and tone of him, quite overcame Marians. "Are you absolutely determined to stay here? Live here?"

"I am. I'm going to be happy . . . and prosperous, too."

"Very well. But I will not stay unless you marry me."

"Dick! Won't that be failing me?"

"Listen, Marian. It won't do. All young women are married out here. I told you once how I felt toward you. Well, if you have no ties, if you really are a poor girl who saved . . . perhaps borrowed . . . enough to come out here . . . why marry me, and I'll make a go of it somehow. Of course, I mean you . . . wife in name only . . . until you care for me a little. Do you think you ever could?"

"It's not beyond the bounds of possibility."

"Then . . . Marian . . . will you?"

"I think I'll accept, Dick."

"When?" he cried, gripping her hands.

"Oh, it needn't be soon."

"Yes, it need be. I must stop this gossip."

"Very well, then, the first time we go to town."

"That might not be soon."

"I promise . . . pretty soon. And now have you anything more to tell me?"

"Yes. And it'll be short and sweet. I was invalided home the last year of the war. Got well, or they thought so. But it seems I wasn't. I went out of my head. And when I came to my senses again I was here on the range . . . one of Black's men. I had helped him steal cattle and horses, so *he* claimed. But I never did it consciously. And I left him to come here with Bates."

"So that was it?" mused Marian, deeply touched. "I believe you, Dick. Let us forget that dark shadow, and pray it never comes again."

"Marian, you are splendid," he ended, and, kissing her hand, he strode away.

The succeeding days for Marian revolved around one sole heart-throbbing question—how soon would she surrender and ride in to Coombs to marry Drake? More and more she wanted to. Yet she toyed with happiness. She had a reluctance to be true to herself.

The days grew hotter, and during the windy hours a fine, sandy dust permeated everything. She rested then, and, if she did not sleep, she thought and dreamed herself nearer to capitulation.

She was not asleep, however, one day when Drake's voice, strangely different, disrupted her reverie. She answered, wondering what had happened.

"Visitors, Miss Hastings," said Drake.

"From where?"

"Melville Station . . . and England," rang out Drake.

"England!" Marian ran out on the porch. Drake stood at the steps, standing tall and straight, white to the lips. Musical voices of women, in gay laughter and speech, petrified Marian. She saw a group behind Drake, emerging from behind the low firs. A tall girl, stylish, beloved, appeared strangely familiar. Then Marian, with a violent start, recognized her. Blanch Maitland! A friend—a friend of her friends in London, although not close, yet she was one Marian would have been glad to see, had she not been pretending.

"You runaway darling," cried Blanch gaily, and rushed up the steps. Marian met her embrace heartily. Blanch reeked of London and home. Then Mrs. Maitland came up.

"Of all wonderful happenings and places!" she ejaculated in a high-pitched voice. "Marian, I rejoice to find you. Yes, indeed, we heard of you in Sydney. Traced you to Melville Station. And here we are."

"I'm amazed . . . but glad, really," replied Marian remorsefully and awfully aware of Drake standing there like a stallion.

"How perfectly stunning you look!" babbled Blanch. "All gold tan . . . Marian, you must remember Eleanor Starett. She has met you."

"Yes, indeed, I do."

And then Marian was being introduced to the elder Melville, a typical English type.

"Delighted to meet you," he said. "My brother's raving seems justified. But he didn't know who you were."

"So I am unearthed," laughed Marian.

The younger Melville approached from behind. The light on his sunburned face was satirical if not resentful. He made a profound bow before Marian. "It was a capital joke. To take us in as you did. The schoolteacher who saved her money to come to Australia."

"No, I said I'd been a clerk," declared Marian, joining in the laugh at her expense.

Melville turned a sardonic smile upon Drake, who had gradually stepped to the side.

"Drake, you must have heard that Rangle River had been left to one of the richest girls in England."

"No, I had not," replied Drake haltingly.

"You hear it now, then."

Drake gave Marian a dark questioning glance that seemed to pierce her like a dagger. Then, wheeling, he strode off. And Marian, if not the others, knew he was leaving. She asked her guests up on the porch. "Please make yourself comfortable. I'll have my housekeeper fetch tea." Marian stopped at Kate's tent only long enough to order the tea made. Farther on she encountered Bates, who told her she had played hell.

"Oh, Jim! Where is Dick?"

"You better hurry, Marian Hastings."

Marian ran in the mud, losing her slippers. She came upon Drake at the corral, where he was leading Blue out of the saddle rack.

"Dick! What are you doing?" she panted.

He bent terrible eyes upon her. "What do you think? I'm stealing Blue. I'm on my way . . . a real thief at last. And *you* made me one."

"You can't steal Blue."

"Can't I? Watch me. And keep out of my way, Miss Hastings."

"You can't . . . because long ago I gave Blue to you."

"You did? Fine! But no matter. I never knew. And I'm stealing him."

Marian got hold of his swift hands, and clung to them so desperately that he would have thrown her had he persisted. Her touch had some subduing effect on the man.

"Let go, Marian. It's all hopeless. Why didn't you tell me? You liar!"

"Dick, it was only in fun, at first, just a romantic idea."

"But *are* you rich at all?" he demanded.

"Yes. I'm sorry. I meant to tell you. Only there was a reason."

"Oh, to fool me that way. When I loved you, trusted you."

He dropped the saddle to the dust. Marian's spirit soared, as she sensed her power over him. She felt it. She saw it in his eyes so black with passion and reproach. She slipped her hands up his arms, clung to him, meaning not to let go now.

"Listen, Dick. Listen to my reason," she pleaded.

"No. You played with me. You'd never have married me."

"I *will!*" she cried eloquently.

And at that a violent shock ran through him. "You will not. I wouldn't marry you now," he declared passionately.

"Very well. Jilt me if you can! But give me back what you took from me."

"I have taken nothing, Marian Hastings."

"Indeed you . . . have," she flushed, and threw her arms around his neck. "Give me back . . . my kisses. Take your own . . . again."

Nonnezoshe, the Rainbow Bridge

John Wetherill, one of the famous Wetherill brothers and trader at Kayenta, Arizona, is the man who discovered Nonnezoshe, which is probably the most beautiful and wonderful natural phenomenon in the world. Wetherill owes the credit to his wife, who, through her influence with the Indians, finally, after years, succeeded in getting the secret of the great bridge.

After three trips to Marsh Pass and Kayenta with my old guide, Al Doyle of Flagstaff, I finally succeeded in getting Wetherill to take me in to Nonnezoshe. This was in the spring of 1913, and my party was the second one, not scientific, to make the trip. Later this same year Wetherill took in the Roosevelt party and after that the Kolb brothers. It is a safe thing to say that this trip is one of the most beautiful in the West. It is a hard one and not for everybody. There is no guide except Wetherill, who knows how to get there. And after Doyle and I came out, we admitted that we would not care to try to return over our back trail. We doubted if we could find the way. This is the only place I have ever visited which I am not sure I could find again alone.

My trip to Nonnezoshe gave me the opportunity to see also Monument Valley, and the mysterious and labyrinthine Cañon Segi with its great prehistoric cliff-dwellings.

The desert beyond Kayenta spread out impressively, bare red flats and plains of sage leading to the rugged, vividly colored, and wind-sculptured sandstone heights typical of the Painted Desert of Arizona. Laguna Creek, at that season, became flooded after every thunderstorm, and it was a treacherous, red-mired quicksand where I convinced myself we would have stuck forever had it not been for Wetherill's Navajos.

We rode all day, for the most part closed in by ridges and bluffs, so that no extended view was possible. It was hot, too, and the sand blew and the dust rose. Travel in northern Arizona is never easy, and this grew harder and steeper. There was one long slope of heavy sand that I felt sure would prove too much for Wetherill's pack mules. But they surmounted it, apparently less breathless than I was. Toward sunset a storm gathered ahead of us to the north with a promise of cooling and sultry air.

At length we turned into a long cañon with straight rugged red walls, and a sandy floor with quite a perceptible ascent. It appeared endless. Far ahead I could see the black storm clouds, and by and by began to hear the rumble of thunder. Darkness had overtaken us by the time we had reached the head of this canon, and my first sight of Monument Valley came with a dazzling flash of lightning. It revealed a vast valley, a strange world of colossal shafts and buttes of rock, magnificently sculptured, standing isolated and aloof, dark, weird, lonely. When the sheet lightning flared across the sky showing the monuments silhouetted black against that strange horizon, the effect was marvelously beautiful. I watched until the storm died away.

Dawn, with the desert sunrise, changed Monument Valley, bereft it of its night gloom and weird shadow, and showed it in another aspect of beauty. It was hard for me to realize that those monuments were not the works of man. The great valley must once have been a plateau of red rock from which the softer strata had eroded, leaving the gentle league-long slopes marked here and there by upstanding pillars and columns of singular shape and beauty. I rode down the sweet-scented sage slopes under the shadow of the lofty Mittens, and around and across the valley, and back again to the height of land. And when I had completed the ride, a story had woven itself into my mind; the spot where I stood was to be the place where Lin Slone taught Lucy Bostil to ride the great stallion Wildfire.

Two days' ride took us across country to the Segi. With this wonderful cañon I was familiar, that is, as familiar as several visits could make a man with such a bewildering place. In fact, I had named it Deception Pass. The Segi had innumerable branches, all more or less the same size, and sometimes it was difficult to tell the main cañon from one of its tributaries. The walls were rugged and crumbling, of a red or yellow hue, upward of a thousand feet in height, and indented by spruce-sided notches.

There were a number of ruined cliff-dwellings, the most accessible of which was Keet Seel. I could imagine no more picturesque spot. A huge, wind-worn cavern with a vast, slanted, stained wall held upon a projecting ledge or shelf the long line of cliff-dwellings. These silent little stone houses with their vacant, black, eye-like windows had strange power to make me ponder, and then dream.

Next day, upon resuming our journey, it pleased me to try to find the trail to Betatakin, the most noted, and surely the most wonderful and beautiful ruin in all the West. In many places there was no trail at all, and I encountered difficulties, but in the end without much loss of time I entered the narrow, ragged entrance of the cañon I had named Surprise Valley. Sight of the great dark cave thrilled me as I thought it might have thrilled Bess and Venters, who had lived for me their imagined lives of loneliness here in this wild spot. With the sight of those lofty walls and the scent of the dry sweet sage there rushed over me a strange feeling that RIDERS OF THE PURPLE SAGE was true. My dream people of romance had really lived there once upon a time. I climbed high upon the huge stones, and along the smooth red walls where Fay Larkin once had glided with swift sure steps, and I entered the musty cliff-dwellings, and called out to hear the weird and sonorous echoes, and I wandered through the thickets and upon the grassy spruce-shaded benches, never for a moment free of the story I had conceived there. Something of awe and sadness abided with me. I could not enter into the merry pranks and investigations of my party. Surprise Valley seemed a part of my past, my dreams, my very self. I left it, haunted by its loneliness and silence and beauty, by the story it had given me.

That night we camped at Bubbling Spring, which once had been a geyser of considerable power. Wetherill told a story of an old Navajo who had lived there. For a long time, according to the Indian tribe, the old chief resided there without complaining of this geyser that was wont to inundate his fields. But one season the unreliable waterspout made great and persistent endeavor to drown him and his people and horses. Whereupon the old Navajo took his gun, and shot repeatedly at the geyser, and thundered aloud his anger to the Great Spirit. The geyser ebbed away, and from that day never burst forth again.

Somewhere under the great bulge of Navajo Mountain I calculated that we were coming to the edge of the plateau. The white, bobbing pack horses disappeared and then our extra mustangs. It is no unusual thing for a man to use three mounts on this trip. Then two of our Indians disappeared. But Wetherill waited for us and so did Nas Ta Bega, the Paiute who first took Wetherill down into Nonnezoshe Boco.

As I came up, I thought we had, indeed, reached the end of the world.

"It's down in there," said Wetherill with a laugh.

Nas Ta Bega made a slow, sweeping gesture. There is always something so significant and impressive about an Indian when he points anywhere. It is as if he says: "There, way beyond, over the ranges, is a place I know, and it is far." The fact was that I looked at the Paiute's dark, inscrutable face before I looked out into the void.

My gaze then seemed impelled and held by things afar, a vast yellow and purple corrugated world of distance, apparently now on a level with my eyes. I was drawn by the beauty and grandeur of that scene, and then I was transfixed, almost by fear, by the realization that I dared to venture down into this wild and upflung fastness. I kept looking afar, sweeping the three-quarter circle of horizon till my judgment of distance was confounded and my sense of proportion dwarfed one moment and magnified the next.

Wetherill was pointing and explaining, but I had not grasped all he said.

"You can see two hundred miles into Utah," he went on. "That bright rough surface, like a washboard, is wind-worn rock. Those little lines of cleavage are cañons. There are a thousand cañons down there, and only a few have we been in. That long, purple, ragged line is the Grand Cañon of the Colorado. And there, that blue fork in the end, that's where the San Juan comes in. And there's Escalante Cañon."

I had to adopt the Indian's method of studying unlimited spaces in the desert—to look with slow, contracted eyes from near to far.

The pack train and the drivers had begun to zigzag down a long slope, bare of rock, with scant strips of green, and here and there a cedar. Half a mile down, the slope merged in what seemed a green level. But I knew it was not level. This level was a rolling plain, growing darker green, with lines of ravines and thin, undefined spaces that might be mirage. Miles and miles it swept and rolled and heaved, to lose its waves in apparent darker level. Round red rocks stood isolated. They resembled huge, grazing cattle. But as I gazed these rocks were strangely magnified. They grew and grew into mounds, castles, domes, crags, great, red, wind-carved buttes. One by one they drew my gaze to the wall of upflung rock. I seemed to see a thousand domes of a thousand shapes and colors, and among them a thousand blue clefts, each of which was a cañon.

Beyond this wide area of curved lines rose another wall, dwarfing the lower, dark, red, horizon-long, magnificent in frowning boldness, and because of its limitless deceiving surfaces incomprehensible to the gaze of man. Away to the eastward began a winding, ragged, blue line, looping back upon itself, and then winding away again, growing wider and bluer. This line was San Juan Cañon. I followed that blue line all its length, a hundred miles, down toward the west where it joined a dark, purple, shadowy cleft. And this was the Grand Cañon of the Colorado. My eye swept along with that winding mark, farther and farther to the west, until the cleft, growing larger and closer, revealed itself as a wild and winding cañon. Still farther westward it split a vast plateau of red peaks and yellow mesas. Here the cañon was full of purple smoke. It turned, it closed, it gaped, it lost itself and showed again in that chaos of a million cliffs. And then it faded, a mere purple line, into deceiving distance.

I imagined there was no scene in all the world to equal this. The tranquility of lesser spaces was here not manifest. This happened to be a place where so much of the desert could be seen, and the effect was stupendous. Sound, movement, life seemed to have no fitness here. Ruin was there and desolation and decay. The meaning of the ages was flung at me. A man became nothing. But when I gazed across that sublime and majestic wilderness, in which the Grand Cañon was only a dim line, I strangely lost my terror, and something came to me across the shining spaces.

Then Nas Ta Bega and Wetherill began the descent of the slope, and the rest of us followed. No sign of a trail showed where the base of the slope rolled out to meet the green plain. There was a level bench a mile wide, then a ravine, and then an ascent, and after that rounded ridge and ravine, one after the other, like huge swells of a monstrous sea. Indian paint brush vied in its scarlet hue with the deep magenta of cactus. There was no sage. Soap weed and meager grass and a bunch of cactus here and there lent the green to that barren, and it was green only at a distance.

Nas Ta Bega kept on at a steady gait. The sun climbed. The wind rose and whipped dust from under the mustangs. There is seldom much talk on a ride of this nature. It is hard work and everybody for himself. Besides, it is enough just to see, and that country is conducive to silence. I looked back often, and the farther out on the plain we rode, the higher loomed the plateau we had descended. As I faced ahead again, the lower sank the red-domed and castled horizon to the fore.

It was a wild place we were approaching. I saw piñon patches under the circled walls. I ceased to feel the dry wind in my face. We were already in the lee of a wall. I saw the rock squirrels scampering to their holes. Then the Indian disappeared between two rounded corners of cliff.

I rode around the corner into a widening space thick with cedars. It ended in a bare slope of smooth rock. Here we dismounted to begin the ascent. It was smooth and hard, although not slippery. There was not a crack. I did not see a broken piece of stone. Nas Ta Bega and Wetherill climbed straight up for a while, and then wound around a swell, to turn this way and that, always going up. I began to see similar mounds of rock all around me, of every shape that could be called a curve. There were yellow domes far above and small red domes far below. Ridges ran from one hill of rock to another. There were no abrupt breaks, but holes and pits and caves were everywhere, and occasionally deep down an amphitheatre green with cedar and piñon. We found no vestige of trail on those bare slopes.

Our guides led to the top of the wall, only to disclose to us another wall beyond, with a ridged, bare, and scalloped depression between. Here footing began to be precarious for both man and beast. Our mustangs were not shod, and it was wonderful to see their slow, short, careful steps. They knew a great deal better than we what the danger was. It has been such experiences as this that have made me see in horses something besides beasts of burden. In the ascent of the second slope it was necessary to zigzag up, slowly and carefully, taking advantage of every bulge and depression.

Then before us twisted and dropped and curved the most dangerous slopes I had ever seen. We had reached the height of the divide, and many of the drops on this side were perpendicular and too steep for us to see the bottom.

At one bad place Wetherill and Nas Ta Bega, with Joe Lee, a Mormon cowboy with us, were helping one of the pack horses, named Chub. On the steepest part of this slope Chub fell and began to slide. His momentum jerked the rope from the hands of Wetherill and the Indian. But Joe Lee held on. Joe was a giant, and being a Mormon he could not let go of anything he had. He began to slide with the horse, holding back with all his might.

It seemed that both man and beast must slide down to where the slope ended in a yawning precipice. Chub was snorting or screaming in terror. Our mustangs were frightened and rearing. It was not a place to have trouble with horses.

I had a moment of horrified fascination, in which Chub turned clear over. Then he slid into a little depression that, with Joe's hold on the lasso, momentarily checked his descent. Quick as thought Joe ran sidewise and down to the bulge of rock and yelled for help. I got to him a little ahead of Wetherill and Nas Ta Bega, and together we pulled Chub up out of danger. At first we thought he had been choked to death. But he came to, and got up, a bloody, skinned horse, but alive and safe. I have never seen a more magnificent effort than Joe Lee's. Those fellows are built that way. Wetherill has lost horses on those treacherous slopes, and that risk is the only thing about the trip that is not splendid.

We got over that bad place without further incident, and presently came to a long swell of naked stone that led down to a narrow green split. This one had straight walls and wound away out of sight. It was the head of a cañon.

"Nonnezoshe Boco," said the Indian.

This, then, was the Cañon of the Rainbow Bridge. When we got down into it, we were a happy crowd. The mode of travel here was a selection of the best levels, the best places to cross the brook, the best places to climb, and it was a process of continual repetition. There was no trail ahead of us, but we certainly left one behind. And as Wetherill picked out the course and the mustangs followed him, I had all freedom to see and feel the beauty, color, wildness, and changing character of Nonnezoshe Boco.

My experiences in the desert did not count much in the trip down this strange, beautiful, lost cañon. All cañons are not alike. This one did not widen, although the walls grew higher. They began to lean and bulge, and the narrow strip of sky above resembled a flowing blue river. Huge caverns had been hollowed out by water or wind. And when the brook ran close under one of these overhanging places, the running water made a singular, indescribable sound. A crack from a hoof on a stone rang like a hollow bell and echoed from wall to wall. And the croak of a frog—the only living creature I noted in the cañon—was a weird and melancholy thing.

"We're sure gettin' deep down," said Joe Lee.

"How do you know?" I asked.

"Here are the pink and yellow sego lilies. Only the white ones are found above."

I dismounted to gather some of these lilies. They were larger than the white ones of higher altitudes, of a most exquisite beauty and fragility, and of such rare pink and yellow hues as I had never seen.

"They bloom only where it's always summer," explained Joe.

That expressed their nature. They were the orchids of the summer cañons. They stood up everywhere star-like out of the green. It was impossible to prevent the mustangs treading them under foot. And as the cañon deepened, and many little springs added their tiny volume to the brook, every grassy bench was dotted with lilies, like a green sky star-spangled. And this increasing luxuriance manifested itself in the banks of purple moss and clumps of lavender daisies and great mounds of yellow violets. The brook was lined by blossoming buck brush; the rocky corners showed the crimson and magenta of cactus; and there were ledges of green with shining moss that sparkled with little white flowers. The hum of bees filled the fragrant, dreamy air.

But by and by this green and colorful and verdant beauty,

the almost level floor of the cañon, the banks of soft earth, the thickets and clumps of cottonwood, the shelving caverns and bulging walls—these features were gradually lost, and Nonnezoshe began to deepen in bare red and white stone steps. The walls sheered away from one another, breaking into sections and ledges, and rising higher and higher, and there began to be manifested a dark and solemn concordance with the nature that had created this old rent in the earth.

There was a stretch of miles where steep steps in hard red rock alternated with long levels of round boulders. Here, one by one, the mustangs went lame, and we had to walk. And we slipped and stumbled along over these loose, treacherous stones. The hours passed; the toll increased; the progress diminished; one of the mustangs failed and was left. All the while the dimensions of Nonnezoshe Boco were magnified and its character changed. It became a thousand-foot walled cañon, leaning, broken, threatening, with great yellow slides, blocking passage, with huge sections split off from the main wall, with immense dark and gloomy caverns. Strangely it had no intersecting cañons. It jealously guarded its secret. Its unusual formations of cavern and pillar and half arch led me to expect any monstrous stone shape left by avalanche or cataclysm.

Down and down we toiled. And now the streambed was bare of boulders and the banks of earth. The floods that had rolled down that cañon had here borne away every loose thing. All the floor, in places, was bare red and white stone, polished, glistening, slippery, affording treacherous foothold. And the time came when Wetherill abandoned the streambed to take to the rock-strewn and cactus-covered ledges above.

The cañon widened ahead into a great, ragged, iron-lined amphitheatre, and then apparently turned abruptly at right angles. Sunset rimmed the walls.

I had been tired for a long time, and now I began to limp and lag. I wondered what on earth would make Wetherill and the Indians tired. It was with great pleasure that I observed the giant Joe Lee plodding slowly along. And when I glanced behind at my straggling party, it was with both admiration for their gameness and glee for their disheveled and weary appearance. Finally I got so that all I could do was to drag myself onward with eyes down on the rough ground. In this way I kept on until I heard Wetherill call me. He had stopped— was waiting for me. The dark and silent Indian stood beside him, looking down the cañon.

I saw past the vast jutting wall that had obstructed my view. A mile beyond, all was bright with the colors of sunset, and spanning the cañon in the graceful shape and beautiful hues of the rainbow was a magnificent natural bridge.

"Nonnezoshe," said Wetherill simply.

This Rainbow Bridge was the one great natural phenomenon, the one grand spectacle that I had ever seen that did not at first give vague disappointment, a confounding of reality, a disenchantment of contrast with what the mind had conceived.

This thing was glorious. It absolutely silenced me. My body and brain, weary and dull from the toil of travel, received a singular and revivifying freshness. I had a strange, mystic perception that this rosy-hued, tremendous arch of stone was a goal I had failed to reach in some former life, but had now found. Here was a rainbow magnified even beyond dreams, a thing not transparent and ethereal, but solidified, a work of ages, sweeping up majestically from the red walls, its iris-hued arch against the blue sky.

Then we plodded on again. Wetherill worked around to circle the huge amphitheatre. The way was a steep slant, rough and loose and dragging. The rocks were as hard and jagged as lava, and cacti hindered progress. Soon the rosy and golden lights had faded. All the walls turned pale and steely, and the bridge loomed darkly.

We were to camp that night under the bridge. Just before we reached it, Nas Ta Bega halted with one of his singular motions. He was saying his prayer to this stone god. Then he began to climb straight up the steep slope. Wetherill told me the Indian would not pass under the arch.

When we got to the bridge and unsaddled and unpacked the lame mustangs, twilight had fallen. The horses were turned loose to fare for what scant grass grew on bench and slope. Firewood was even harder to find than grass. When our simple meal had been eaten, there was gloom gathering in the canon, and stars had begun to blink in the pale strip of blue above the lofty walls. The place was oppressive, and we were mostly silent.

Presently I moved away into the strange, dark shadow cast by the bridge. It was a weird black belt, where I imagined I was invisible, but out of which I could see. There was a slab of rock upon which I composed myself, to watch, to feel.

A stiffening of my neck made me aware that I had been continually looking up at the looming arch. I found that it never seemed the same any two moments. Near at hand it was too vast a thing for immediate comprehension. I wanted to ponder on what had formed it—to reflect upon its meaning as to age and force of nature. Yet it seemed that all I could do was to see. White stars hung along the dark, curved line. The rim of the arch appeared to shine. The moon was up there somewhere. The far side of the cañon was now a blank black wall. Over its towering rim showed a pale glow. It brightened. The shades in the cañon lightened, then a white disk of moon peeped over the dark line. The bridge turned to silver.

It was then that I became aware of the presence of Nas Ta Bega. Dark, silent, statuesque, with inscrutable face uplifted, with all that was spiritual of the Indian suggested by a somber and tranquil knowledge of his place there, he represented to me that which a solitary figure of human life represents in a great painting. Nonnezoshe needed life, wild life, life of its millions of years—and here stood the dark and silent Indian.

Long afterward I walked there alone, to and fro, under the bridge. The moon had long since crossed the streak of star-fired blue above, and the cañon was black in shadow. At times a current of wind, with all the strangeness of that strange country in its moan, rushed through the great stone arch. At other times there was silence such as I imagined might have dwelt deep in the center of the earth. And again an owl hooted, and the sound was nameless. It had a mocking echo. An echo of night, silence, gloom, melancholy, death, age, eternity!

The Indian lay asleep with his dark face upturned, and the other sleepers lay calm and white in the starlight. I seemed to see in them the meaning of life and the past—the illimitable train of faces that had shone under the stars. There was something nameless in that cañon, and whether or not it was what the Indian embodied in the great Nonnezoshe, or the life of the present, or the death of the ages, or the nature so magnificently manifested in those silent, dreaming, waiting walls—the truth was that there was a spirit.

I did sleep a few hours under Nonnezoshe, and, when I awoke, the tip of the arch was losing its cold darkness and beginning to shine. The sun had just risen high enough over some low break in the wall to reach the bridge. I watched. Slowly, in wondrous transformation, the gold and blue and rose and pink and purple blended their hues, softly, mistily, cloudily, until once more the arch was a rainbow.

I realized that long before life had evolved upon the earth this bridge had spread its grand arch from wall to wall, black and mystic at night, transparent and rosy in the sunrise, at sunset a flaming curve limned against the heavens. When the race of man had passed, it would, perhaps, stand there still. It was not for many eyes to see. The tourist, the leisurely traveler, the comfort-loving motorist would never behold it. Only by toil, sweat, endurance, and pain could any man ever look at Nonnezoshe. It seemed well to realize that the great things of life had to be earned. Nonnezoshe would always be alone, grand, silent, beautiful, unintelligible; and as such I bade it a mute, reverent farewell.

About the Author

Zane Grey was born Pearl Zane Gray at Zanesville, Ohio in 1872. He was graduated from the University of Pennsylvania in 1896 with a degree in dentistry. He practiced in New York City while striving to make a living by writing. He married Lina Elise Roth in 1905 and with her financial assistance he published his first novel himself, BETTY ZANE (1903). Closing his dental office, the Greys moved into a cottage on the Delaware River, near Lackawaxen, Pennsylvania. Grey took his first trip to Arizona in 1907 and, following his return, wrote THE HERITAGE OF THE DESERT (1910). The profound effect that the desert had had on him was so vibrantly captured that it still comes alive for a reader. Grey couldn't have been more fortunate in his choice of a mate. Trained in English at Hunter College, Lina Grey proofread every manuscript Grey wrote, polished his prose, and she effectively managed their financial affairs. Grey's early novels were serialized in pulp magazines, but by 1918 he had graduated to the slick magazine market. Motion picture rights brought in a fortune and, with 109 films based on his work, Grey set a record yet to be equaled by any other author. Zane Grey was not a realistic writer, but rather one who charted the interiors of the soul through encounters with the wilderness. He provided characters no more realistic than one finds in Balzac, Dickens, or Thomas Mann, but nonetheless they have a vital story to tell. "There was so much unexpressed feeling that could not be entirely portrayed," Loren Grey, Grey's younger son and a noted psychologist, once recalled, "that, in later years, he would weep when re-reading one of his own books." More than stories, Grey fashioned psychodramas about the odyssey of the human soul. They may not be the stuff of the real world, but without them the real world has no meaning—which may go a long way to explain the hold he has had on an enraptured reading public ever since his first Western romance in 1910.

ZANE GREY
TOP HAND

All of the magic of the Southwest's open range can be found in this Zane Grey novel of a young man achieving his life-long ambition of becoming a top ranch hand. But his nomadic life has taken Panhandle Smith far from home. When he finally returns for a visit, he finds that his family has moved to New Mexico, his father has been cheated by an unscrupulous rancher named Hardman, and his boyhood sweetheart, Lucy Blake, is being forced to marry Hardman's son. There's only one way out of this for everybody—and it all depends on Panhandle. But Hardman has no intention of allowing Panhandle to succeed!

THE WESTERNERS
ZANE GREY

The very essence of the American West is in the stories of Zane Grey, an author whose popularity has not flagged since his first Western novel was published in 1910. He wrote more than sixty novels, including the classic *Riders of the Purple Sage*, and the stories collected here for the first time in paperback are shining examples of his best. Included in this volume is "The Ranger," first published in 1929 but never before in the form Grey himself intended. Here is a rare opportunity to experience the short stories of Zane Grey, restored and corrected to the author's original vision, a vision that has remained unmatched for nearly a century!

Dorchester Publishing Co., Inc.
P.O. Box 6640   **$5.99 US/$7.99 CAN**
Wayne, PA 19087-8640   __ 5192-3
Please add $2.50 for shipping and handling for the first book and $.75 for each book thereafter. NY and PA residents, please add appropriate sales tax. No cash, stamps, or C.O.D.s. Prices and availability subject to change.
Canadian orders require $2.00 extra postage and must be paid in U.S. dollars through a U.S. banking facility.

Name_____
Address_____
City_____ State_____ Zip_____
E-mail _____
I have enclosed $_____ in payment for the checked book(s).
Payment <u>must</u> accompany all orders. __ Check here for a free catalog.

CHECK OUT OUR WEBSITE! www.dorchesterpub.com

WINTER SHADOWS

Will Henry

From the very beginning of his long and illustrious career, Will Henry wrote from the Native American viewpoint with authenticity and compassion. This volume collects two of his finest short novels, each focused on the American Indian. The title novel finds a band of Mandan Indians facing the harshest winter in their history, while having to deal with an unscrupulous medicine man. *Lapwai Winter* is set in Northeastern Oregon at the time of Chief Joseph of the Nez Perce. A treaty is violated, the territorial rights of the tribe are revoked . . . and the threat of war hangs ominously in the air.

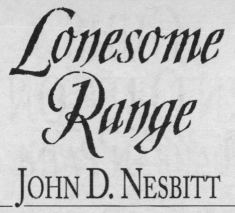

Lonesome Range

JOHN D. NESBITT

Lyle McGavin is a very dangerous man. He's one of the most powerful land developers in the area, an overbearing bully who's used to having his own way and who's definitely not above using threats and physical harm to get what he wants or protect what's his. Too bad he has such an attractive wife. It's especially too bad for Lane Weller, a sometime ranch hand who's fallen in love with Cora McGavin. She says she loves him too, but she never should have left Lane's love letters where her jealous husband could find them…

Dorchester Publishing Co., Inc.
P.O. Box 6640   ___5541-4
Wayne, PA 19087-8640 $5.99 US/$7.99 CAN
Please add $2.50 for shipping and handling for the first book and $.75 for each additional book. NY and PA residents, add appropriate sales tax. No cash, stamps, or CODs. Canadian orders require an extra $2.00 for shipping and handling and must be paid in U.S. dollars. Prices and availability subject to change. **Payment must accompany all orders.**

Name: _____

Address: _____

City: _____ State: _____ Zip: _____

E-mail: _____

I have enclosed $_____ in payment for the checked book(s).

CHECK OUT OUR WEBSITE! www.dorchesterpub.com
_____ Please send me a free catalog.

GUNS
IN OREGON
LAURAN PAINE

Nobody ever ended up in Younger, Oregon, unless he had specific business there. Which was why Deputy Sheriff Jim Crawford was so suspicious when Edward Given rode into town. Folks had no idea why he was there, but they did know Given had the fastest draw they'd ever seen. And those skills came in mighty handy when a group of well-organized cowboys attacked their town and rode off with all the money in their safe. Now Crawford has no choice but to trust this stranger if he wants to catch the thieves. Yet the unlikely pair soon discovers that the robbery was just a cover for an even bigger operation—and that Given is not the only one in town with secrets.

Dorchester Publishing Co., Inc.
P.O. Box 6640
_____5726-3
Wayne, PA 19087-8640
$5.99 US/$7.99 CAN

Name: _____

Address: _____

City: _____ State: _____ Zip: _____

E-mail: _____

I have enclosed $_____ in payment for the checked book(s).

CHECK OUT OUR WEBSITE! www.dorchesterpub.com
_____ Please send me a free catalog

LOUIS L'AMOUR

A MAN CALLED TRENT

Louis L'Amour is one of the most popular, beloved and honored of all American authors. For many readers, his novels and stories have become the very definition of the Old West. Collected here are two of L'Amour's classic novellas, both featuring enigmatic gunfighter Lance Kilkenny. "The Rider of Lost Creek" was first published in a magazine as a novella, then, nearly thirty years later, expanded by L'Amour to novel length. This book presents, for the first time ever in paperback, the original version, as L'Amour first wrote it. "A Man Called Trent" was also written initially as a novella, only to be expanded many years later. Readers can once again enjoy it, restored to its original glory.

SONS OF THUNDER
COTTON SMITH

No one in the small Texas town of Clark Springs knows that their minister's real name is Rule Cordell, or that he used to be one of the most notorious outlaws the Confederacy had ever seen. He's been trying very hard to put his days as a pistol-fighter behind him, but that's getting harder to do lately. When his friends and neighbors are threatened with losing their family spreads to a cunning carpetbagger, Rule realizes it's time for his preacher's collar to be replaced by a pair of .44s. But he won't be able to do it alone. If he's going to rid the town of this ruthless evil, he'll need to call on a very special group of warriors—the Sons of Thunder!
